SCALA SPECIAL EDITION

BOOK TWO OF THE ANGELBOUND ORIGINS SERIES

CHRISTINA BAUER

COPYRIGHT

Monster House Books
Brighton, MA 02135
ISBN 9781945723919
Second Edition

DEDICATION

Dedicated to Prince Lincoln Brezina,
Heaven's Sweetest Angel

AUTHOR'S NOTE

Dear Readers,

Here are some thingy-things to know about this special edition:

Why I did this

Short answer: I'm changing distributors.

Long answer: Because of that switch, my first seven books need new back-end tracking numbers. In other words, I must deactivate the original SCALA (as well as some other books) and then republish it.

As in, the exact same book.

So there will be two versions floating around.

Again, of the exact same book.

Which will be hella confusing.

Now for some context. My day job used to be in software, and we have a saying: *it's not a bug, it's a feature.* So, I figured that if I must have two versions, one of them might as well include new content.

The special edition series was born.

What's in this special edition

An all-new honeymoon story! Boom. Mic drop.

More special editions ahoy

As I mentioned above, my first seven books need new product numbers, so they're also getting extra content. Here's an overview of all seven new special editions (SE):

- ANGELBOUND SE, Angelbound Origins Book 1
- SCALA SE, Angelbound Origins Book 2
- ARMAGEDDON, Angelbound Origins Book 7
- MAXON SE, Angelbound Offspring Book 1
- PORTIA SE, Angelbound Offspring Book 2
- CURSED SE, Beholder Book 1
- CONCEALED SE, Beholder Book 2

So there you have it: why I wrote this special edition and some other semi-random stuff. Hope you enjoy this new edition!

Thanks for reading and being you,

Christina

AUTHOR'S NOTE PART DEUX

Dear Readers,

This note contains my suggested reading order for all things Angelbound. So if you want to skip ahead to that part, feel free! Bottom line: I'm a non-linear thinker and my books sometimes come out in an odd order. I try to stop this, but then the writing stops. Eek. That said, let's get to the good stuff.

My Suggested Angelbound Reading Order

Below please find the suggested reading order for my current Angelbound titles:

1. ANGELBOUND
2. DUTY BOUND (Book 1 in the new Lincoln POV series)
3. LINCOLN (Book 2 in the new Lincoln POV series)
4. SCALA

5. ACCA and the rest of the current Angelbound Origins series

6. The current Angelbound Offspring series (*MAXON* Special Edition and so on)

In case you're wondering, I still plan to release books about Xavier, Cissy and Walker. However, Author Me needs to get more Lincoln POV novels out of my head first. In the meantime, I hope you enjoy all things Angelbound!

Thanks (again!) for reading and being you,

Christina

SCALA

1

Ring, ring, ring. Five o'clock in the morning and my kitchen phone won't shut the Hell up.

A dull ache of worry pulses through my drowsy brain. Someone calling at this hour? Most likely, it's bad news.

I sleep-shuffle into the kitchen. Yawning, I pick up the receiver and set it to my ear. "Myla Lewis speaking."

"Is this the Great Scala?" The voice is young, female, and borderline hysterical.

My anxiety level kicks up a notch. Based on that tone? Definitely bad news.

"Yup. That's me." I only gained my Scala powers a few months ago, but already, my old Myla Lewis self is fading into the background. People only want to talk to the Great Scala, the sole being who can move souls to Heaven or Hell. Most assume that Myla's my nineteen-year-old secretary or something. It's really weird.

I stifle another yawn. "What's going on?"

"I'm calling about the eighteen million souls in Ghost Tower Six."

"No, you're not. There are 3,325,932 souls in Ghost Tower Six. 18,873,264 in all of Purgatory." Give or take a few. Since it's my job to move them all to Heaven or Hell, I like to keep tabs on these things. "Still, that didn't answer my question. What's the problem?"

"Code-red failure, Great Scala. Ghost Tower Six is ready to blow."

Now, I'm wide-the-fuck-awake. Ghost Towers keep angry, confused and homicidal spirits off the streets while we sort them into Heaven or Hell. There hasn't been a code-red failure in ten years. Electric jolts of panic course along every nerve ending I've got. I grip the receiver so tightly, I'm surprised it doesn't snap in two.

"When did this start?"

"Thirty minutes ago. Your phone rang and rang."

My mouth falls open with a mixture of rage and shock. "A half-hour ago? Why didn't you send a runner to my house? I live two blocks from your Tower."

"The rules say to call you on a code-red. Please don't be angry with me. Please don't—"

"Send you to Hell? No, I won't." Though, I'm sorely tempted. "I'll be right over."

"Thank you, Great Scala, thank you, thank you. May I say how honored I am to have been able to—"

Thus begins the usual kiss-assery that comes with being a demi-goddess. For the first few weeks it was fun, now it's a major time suck. And I have a Ghost Tower about to explode and release three million homicidal spirits all over Purgatory. I hang up without saying goodbye and high-tail over to the Tower.

The building is almost in my backyard, but even if it wasn't, Ghost Tower Six would still be easy to find. The place is massive, rectangular, windowless and made of concrete. I rush towards the only door, a round metal portal. A stocky guard in ninja-style body armor stands nearby. Like all natives of Purgatory, the guard and I are quasis, a mix of human and demon.

I shoot him a quick wave. "Hey, Harold."

"Great Scala, thank Heavens you've come." Harold sets his bare palm onto an input pad by the door. A series of clicks sound as the locks release. "It's a code-red failure."

"I know, buddy. I'm on it."

A muscle twitches by Harold's eye. "The Cloud Carriers are close to rupture. Maybe we should follow the ghoul-rules and—"

"If you say move the souls to Hell, I'll kick you in the kneecaps." Since I grew up fighting demons gladiator-style in Purgatory's Arena, those kicks would hurt, too.

Harold's face takes on a terrified look that I can only describe as 'please don't send me to Hell'. "I meant no disrespect, Great Scala." He keeps standing there, cowering and not opening the door.

"You. Open. Portal. Now."

"Yes, Great Scala. Right away, Great Scala."

Sure, I could scold Harold for even suggesting Hell, but it wouldn't do any good. Twenty years ago, the King of

Hell invaded our lands, toppled the Quasi Republic, killed off anyone with a brain or spine, and set up ghouls as a puppet government. For the next two decades, the ghouls brainwashed quasis like Harold into mindless, submissive, rule-worshiping slaves. I kicked the ghouls out, but their brainwashing has stayed.

At last, the round portal swings open. I hurry inside.

The interior of the Ghost Tower is a concrete shell, noisy as Hell and empty of anything solid. There's a Control Room about halfway up the wall. Wardens stand at each corner, all of them in simple white uniforms. It's what fills this empty space that always takes my breath away. From floor to ceiling, the open air holds a shifting array of what look like clouds. They're actually huge vessels that enclose souls in a misty containment field. We call them Cloud Carriers.

The Lead Warden, Celia, steps to my side, her lion's tail twitching anxiously behind her. All quasis have an animal tail along with a power across the seven deadly sins. Celia's is wrath. I have two deadly-sin powers—lust and wrath—as well as a long, thin dragon-scale tail. Totes badass.

Celia yells to me over the din of our power generators. "So sorry to drag you in here again."

I shout back my reply. "No worries."

Total Lie. In truth, there's a ton to worry about. The Towers have had nine code-orange failures in the last week alone.

"The Carriers are unstable again," explains Celia quickly. "It's never been this bad."

"How do the reports look?"

"Fine." Celia pulls an electronic tablet from her pocket. "Perfect, even." Her features turn wide-eyed and pleading. "Are you sure you won't follow the ghoul-rules? Our old Masters were often very wise. Maybe the ghouls left the Orb here for a reason."

At the very mention of Lucifer's Orb, my hands ball into angry fists. I kick the ghouls out of Purgatory and what do they do? Hide the ultimate source of demonic magic in my homeland so I can only send souls to Hell. Screw them.

"We've been through this before," I reply. Celia opens her mouth, but I shut off her standard speech before she starts. "I know what you're about to say. A million new souls enter Purgatory each month. We're running out of places to put them, and that's why the Towers are ready to burst. But once I send a soul somewhere, even I can't take it back." I fold my arms over my chest. "I won't send innocents to Hell."

"Yes, Great Scala. As you say, Great Scala." Celia starts rapid-fire bowing, which is a new and somewhat cringeworthy move.

"We need to stop rehashing old territory and focus on the code-red. Which Carrier's at risk this time?"

Celia points to a cloud that's resting on the floor. "That one."

I scan the Tower from floor to ceiling. "No, I don't think so." Lately, I can tell at a glance if a Carrier's at risk.

Halfway up the walls, one cloud vibrates ominously. "Show me number thirteen."

Celia pulls up her tablet and starts pressing buttons. Above me, the clouds shift places until a new one takes up the entire mile-long concrete floor. Number Thirteen. Celia presses more buttons and the puffy structure solidifies into a rectangular shape, ready for inspection.

I walk up to the closest wall of mist; Celia follows right behind. We could easily step inside the Cloud Carrier itself, but that's not a safe thing to do. Purgatory isn't exactly happy-fun-time for these souls, and angry ghosts can kick some major ass.

"What level are we on?" Carriers are like cruise ships, only with levels instead of decks.

"A-Level."

"And how many levels are at risk in this Carrier?"

"All of them."

Yipes. "That's not good."

Our Carriers are driven by quantum theory. Dozens of levels jammed into different dimensions of the same cloud, that kind of thing. Saves us room, but it makes everything dangerously interconnected.

I move in closer until my nose almost touches the containment wall. The interior of the Carrier comes into view. It's a semi-transparent dream world. Soft grass, rolling fields, sunny sky. Spirits are sleeping under trees or curled onto blankets. Inches of space separate them from each other.

I exhale a satisfied breath. The field's crowded, sure, but

the souls are calm, comfortable and safe. This is the way it's supposed to work. Unfortunately, A-Level doesn't tell me why this Carrier was moving so strangely. A memory appears in my mind's eye. We've had trouble on this cloud before.

"Show me K-Level."

Celia clicks more buttons and a new scene appears. This time, it's a group of men and women, all ghosts, and all losing their freaking minds. Punching, clawing, pulling hair, tearing shirts, hanging from trees. Screaming incredibly inappropriate crap at each other. I can't hear what they say, but I read lips well enough to get the gist. Rough stuff.

An anxious weight settles onto my back. All these folks should be sleeping peacefully, like the souls on A-Level. Instead, they're wide-awake, crowded on top of each other, and pissed.

Before me, a pair of ghost fighters slams into the containment wall. The exterior of the whole Carrier shakes with the impact, sending shock waves through the rest of the clouds. If the ghosts break out here, it can cause a chain reaction across the whole Tower. At this point, my only consolation is that they're fighting with each other, and not trying to break out of the Carrier itself.

"What's the spirit density on this cloud, anyway?"

"Four hundred thousand souls."

I let out a low whistle. "That'll do it."

It's the same story everywhere, though. All the Carriers are packed-to-bursting, and the dead don't like being crowded any more than the living. It only takes one ghost to wake up, flip out, and start fighting. After that, the whole Carrier's at risk.

The battle inside the cloud gets vicious. Spectral bodies are hurled into the misty walls. The hazy barriers of the Carrier shake more violently.

Another body hits the containment wall. This time, a spider-web of white lines spread out from the impact point.

My breath catches. The walls are starting to break apart. It's never been this serious before. My mind races through ways to stop the damage. "Did you try lowering the charge on the containment field? The electricity might be zapping them awake."

"We tried that. No effect."

Another blow strikes the wall before me. The fracture lines spread. Some of the nearby Carriers start to vibrate as well. My pulse shoots through the roof.

"How about the concentration of mist?" That's what keeps the souls sedated and calm.

Celia taps on her tablet. "They look fine."

"Have a testing rod?"

Celia pulls what looks like a long silver nail from inside her jacket. "Sure."

I take the rod from her hands and gently move it into the cloud. Meanwhile, the ghosts inside get even more out of control. Bodies smash along the length of the Carrier wall. More fractures appear. Tension spreads up my neck and around my temples.

This could be it. The day we release millions of angry

ghosts into Purgatory, where they'll do what all mobs do. Tear everyone and everything apart.

I pull out the testing rod and check the surface. One-third of it now glows. "The mist levels in this cloud are only at thirty percent."

"That's impossible." All the blood drains from Celia's face. "We cranked everything up to maximum."

"The Towers were never designed to hold this many souls, Celia. I've seen it before. The systems get overloaded and downright glitchy."

More ghosts pound into the wall. This time, they see the fractures, too. It gives them bad ideas, as in: 'let's not fight each other, let's break out of here'. Long cracks form in the containment wall closest to us. Thin lines of mist leak out into the Ghost Tower.

Celia hugs her elbows. "What do we do?"

"Go to the Control Room. Have them call the Minister of Infrastructure. If anyone knows how to override whatever's holding back the mist, he will." The Minister's my old friend Walker. A super-talented engineer, Walker can always get the Ghost Towers working.

"Yes, Great Scala."

Celia races off to the Control Room. Meanwhile, I pace back and forth before the containment wall, thinking through my options. They aren't good. More cracks appear, deeper and longer this time. If the ghosts escape, the protocol's to flood the Tower with mist. Which probably won't be possible, considering that we can't fill the Carriers with enough mist. And if the ghosts get out, that's a worst-case scenario for yours truly. I'll be forced to move the escapees to Hell.

Come ooooooon, Walker.

Seconds drag by. The ghosts are hysterical now, clawing at the walls and crawling on top of each other. I start screaming at them, not that they can hear me.

"Calm down! Trust me, this isn't what you want!"

The fight inside the Carrier takes on a new edge. Weapons are added into the mix. Someone's broken off branches from the nearby trees, and the walls suffer a new level of pounding. One of the cracks opens wider. A misty hand pokes through and into the Tower beyond. A sense of heavy dread settles into my bones.

That's it. I've run out of time.

In my mind, I summon igni. Instantly, little lightning bolts of power swirl and dive around my palms like tiny silver fish. I can feel their excitement. This is what they're meant to do. Move souls. They form a whirlpool on the floor, the first step in creating a Soul Column that will send these spirits to their afterlife. Unfortunately, that afterlife will be in Hell.

My heart sinks. I've failed them.

With a great whoosh, the Cloud Carrier fills with mist, a thicker haze than I've ever seen before. The combatants drop their weapons, close their eyes, and slump over into a deep sleep. Exhaling a relieved breath, I command my igni to disappear.

At last. The mist levels are fixed. The souls are safe.

Wherever you are, Walker, I owe you one.

As Minister of Infrastructure, Walker does more than save my butt every time the Ghost Towers break down. He's also searching for Lucifer's Orb, and is pretty close to finding it, too. Once the Orb's out of Purgatory, I'll be free to move souls again. Whew.

Celia rushes back. "It worked." She pauses before me, her mouth thinning to a fierce line. "Look, I know you don't want to hear this, but we should follow the ghoul-rules here, and the ghouls wanted to send these souls to Hell. Who cares about a bunch of dead people when live quasis are at risk? If these ghosts escape, they'll tear Purgatory apart."

My eyebrows rise with surprise. My, my, myyyyyyy. What's with the sassy mouth? Say what you want about ghoul brainwashing, it usually makes my people cower versus confront. Fighting with a newly-feisty Celia is the last thing I need.

I lower my voice an octave, just to show I mean business. "No good souls go to Hell on my watch. Not unless we've no other choice."

Celia's entire body quivers as she speaks. "Our choice was already made for us. By the ghouls. All we have to do is act on it."

I watch Celia tremble; all the irritation drains right out of me. The ghouls spent twenty years brainwashing her. Her so-called Masters left only two months ago. I can't expect to erase years of conditioning in a matter of weeks. "When was the last time you slept, Celia?"

"Two days ago, Great Scala."

I rest my hand gently on her upper arm. "Go home. Take the day off. We'll talk about this later."

After a fast nod, Celia slowly walks away.

Suddenly, the power generators stop. Green lights flicker along the top of the Tower, showing that we're now running on back-up energy from Upper Purgatory. Everything turns eerily quiet.

My body goes on alert. Shutdowns like this only happen if the containment walls crash or if there's some serious diplomatic gunk going on. Maybe we're about to get an emergency visit from my mother, who's now Purgatory's President.

I cross my fingers, hoping it's Mom.

From across the concrete floor, my best friend Cissy appears in the doorway. She's our new Senator for Diplomacy, so that puts things solidly into the 'diplomatic gunk category' of shutdown. I exhale a shaky breath. I don't need any more adrenaline rushes today.

My best friend runs at me at full speed, her golden retriever tail wagging busily behind her. Cissy is tall and willowy with tawny brown eyes and blonde hair that falls in neat ringlets. Today, she wears purple Senatorial robes and a worried look on her face. She stops to a skid at my side.

"You're in your Scala robes, good."

Huh. Cissy wants me to look all official. Must be an ultra-important diplomatic thingy going on.

"What's up, Cis? Is Mom coming over?" I wouldn't be

surprised if she's been monitoring this whole scene from her office via the Control Room.

"No. Do you want the bad news, or the really-bad news?"

"Let's start with the bad."

"Adair's coming over with all the other inter-realm Diplomats."

I let out a long groan. *Fuuuuuuuuuuck.*

That's Adair as in Lady Adair, the nutjob who wants to marry my very-much-in-love-with-me boyfriend Lincoln, the High Prince of the demon-fighting thrax. A few months ago, Adair became Thrax Diplomat to Purgatory. Since then, she hasn't done dick as a diplomat. Her sole purpose seems to be following me around, trying to cause trouble. Last week alone, she started three petitions about my supposed incompetence as a leader. No one signed them, but still. Sheesh.

"What's my personal stalker up to this time?"

"Adair's performing an official emergency inspection of this Ghost Tower, followed by some kind of formal announcement."

"Ugh. That could be a problem." Especially since one of my Cloud Carriers looks like Swiss cheese. Not exactly inspection-friendly.

Cissy shakes her head sadly. "I'm so sorry, Myla. I've been trying to run interference for you."

"Hey, just because you're the Senator for Diplomacy doesn't mean you have to be Adair's babysitter. It's bad enough that she took over your day with her *emergency*." I make little quotation marks with my fingertips when I say that last word.

"Goes with the job," retorts Cissy with a shrug. "Diplomats can't go around inspecting Purgatory's buildings without having our Senator for Diplomacy along."

"Still, you've better stuff to do." I give the floor a frustrated kick with my sandal. "When will she be here, anyway?"

"In a few minutes," says Cissy. "I just found out about this myself. You know how Adair's been grilling me about the Ghost Towers. I told her it's classified, but she interviewed some Wardens in this tower and heard all about our problems."

"Man, I hope it wasn't Celia."

"Who's Celia?"

"My Lead Warden. She's been a little twitchy lately."

"Well, whoever it was, Adair's now in a big huff."

Unfortunately, as Thrax Diplomat, Adair has every right to huff. If the ghosts break free, her people will be called into Purgatory to clean up the mess. And if Adair uses her Diplomatic role to make noise about our Tower problems, there'll be a ton more pressure on me to move souls to Hell. My people tolerate my changing the ghoul-rules—they're even excited to get rid of the Orb—but that's only because they don't know they have Ghost-Tower-pressure-cookers in their back yards.

"Can you stall her for a bit? I need to fix up this Carrier." The ghosts are already sleepwalking around, finding comfy spots to snooze, but the containment walls look B-A-D.

Cissy stares at the spider web of fractures along the Carrier wall, noticing them for the first time. "Myla, this thing almost broke wide open. I've seen smashed windshields that look better."

"I know. That's why I need some time. Can you get me an hour? We'll do a quick patch job."

"Sure, girlfriend. I'll run some fresh interference for you, too. Try to neutralize Adair."

"Thanks, but I still say you should be doing your day job. Or, better yet, hanging with Zeke." Since Cissy became Senator, she hasn't seen too much of her boyfriend, Zeke.

"First of all, you are my day job. Second, I spent years chasing after Zeke from afar. It won't hurt him to be in the background for a little while. And third, neutralizing Adair is fun."

"You're the best, Cis."

"Stay safe." She gives me a big hug and then walks away at double-speed.

For a time, I watch the Cloud Carriers drift lazily about the Tower.

"You guys stay safe, too."

2

Over the next hour, we do the sketchiest patch job on a Cloud Carrier, ever. It won't be a solid fix until Walker comes by, but it should be enough for Adair's inspection. In fact, my repair team has just left the Tower when Adair appears in the doorway.

"Greetings, Great Scala."

She's a pale girl with pinched features, long blonde hair and the mismatched eyes that mark every thrax. She wears a butter-yellow gown, which is the color of her House, Acca. Behind her steps the Ghoul Delegate, a seven-foot-tall man in a flowing black robe. He has a colorless, scarred face and pronounced limp. The Angelic Delegate is with them, too. She's an elderly grandma-type with ebony skin and a shock of white hair. We aren't on diplomatic terms with Hell anymore, so there's no demon representative.

Adair marches across the floor, her mismatched eyes

glaring red-hot death in my direction. Meh. She can kiss my ass.

The group stops before me. Cissy steps forward, looking very official in her Senatorial robes. There's a glimmer in her eye that I like very much, indeed. I've known Cissy since we were kids, and that look means one thing: whatever interference she ran for me with Adair, it's gooooooooooood.

"Greetings, Great Scala," says Cissy smoothly. "As the Thrax Senator for Diplomacy, I'm here to witness the inspection of this Ghost Tower followed by an official announcement from the Thrax Dele—" Cissy pauses dramatically, tapping her chin. "Ah, how silly of me to forget. Before we begin, I've had a rush communiqué from Antrum. A special message for the Great Scala." She reaches into her robes and pulls out a small silver envelope. Lincoln's seal is mighty visible. Nice.

Cissy is a genius. Now, Adair will spend her time obsessing over that message and—with any luck—not inspect anything during her inspection of the Cloud Carriers. I could kiss Cissy right now.

"Here's the message." My best friend offers me the envelope with a flourish. "There's been a demon sighting in Purgatory. The High Prince will be taking care of this personally. He requests that you join him for the battle." She looks meaningfully to Adair. "Details are in this letter."

I take the envelope and smile, smile, smile. "Thank you, Senator." I could do my happy dance, I'm so pumped. Cissy must've pulled some strings to find a demon to kill and get a rush courier over to Antrum, all in an hour. What a girl. And demon fighting with Lincoln? Today is definitely on the upswing.

Adair stares at the envelope in my hands, and then looks to Cissy. "Weren't there any messages from Prince Lincoln for me?"

"Nothing for you," says Cissy slyly. "Now, you wanted to perform an inspection that would be followed by a formal announcement. What in the Tower would you like to inspect?"

Adair looks around the Tower floor. "Is Lead Warden Celia here? She could give me some guidance."

"No, she's got the day off." Glad I gave it to her, too, considering that Adair's asking for guidance from her. Unfortunately, that means my Celia may be Adair's source about our troubles with the Ghost Towers. Note to self: look into this situation ASAP. I hate the thought of firing Celia, but it may come to that.

Adair glances at the Cloud Carriers, but her gaze keeps flickering back to the silver envelope, which I've decided to use as a fan.

Cissy rocks on her heels. "We're waiting."

"Everything seems fine," says Adair quickly. "Thank you, Senator."

"You're most welcome. And now, you have an announcement for us?"

"That I do." Adair straightens the neckline of her medieval-style gown. "My esteemed colleagues, I'm here today to announce that as Thrax Delegate to Purgatory, I've launched a formal investigation of the Ghost Towers. I have it on good authority that these things are ready to explode, releasing millions of angry ghosts onto Purgatory's streets. And when spirits are this furious, they can tear down buildings, break through walls, even kill people." She makes a stabbing motion with her arm, miming murder.

"We all know what angry ghosts can do, Adair." *But thanks for the theatrics.*

She rounds on me. "It's a catastrophe waiting to happen, and it's all due to your mismanagement. These Towers ran fine when the ghouls were here."

"The ghouls didn't have to deal with Lucifer's Orb," I say. "Do you know what the Orb does?"

"Please. Per Inter-Realm law, it's my role to ask questions in a formal investigation." Adair pulls a sheet of paper from her pocket. "Let's begin. The souls in this Ghost Tower seem perfectly ready for Heaven or Hell. Why don't you use your Scala powers and move them all at once, in a big iconigration?"

"I tried. I could only move them all to Hell." *In fact, I barely stopped the iconigration in time, not that I'm telling her that.* "As I started to say before, Lucifer's Orb is now in Purgatory. You know what that means, right?"

"No." Adair shrugs. "Should I?"

I stare at her for a long minute. Could she really be that oblivious to the challenges facing Soul Processing in Purgatory? She is our Thrax Diplomat, after all. There's a smug, know-it-all look in her eyes that confirms my worst suspicions. She's absolutely and blissfully oblivious.

"Here's the deal. The Orb is the ultimate source of demonic power in the after-realms. Right now, it's forcing me to send all souls to Hell. Long story short, I'm not sending spirits anywhere until the Orb is gone."

Adair taps her chin. "And there are no other reasons preventing you from moving souls?"

"Like what?"

"Your grip on igni, for instance. Maybe the problem isn't that Lucifer's Orb is too strong. Could be, you're too weak."

"Weak? I sent Armageddon to Hell with my powers."

"You were strong at one time, sure. But now? I see it as my job to use my unique knowledge of igni to assess your current state. After all, I was initiated Scala Heir by Verus, the Queen of the Angels."

I set my fist on my hip. I can't believe she's bringing up that sham initiation. Verus only did a fake ceremony with Adair in order to activate my real powers. Adair even admitted as much herself.

"Come on. Don't you remember? We were all in a bunker, right before my battle with Armageddon. That's when you came clean that your initiation was a sham. You even confessed how your witch-friend Gianna faked your power over igni."

Adair does an awesome job of looking totally shocked. "I don't remember that at all."

"Senator Frederickson was in the bunker with us." I

turn to Cissy. "Do you remember the Diplomat's confession?"

"Vividly."

Adair rests her fingertips against her throat and sighs. "The friendship between the two of you is touching, really touching. But it won't stop this investigation." Translation: she's saying that Cissy's lying for me. My blood starts to boil with rage.

The Ghoul Delegate raises his hand. "What should we do about the Ghost Towers? I, for one, am very concerned. I'd appreciate some insight from the Thrax Delegate."

Note to self: hate that guy.

"I don't know yet," Adair says with a sad shake of her head. "The mismanagement issues here are pretty severe. I need time to complete my investigation."

My hands ball into angry fists. Mismanagement issues? This has gone too far. Either I bash Adair on her turned-up nose, or I call an end to this meeting.

Le sigh. As satisfying as a punch would be, it would only give Adair more fodder to make trouble.

"Great idea to investigate," I say sternly. "Why don't you go do that? Like, somewhere else?" I point to the door. "And right now?"

Adair neatly refolds her paper and resets it into her pocket. "Agreed. I'll depart, if that's acceptable to you, Senator."

Cissy waves her hand towards the exit portal. "You're all free to go."

"Thank you for your time today." Adair grips my hands in her own. "Good luck."

I wince. Adair's palms feel cold, clammy and stomach-churningly gross. I release them quickly. "Good-bye, Adair."

"Follow me, people." Adair finally walks away, happily chatting with her two diplomatic colleagues. No doubt, she's telling them horror stories about how the Ghost Towers will explode any second.

Once they're gone, I lean my head back and groan. "Oy. I really need to kill me some demons." I raise the silver envelope. "This was your handiwork, wasn't it?"

"Yeah. I thought it would keep her inspection short, at least."

"It totally did. She'd have actually inspected something if it weren't for you. By the way, how'd you find the demon so quickly?" Only a real sighting would've called out a thrax warrior.

A mischievous look crosses Cissy's face. "I might have imported it. Let's just say I owe the Furor Delegate a big favor."

"Damn, girlfriend. You wheeler-dealer you. Thanks."

"You're welcome." Cissy frowns. "Now, are you ready for the really-bad news?"

That's right. When I first saw Cissy, she said she had bad news and really-bad news.

"Oops, I forgot about that part. Spill."

"You know how Walker had almost found Lucifer's Orb?"

My stomach sinks to my toes. I don't like where this is going. "Yeeeeeeeeah. He was digging up a crypt in Lower Purgatory."

"Well, the Orb wasn't in the crypt. They finally got it open. There was a coffin inside, but it was empty."

"Not good."

"Well, not entirely empty. A riddle was carved inside it."

"Better. What does it say?"

"No idea. Walker's trying to figure it out."

My tail pounds my thigh in frustration. "Does Walker have any idea when he'll find the Orb?"

Cissy shakes her head. "I'm sorry, Myla."

"Damn. If we run out of Soul Storage, I don't have a lot of options. I can't send these folks to Hell."

"Hang in there. You're doing the right thing. Look, I can stall on the announcement of Adair's investigation. The office of the President is the only group that has to know for now. That'll keep things quiet from the public, at least for a little while longer."

"Good idea. With any luck, we keep this under the radar until the Orb is history."

Cissy wraps her arm around my shoulder. "Besides, Walker's brilliant. If anyone can find the Orb quickly, he can." She points towards the door. "Plus, your old station wagon's already waiting outside."

"Betsy?"

"None other."

What a great idea for Cissy to drop off my old wagon. Betsy's such a piece of crap; no one would suspect the

Great Scala would tool around in it. I drive her when I want to go incognito.

"Come on, quasi girl," says Cissy. "I know you've been fixing Ghost Tower emergencies all day. Go kill stuff. You'll feel better."

"Thanks." I grin from ear to ear. "You know what? I definitely will."

3

I pace the dusty floor of an abandoned auto plant in Middle Purgatory. Lincoln's note was most specific. Any second now, he'll show up so we can kill us a Durus demon, a metal-loving monster that I've never had the fun of skewering before. Nice. After the unpleasantness with Adair at the Ghost Tower, I could sure use the break.

I scan the dimly-lit factory, my senses on high alert for any sign of the Durus. All I find is a huge building whose tiled floor is covered in a maze of winding conveyor belts. Random auto parts are stacked into towering piles. No Durus, though.

Bummer.

A strange noise sounds a few feet behind me: a low half-cough.

Spinning about, I find a familiar outline waiting for me in the shadows. Someone tall with broad shoulders, military bearing, and a mop of loose brown hair. His black body armor has the Rixa eagle crest emblazoned on his chest. Even in the pale light, I can see his mismatched irises: one's wheat brown, while the other's slate-gray. Joy bubbles through my chest.

Rushing over, I wrap my arms around Lincoln's neck, my tail swaying contentedly behind me. He tightens our embrace, his body feeling all warm and firm against mine. I inhale a long breath, catching his yummy scent of forest pine and leather. A deep part of me, some place that always feels lost and empty without him, starts to overflow with his touch and love. I nuzzle my head into his shoulder. "Lincoln."

"Hello, Myla." Lincoln leans back and eyes me from head to toe. The intensity of his gaze makes me suddenly self-conscious of how I look in my Scala robes. Curvy figure, full mouth, bright blue eyes and long auburn hair that hangs in waves down my back. He pulls me close once again. "You look lovely."

"You're not so bad yourself." I am a big fan of his black body armor. Yum.

Lincoln rests his left hand against my cheek, his thumb brushing my skin in gentle arcs. "It's been too long."

"Another busy week for both of us."

I rule the quasi-demons of Purgatory while Lincoln does the same with the thrax of Antrum. Our two realms could literally not be farther apart, or more complex to manage. We're lucky if we catch each other for an hour or two each week. And if Walker says he won't schlep us around anymore with his secret ghoul portals, we won't even have that. Today's a rare occurrence, an official visit from Antrum using transfer stations. Normally, it takes days to get all the paperwork and approvals, even for royalty. Demon-related stuff gets special treatment.

"I missed you, too." I slowly raise my mouth to his. Lincoln's lips are soft and warm. My body goes tingly all over. I feel like someone who hasn't breathed easily in ages and then, inhales pure oxygen.

Lincoln presses his forehead to mine. "What's going on? Cissy's message said it was urgent."

There's a lot to tell, but I'll hit the most important topic first. "Remember how I thought Walker had almost found Lucifer's Orb?"

"I remember. Wasn't he digging up a crypt last week?"

"Yup."

Lucifer was the King of the Angels; he even outranked Dad. Then, the guy went nuts and got imprisoned. His Crown holds angelic magic, while his Orb contains demonic power. Man, I want that thing out of my backyard.

I shake my head. "Walker's been tracking down leads on the Orb for months. We really thought this crypt was the end of the line. But all Walker found inside was a coffin with a riddle carved inside."

"What did the riddle say?"

"Walker's working on it." My voice lowers to a whisper. "I've no idea when we can restart Soul Processing. And in the meantime, the Cloud Carriers are getting more packed every day. I won't send those innocents to Hell, though. I can't."

Lincoln examines me carefully. "There's something else bothering you, though."

Wow. He nailed that one, for sure. Despite my worries, a warm and happy feeling rolls down to my toes. No one reads me the way Lincoln does.

"Tell me what's wrong." His voice is low, soft and comforting.

"Adair is getting worse, too. Today, she launched an official investigation about the overcrowding in our Carriers. If Purgatory finds out those Towers could blow, my people will lose it."

Lincoln rakes his left hand through his mop of brown hair. "This is all my fault. Adair's been asking me to play King and Queen since we were kids. I should never have even considered a marriage contract with her. Mother warned me not to, but their damned army—"

"Hey, there's more to the Adair-problem than just you. Look at Verus. She's the Queen of the Angels and a freaking oracle. You'd think she'd have known better than to give Adair a sham initiation as Scala Heir. But she did, complete with Gianna using witchcraft to create fake igni. Now, Adair is saying that the ceremony was real."

Lincoln's quiet for a while, his eyes lost in thought. "Tell you what." He tightens his grip around my waist. "I'm staying."

"Here? In Purgatory?" Official visits are typically less than an hour. "How long?"

"As long as it takes. This is serious, Myla. We should tackle it as a team."

That awesome warm-happy-tingly feeling rolls through me again, only even stronger this time. I wrap my arms around his neck. "You're amazing."

Lincoln whispers in my ear. "How about we go kill this thing, then head over to your house?"

"You and Cissy are spoiling me today."

"Don't say that. You've made a really brave choice to stand by those souls. You're carrying a huge responsibility right now. This is the least I can do. Cissy feels the same way."

A great roar echoes through the darkened factory, breaking the moment. The cry is so deep and powerful, bits of dingy wall-glass tumble from their rusted window frames.

Hellooooo, Durus demon.

Battle energy careens through my muscles. "You're right. Let's go take down this Durus."

I snap into fighting mode, my mind zooming through different approaches and scenarios. "How about we start with long-swords, and then finish with a net?"

"Excellent."

We take out our baculum, igniting the silver rods as long-swords made of angelfire. Once the flames begins to crackle, the threads of my Scala robes instantly realign into white battle armor. I have to admit, dynamic robe re-alignment is one of the cooler benefits of being the Great Scala.

Before us, garbage heaps scrape across the floor, combining into a larger shape.

"Guess someone's decided to come to us," says Lincoln. "So thoughtful for a demon."

On the ground nearby, the trash-pile shifts at a faster rate: melting, reforming, rising. The sour smell of burned rubber and engine grease fills the air. Within seconds, the metal refuse resolidifies as a massive man that's eight feet tall and almost as broad.

The Durus is here.

The demon's arms are a mash-up of jackhammers and belt riveters. It stands on legs made of massive steel beams; strange smokes and acids spew from its torso of engine parts. The head's the nastiest bit of all, a crazy mix of punch-needles and round-saws with crushed-glass eyes and a huge, gaping mouth full of moving-piston teeth.

My breath catches. I have to admit, this thing is way cool.

The Durus speaks in a deep and rusty voice. "Leave my lair."

Lincoln moves into battle stance: feet wide apart, his long-sword raised high. "That's not going to happen, buddy."

With lightning speed, the demon raises its arm to strike Lincoln. I get ready to leap into a counter-attack. However, the demon does something unexpected. It stops, actually freezing in place for a few seconds. After that, its crushed-glass eyes begin to glow with demonic fire.

Lincoln and I share a confused look. That's strange.

Durus demons are one of the few breeds whose eyes don't light up.

The Durus rounds on me. "Show me how you move souls, Great Scala." With clunky movements, he rips a length of conveyor belt off the floor and chucks it at me; I easily leap out of the way. The broken machinery lands on the floor with a room-shaking crash. The Durus takes a lumbering step closer. "Fight me like you fought Armageddon."

I frown, considering. Two months ago, I blasted Armageddon and his ghoul cronies out of Purgatory. It took a bit to figure out my brand-spanking-new igni power, but eventually, I trapped the King of Hell in a Soul Column. I can still picture him howling with bone-crunching rage as he plummeted under the earth, to be forever locked into Hell. Fun times.

Beside me, Lincoln speaks in a low voice. "Your call, Myla. If you send him back to Hell, he'll be locked down there forever, but he'll still be alive."

"That's true." However, I can't move any souls right now, so I've been itching to use my igni. "But I could use the practice with my powers." I turn to the demon. "You've got yourself a deal."

I raise my arms high above my head. Closing my eyes, I reach out with my thoughts to the dark igni, the tiny bolts of power and light that transport evil souls to Hell. *Come to me, my little ones.* Instantly, their grating voices fill my mind, a cacophony of rasps and whispers that only I can hear.

Opening my eyes, I watch the tiny white lightning bolts materialize before my outstretched palms. More come into existence, soaring and diving about my hands like tiny silver fish. Soon, hundreds have arrived, their bodies making intricate flow-patterns that wind up my arms.

My sweet igni. A sense of peace and power rolls through me. I am the Great Scala, and this is what I'm meant to do.

Sensing the igni's power, the Durus leans back on its heels, beating his chest with his great fists. Opening his piston-mouth, the demon lets out another ear-splitting roar.

At the sound of this cry, my inner wrath demon kicks into high gear, electrifying my nervous system with rage. *Time to go home, buddy.* I lower my arms and command the igni to slide onto the floor and create a Soul Column, the vehicle that will send the Durus to Hell.

Only, the igni don't move.

I frown, my forehead creased with confusion. This can't be right.

The igni keep whirling around my arms. Inside my head, they start rasping out an odd song that makes me wince. I catch the words 'dragon' and 'must get' in there, but otherwise, it's a bunch of nonsense.

I mentally command the igni with more force. It makes no difference. Their voices keep chattering away in their strange cacophony, their sounds faster and harsher by the second. Finally, I resort to speaking out loud, something I've never had to do before.

"I order you! Send the Durus to Hell!"

In reply, the igni's song turns furious in its intensity. I've no idea what they're saying anymore, only that the sounds are super-painful to hear. I set my hands over my ears. "Enough!"

Instantly, the igni disappear. It takes me a full minute to regain my focus and senses. Damn, those dark igni can take over your brain when they want to.

I scan the factory floor for Lincoln. He's fighting the Durus, and probably has been for some time. The demon's now missing a riveter-arm; half its face is gone. The Durus swings its remaining band-saw arm at Lincoln, who leaps away while changing his baculum into a net of white flame. Tossing it high, Lincoln encases the demon in his angelfire web.

A pause follows. In a moment that lasts forever, Lincoln and the Durus stare at each other. The demon's face droops with an unasked question: what can this thrax possibly do with a net?

In one swift movement, Lincoln cinches the net-cords into a tight ball. The angelfire strands are razor-sharp, tearing easily through the demon, slicing its metal body into thousands of tiny shards. The bits tumble to the floor, softly jingling as they fall. The place where the demon once stood is now a shredded pile of scrap metal.

The Durus is dead.

I should cheer, but I'm still a little freaked out my impromptu igni concert.

Lincoln steps up to my side. "What happened? Are you alright?"

"Yeah, I'm fine. My igni wouldn't listen to my commands, though. They were singing some kind of message to me instead. Weird." I punch his upper arm. "By the way, nice job, you."

"I've fought Durus before. Normally, they're incredibly fast. The eyes shouldn't light up, either. Something was wrong with this one." He frowns, resetting his baculum into their holster on his thigh. "Not that there's anything wrong with an easy battle every once in awhile." A crafty look lights up his eyes. "Ready to head out? I want to hear all about what's going on."

Happiness bubbles up inside me. That's right. Lincoln's staying for days now. Awesome. Whatever other plans I had, I'm clearing my schedule and enjoying our time together. I take his hand in mine and head for the door.

Betsy's still waiting outside.

4

Lincoln and I hunt through the contents of my fridge, looking to scrounge up a quick snack before dinner. Like most nights, my parents are off running Purgatory as Madame President and First Man, so it's fend for yourself time. Turns out, killing a Durus makes you hungry. Plus, that weird-igni-concert was no-fun. I need me some grub.

Lincoln digs through a shelf loaded with plastic containers. "I still can't get over this place. So much nicer than Arx Hall."

My new house is nicer than Lincoln's underground castle in Antrum?

"I don't know. Arx Hall's pretty sweet."

"Sure, it all looks good," says Lincoln. "But we've no electricity, no phones, no computers. Our kitchens are still stuck in the Middle Ages. There's a larder, a buttery, an icehouse, and a guy whose only job is to ensure that meats roast properly. I kid you not; I pay someone to be my Master of Turning Spits. It takes a legion of people two days to make me a sandwich." He gestures open-armed at the fridge. "Now, this is so much better."

"The kitchen here's pretty kick-ass, I'll grant you that."

Once I got to be the Great Scala—and Mom became Purgatory's President—I knew we'd get an upgrade in housing. The place we ended up in was recently abandoned by a wealthy ghoul collective (they don't use the term 'family') so it's essentially a mash-up of Goth haunted house and high-tech superstore. And for once, the ghouls didn't cheap out on the electronics, either. The kitchen's the nicest spot, a huge space covered in stainless steel and the latest gadgetry from Earth. There's a long shiny table on the right-hand side of the room. On the left is where all the inscrutable appliances hang out.

Lincoln slides out a plastic container filled with multicolored goop. "What in blazes is this?"

"One of Dad's creations." As an archangel General, my father has a list of superpowers a mile long. Expertise in demon lore and battle strategy rank up at the top. Being a decent cook isn't on the list, period. "Dad doesn't have to eat, but he still likes combining random stuff in a pan. Lately, he's been stashing it in the fridge, too."

"Should I open it?"

"Don't, really. It'll be the most disgusting thing you've ever smelled."

"Now, I've got to open it." Lincoln lifts the lid a crack. The scent of rotten eggs and dumpster juice slams into our faces. “Damn, that’s nasty.” He closes the lid quickly and shoves it back into the fridge.

“Told you so.” Giving up on the fridge, I go to the stainless steel cabinet where all the Demon bars are stored. Along the way, I notice a pile of written sheets on the countertop. I’d know that handwriting anywhere. It’s Walker’s. As a ghoul and family friend, Walker portals in and out of our kitchen daily. Lately, he’s taken to leaving notes behind, especially if he needs to update us on sensitive stuff.

“Hey, there’s something here from Walker. I bet it’s about the Orb.” My heart rate kicks up a notch. Walker wouldn’t leave a note unless something big had happened. Hopefully, it’s something super-awesome.

“Anything good?” asks Lincoln.

I scan the letter. “Depends how you define good. This is all about Walker’s search for the Orb. He figured out the riddle in the crypt, which is amazing, but it led him to a warehouse in Lower Purgatory that’s filled with magical junk.” I skim through more pages filled with long equations and notes on stuff like probability theory. I flash the sheets at Lincoln. “Any idea what this means?”

“Got me. Walker knows his stuff, though.”

“Well, the bottom line’s that the Orb’s definitely in the warehouse, but Walker has no idea when he’ll find it.” I toss the sheets onto the countertop. “So, we’re back to where we were before. No clue when I can start moving souls again.” I return my attention to the stainless steel cabinets. “Time for comfort food.” I grab a

Demon bar, rip it open, and bite into the chocolate-y goodness.

Lincoln slides out a bag of carrots from the fridge and starts to munch. "You know, what you're eating there is a tiny smidgeon of granola and a whole bunch of chocolate."

"Hence the name Demon bar." I bite off another chunk. "I'm at peace with that."

"Only you, Myla."

I polish off the bar. "So, I can't get over how my igni acted around that Durus. They wouldn't do what I told them. They only wanted to sing. And it was the dark igni too, so their music was a bunch of screeching. Think about two-dozen Yoko Ono clones doing speed metal covers. That's pretty much the idea."

Lincoln starts laughing so hard, he almost chokes on a carrot. "What were they singing about?"

"Something about dragons and finding someone. I don't know. Finally, I told them to shut up and they went away. It was so strange."

"Doesn't sound like a big deal to me. Don't they pop in every so often with odd messages, anyway? This is just the first time they did it when you were telling them to do something else."

"That's true." The igni are notorious for chattering on about cryptic nonsense.

"I wouldn't worry about it, not unless it happens again." Lincoln bites off more carrot. "Now, tell me more about Adair. Let's start with the investigation. What's she looking into, specifically?"

"How the Ghost Towers are overcrowded and ready to blow. It's an official inquiry, so there's no way to bury it. Cissy said she could stall the news getting out, though. So, that's a help."

"Nice to have friends in high places."

"You're telling me." I frown. "But after announcing her investigation, Adair asked if I couldn't move souls to Heaven because I've lost some of my powers. I hate to admit it, but after the igni ignored me with the Durus, her words have really gotten under my skin."

"You losing your powers? That's impossible."

"No, it's possible, alright. There's one disease where a Scala loses their igni. It's called the Bloodstone Curse." I'm tempted to discuss the symptoms, but I've had enough nastiness to contemplate for one day.

"So there's one disease where a Scala loses igni. Whatever. You're the most powerful Scala in a thousand years. Adair's just trying to rile you up."

"Most likely." I raise my pointer finger, as if an idea's just occurred to me. "Hey, why can't she stalk you for a change?"

"Antrum's totally locked-down. If she got within fifty yards of me without an official reason to be there, my guards would chuck her in the dungeons like that." Lincoln snaps his fingers. "So, unfortunately, you have to be the focus of her mania." He bows slightly at the waist. "My sincere apologies."

"Well, now that you're here, I'm sure we can share the load." I tear open another Demon bar.

Lincoln's right eyebrow lifts in disbelief. "Aren't you going to ruin your dinner?"

"What are you, my mom? Besides, my parents won't be back for hours. Dinner is late-night thing around here, if we get to it at all."

Lincoln sets aside his carrots, a sudden gleam in his eyes. "So, I've been thinking about your warehouse problem."

"And?"

"What if I call in the thrax Alchemists?"

I munch more Demon bar and ponder. For thrax royalty, Alchemists are like food tasters, only with magic. Everyone wants to control the King and Queen of the Thrax, and lots of bad-minded folks try enchantments, potions, you name it. Thrax Alchemists test stuff for evil magic.

"It's a thought at that," I say.

"Do you think Walker would be insulted? He's been running this operation all along and you'll be bringing in new faces."

"No, he's a practical guy. There's a huge warehouse of magical stuff to search through. I'm sure he'd love all the help he can get."

"Well, he'll love the Alchemists, that's for certain. They're more scientists than sorcerers."

"But do they know a lot about enchantments and stuff on machines? Looking at Walker's note, I guess the warehouse is full of them."

"Sure." He gestures to the mixer. "Let me show you."

Our gazes lock, and the world seems to freeze for a full minute. I'm suddenly very aware that we're all alone in my house. No parents. Nowhere to be. Just time, quiet and each other…Something that hasn't happened in weeks. The air crackles with electricity and anticipation. The lust demon side of my lust-and-wrath combo powers awakens within me.

A sneaky smile rounds my lips. "What are you going to show me?"

"Why, the mixer, of course."

My heart kicks harder as I wonder what Lincoln really plans to do. I turn to face the bizarre contraption on the countertop. "Okay, I'm listening."

Lincoln slips up behind me, the firm contours of his chest brushing against my back in a way that's most distracting, especially for someone who's supposedly demonstrating household appliances. He firmly grips the countertop on either side of my body, and then speaks into my ear, his voice all low, slow and growly. "Almost every group in the after-realms has magic users. Thrax and the House of Striga, Furor and the Hexenwings, even humans. Any one of them could place different hexes and spells on each of the buttons here."

"Why is it that everything you say sounds sexy?" My voice comes out a bit husky, as well. "This is a mixer."

He nuzzles into my neck, sending pleasant shivers down my torso. "I don't know what you're talking about. As I was saying. My Alchemists know how to detect that magic, and then undo it. For you, they could change it. Make it do whatever you want. Even find the Orb."

"Whatever I want? That could work." I grin and lean backwards, allowing my body to press more tightly against his. Damn, that feels niiiiiiiiiice. "We have to be careful, though. After the ghouls, my people freak about outsiders doing anything major in our government."

"Walker has his secret portals in and out of Antrum. No one would ever have to know."

"There could be other problems, too." My mouth starts talking without any conscious direction from my brain. "Quasis have inner demons. They can be hard to control. Maybe even frightening."

"I'm not worried." He leans in closer, his voice turning growly again. "Inner demons are rather intriguing, don't you think?"

I pause, a realization appearing in my mind. "We've stopped talking about Alchemy, haven't we?"

"Yes. I believe we've begun discussing your inner lust demon."

Crap, I think he's right. Somewhere between Walker's portals and the words 'don't you think?' I totally segued onto my adjustment issues with my inner lust demon. As in, I'm actively avoiding dealing with her presence.

Lincoln nuzzles my ear. "You haven't shown her to me since the night of the ball in Purgatory."

"Yup." For a reason. That was the night of the infamous 'hedgerow maze incident'. Whenever my inner lust demon gets out, she makes me go nuts and do crazy stuff. On that fateful night, I almost stripped down naked and tackled Lincoln in a hedgerow maze, with all of thrax nobility hanging out at a Ball nearby. That sure was classy.

Lincoln shifts his weight, so his upper thigh presses between my legs from behind. "I'd like to see that part of you again, when you're ready."

And, yow, that feels good. I start to reconsider my avoidance strategy. Maybe my lust demon and I only need to spend more time together. After all, Lincoln and I see each other so rarely, and then mostly in public. Not a lot of bonding opportunities, there.

From across the mansion, I hear the unmistakable sound of the front door opening.

Someone's home. Huh. Can't decide if that's a good thing or a bad thing.

"Myla, is that you?"

I cup my hand by my mouth. "Yeah, Mom. I'm in the kitchen."

Dad's voice sounds next. "We brought pizza!"

Lincoln nips my ear with his teeth, sending one last shiver of desire down my belly. "We'll have to continue this discussion later." He steps away and leans against the opposite counter. We share an awkward smile while my inner lust demon coils and fumes inside my soul. She isn't happy about this situation. Not one bit.

But for now, there's nothing either of us can do about it.

5

My parents, Lincoln and I sit around the kitchen table, polishing off our second pepperoni pizza. Dad nibbles at his slice for show; the rest of us chow down.

Mom positively beams at Lincoln. "It's such a treat to see you." With her auburn hair, curvy body, and long dragon-scale tail, my mother looks like an older version of me, only in a purple suit.

"Good to be seen," says Lincoln.

Mom glances at the wall clock. "Aren't you usually back in Antrum by now?"

"Yes, but I'd like to stay for a while, if that's alright with you."

"Of course," says Mom. "It's kind of your parents to spare you."

"Mother will have her price, as always."

I stop mid-chew. If Queen Octavia has a price, I'm probably not going to like it. "What is it?"

Lincoln stares at me out of his right eye. "You know what she wants, Myla."

Oh, crap. Now, I remember.

There's one thing Lincoln's Mom has been going on about for weeks: a Ball of Welcome in my honor. So far, I've been dodging her, saying that a Ball would take me away from Purgatory for too long. But now that Lincoln is MIA from Antrum to help me, I can't really say I won't leave Purgatory for her. I make my yuck-face. "Yeah, I know what she wants, alright."

Mom's eyes sparkle with hidden laughter. "She already contacted me about it. Requested that your father and I attend as well."

Dad leans back in his chair. "You're not alone, Myla. Formal events aren't my favorite thing, either."

My father and I share a smile. He has handsome features, a chiseled jawline, cocoa-colored skin, and bright blue eyes. His gray suit hangs a little loose on his once-buff frame. Armageddon imprisoned Dad in Hell for nearly two decades. I freed my father a few months ago, but Dad's still not back to full strength.

"Let's move onto more pleasant topics." Dad rubs his palms together. "Anything in particular you two want to discuss tonight? Future plans, maybe?"

I roll my eyes. No question what Dad's hinting around about. As an archangel, my father's been alive since the beginning of time. Until I came along, he never had a child. Now that he's got the hang of it, he wants me married and giving him a grandkid, pronto.

I'm having none of it. "We're not talking about weddings right now."

"Then, I'll ask someone else." Dad turns to Lincoln. "Anything you want to say?"

"If I were enacting the thrax betrothal ceremony for a High Prince," says Lincoln. "I wouldn't do it over pizza. To begin with, it takes time to get the betrothal jewels out of the Royal Vaults." He sets his hand on mine. "And it all requires far more of a sense of occasion."

Marriage. The thought buzzes through my nervous system, charging every inch of me with all kinds of happy. How awesome would it be to wake up next to Lincoln every day? Quite awesome, indeed.

Under the table, my tail twists lovingly around Lincoln's ankle. He peeps over in my direction, his mismatched eyes alive with excitement. We'll really do this one day. Get married and be together.

My pulse races with anticipation. Seems like Lincoln's already got plans in the works, too. And a betrothal ritual? Jewels? Those thrax have ceremonies and sparkly stuff for everything. Not that I'm complaining. This is one situation where the extra falderal and romance would be much appreciated.

Dad's grin gets larger, if that's possible. "Fair enough."

Mom kicks her feet up onto a nearby chair. "Mind if I talk shop for a bit?"

"Go ahead," I reply. "What's on your mind?"

"I received a message from Cissy's office tonight. Adair's launching an official investigation into the Ghost Towers. I'd heard about the trouble with Ghost Tower Six today. What's the latest?"

I picture the fractured containment wall at the Ghost Tower, complete with that spectral hand reaching through the break. A shiver of dread twists up my spine. "The Tower's now stable, but we've got a million new souls coming into Purgatory each month. I don't know how much more storage we have."

"We can't stop souls from entering Purgatory, that's for sure," says Mom. "Besides, isn't Walker close to finding the Orb anyway?"

I tear apart my pizza crust into small bits. "We've some bad news on that front. Turns out, the Orb is actually hidden in a huge warehouse filled with magical junk. Lincoln's bringing in some specialists from Antrum to help us find it, but we've no idea how long it will take."

"You're bringing in the Alchemists, then," says Dad. "That's a first-class idea."

"I agree, excellent thinking from both of you," adds Mom. "You'll get Soul Processing back on track in no time."

"Thanks, Mom." A sunny sense of pride radiates through me. "I certainly hope so."

With that complement, I'm feeling downright awesome and in control. Then, my gaze runs across the old-fashioned phone set onto our kitchen wall. Any second now, that thing could ring again, not with a code-red failure this time, but with a full Tower meltdown. My chest tightens with worry and doubt. "Sometimes, though, I wonder what would've happened if I hadn't stopped my first iconigration. I mean, the Old Scala would never have questioned sending everyone to Hell."

"Nonsense," says Mom quickly. "You know how your father and I feel about what you're doing. It's a very brave move to shut down Soul Processing. You have our full support. And we'll help keep Adair's investigation quiet for as long as possible. Don't let the nay-sayers get you down, honey."

Huh. Mom's been warning me about the dangers of nay-sayers since I was two years old. Now, her words wrap around me once again, comforting as a blanket. "With you as my Mom, the nay-sayers don't stand a chance."

Dad's features firm up. I know this look; he's going into what I call Father-General-mode. "We've got you covered from the military side, as well." His voice carries a note of grim determination. "If there's rioting again, I'll call in troops from Heaven, no problem."

My father means for that statement to be reassuring, but it's not. At all. Instead, I start thinking about Purgatory's infamous Ghost Riots. The tightness and anxiety in my chest grow downright painful. Thoughts of those bloodthirsty mobs have been torturing me for weeks.

"Riots?" My voice comes out a little shaky. "I hope it doesn't come to that."

A memory appears in my mind's eye. I'm nine years old, sitting on our old ratty couch back in Lower Purgatory. Far-off explosions and screams rip through the night air. I curl into Mom's shoulder, my entire body trembling with fear. Walker sits in the armchair across from us, his colorless face set into grim lines. If the mobs reach our street, he's here to portal us away to safety. Outside our living room window, the night sky's horizon is lined with shifting shades of red. Purgatory is burning.

Mom guesses my thoughts and worries. "Don't get too concerned about rioting for now," she says soothingly. "You two focus on working with Walker and getting things going again. Just, you know, quickly. Like a few days. Maybe a week, tops."

"Sure, Mom. We'll do the best we—"

All of a sudden, the sound of ethereal singing fills my head. It's high-pitched, childlike and lovely. I press my fingertips to my temples. This shouldn't be happening now. I didn't summon any igni.

Still, the music continues. My brain fills with sweet voices that only I can hear. These are the light igni, the power that draws souls to Heaven. Evidently, they've decided that now is a good time to converse via somewhat-sappy music inside my brain. I exhale a slow breath. At least, unlike the dark igni, I can listen to their singing without wanting to scream.

Lincoln gives my hand a gentle squeeze. "What's going on?"

"The igni have a message for me. They're singing, right now, inside my head."

Mom leans across the table, her eyes widening. "What are they saying?"

I close my eyes to better focus. "They're saying something about the Furor. A Furor necklace. And the Furor Empress, too. It's her amulet. They want me to find it. I think the dark igni were singing about this before." I open my eyes, and the music fades from my mind. "Does anyone know what they're talking about?"

Mom shakes her head. "Never heard of it."

Dad's face becomes still as stone. "What do you know about the Furor?"

"Not much. All I learned in High School was sucking up to ghouls."

"Furor have magic casters," explains Dad. "They're a tribe called the Hexenwings. They create enchanted stones; no one really knows how they manage it. Royalty have specific stones associated with them, to give them special powers. Rubies for the Emperor, Opal for the first-born daughter, Obsidian for the first-born Prince..."

I can see where this is going, and I don't like the destination one bit. A tension headache crawls around my temples. "And the Empress?"

"Bloodstone."

My world freezes for a moment. Don't panic, Myla. It could be a coincidence.

Mom lets out a soft gasp. "I heard about this thing called the Bloodstone Curse. It sucks away a Scala's powers and gives it to someone else. Are the Curse and this neck-lace related?"

"I'm afraid so," says Dad.

Okay, time to panic. My heart starts pumping a mile a minute. The igni asked me to find something associated with the Bloodstone Curse. Is this their way of telling me that I have it? Could they possibly be giving my powers to someone else?

"The last time a Scala couldn't move souls, I was there," explains Dad. "I've a broad knowledge of demon lore, so whenever someone's stuck with a mystery ailment, they call me in. We didn't know what was wrong until we borrowed the Bloodstone Amulet. It's unique. Shows the Empress the status of her powers. We tried it with the patient and discovered that his igni were slipping away, moving to the Scala Heir on their own. That was, oh, two thousand years ago now. Today, most people probably remember the Curse and not how it got its name."

"I've read everything I can find on Scalas," I say. "There's always something about the Bloodstone Curse, but no mention of any amulet."

"Those damned ghouls," exclaims Mom. "They wiped out all our libraries, all our records, especially anything to do with the Scala."

The firm lines of Dad's face soften with sympathy. "This isn't the first time someone's talked to you about the Curse, is it?"

"No. Well, not directly anyway. Today, Adair asked me

if I wasn't moving souls because I didn't have the power anymore. I think she was hinting around about the Curse."

Dad's eyes glow angel-blue. "How dare she? I saw you send Armageddon straight into Hell with your powers. You freed me from his prison, something I never thought could happen. You're strong, Myla. And your bond with your igni is strong. There must be another reason why they want you to have the necklace. We'll figure it out." He reaches across the table and sets his hand on mine.

I stare at Dad's wide, muscular hand wrapped around my smaller one. All my life, I'd wondered who my father was, and if I'd ever find him. Now, he's here and more supportive and awesome than I ever dreamed of. My eyes sting with a mixture of love, awe, and gratitude. "Thanks, Dad."

Mom pulls out one of her ever-present notepads and starts scribbling orders for her staff. "We'll need to make a diplomatic request for the necklace." She pauses, tapping her pen against her chin. "However, it might not work coming from Purgatory. Unfortunately, under the ghouls, we ignored the Furor for decades. Cissy's only starting to rebuild ties there."

"I can ask them," says Lincoln. "I saved a Furor child at the Winter tournament. They were very grateful."

"Let me take this one," counters Dad. "I killed the father of the current Furor Emperor. He was downright ecstatic. I'll go to Furonium tomorrow and make a personal request for the amulet."

"And I'll call in the Alchemists," says Lincoln. "They'll be here first thing in the morning." His confident gaze meets mine. "Together, we'll find the Orb and restart Soul Processing. I know it."

And seeing that fearless look in his eyes, I think he may just be right.

6

Cissy, Walker, and I step into my stainless-steel kitchen, large boxes balanced in our arms. It's been two days since Lincoln's Alchemists showed up. Since then, they've kept the three of us busy with regular warehouse-runs to grab magical stuff for them to examine in my kitchen, aka our new Alchemy HQ. There are too many spells and enchantments in the warehouse for the Alchemists to work quickly—plus my kitchen has lots of gadgets and snacks—so they've taken up residence here.

Cissy and Walker speed into the kitchen, setting down their boxes on a nearby countertop. I pause inside the threshold, scoping things out. On the right-hand side of the room, Lincoln's seated at the head of our long steel table, while his Alchemists fill up the other chairs. They're six handsome guys with mismatched eyes, all of them wearing white lab coats that have silver eagles stitched on the right front pocket. The group's super-engrossed in the piles of odd junk that cover the tabletop, everything from typewriters to compasses to chia pets. They don't notice when we come in.

I set my box onto an obliging counter. "Hey, everyone."

Lincoln looks up, his mouth winding into a huge smile. "Hi, Myla."

At his words, all the other guys snap to attention as well. Six bodies immediately stand straight and tall with their fists gripped firmly behind their backs. Military stance. The thrax must start training that particular move in Kindergarten. Unfortunately, it makes me feel a little awkward.

"Guys, you really don't have to do that."

The Head Alchemist, Erik, has white blonde hair and wildly mismatched eyes of dark brown and ice blue. "But that's a proper greeting for the Great Scala."

"Well, honestly, it's creeping me out. As the Great Scala, I hereby order you to call me Myla and not hop around when I enter the room."

"As you command, Great Scala."

I shoot him a dry look.

"I mean, that's cool, Myla."

"Thanks."

Erik and the rest of the Alchemists retake their seats. Over the last two days, they've been working non-stop, trying to figure out what's up with the warehouse. Walker's certain the Orb is in there; the only question's where.

Lincoln steps over and takes his hands in mine. Today, he's wearing faded jeans and a black Elvis T-shirt, which I find hilarious. Everyone in Antrum knows who the real King is, even without the shirt. "How are you feeling?"

"Good," I reply. "No more igni concerts. And I've been doing some practicing, too. Remember when we were in the bunker, right before we fought Armageddon?"

"How could I forget?"

"Back then, the Old Scala did this thing where he cast igni ropes around us. I can't make Soul Columns, so I've been practicing those, just to see if they're listening to me."

"And?"

"Working like a charm. How're things in here?"

"The guys are having a blast." He turns to the team. "Can you report out, Erik?"

"Sure, Linc." I'm still adjusting to Lincoln having a nickname, but I guess these guys are buddies of his from when they were all ten years old. Erik turns towards Walker and Cissy. "I didn't see you two come in."

Walker shoots them a friendly wave. "You were busy playing with the last round of toys I brought you." As a ghoul, Walker's well over six feet tall with pale, colorless skin. As a cool guy, he has a brush-cut, sideburns, and fairly decent muscle tone.

Cissy rattles one of the boxes on the countertop. "We found even better stuff this time around."

Erik rubs his palms together and scans the table, his mismatched eyes glittering with excitement. "Here's what we've figured out so far." He picks up a plate-looking thing made out of metal. "This is a torquetum from the 1400's. It belongs in a museum, not a warehouse. It's the first step in a magical path that leads to this." He sets down the torquetum and picks of a pair of old-fashioned wire-rimmed glasses. "And then, the spectacles are connected to yet another enchanted thing." He holds up a wound-up piece of plastic shaped like a figure eight. "This one's from the Earth."

I can't help but laugh. "That's a Thigh Master. I've seen commercials for them on the Human Channel."

"Crazy, right?" Erik sets the item back onto the tabletop. "The connections go on and on and on. It's like a long magical chain that links every item in the warehouse. The Orb is at the end of the line, but it could take months to find the end by hand. Maybe even years."

I rub my neck with my right hand and frown. "So, any options?"

"Yes, we have an idea right here." Erik picks up a little tin bird from the 1800's. It's blue with mechanical wings and a winding key in its side. "We think we can alter the spell on this toy so it will fly through the exact path the magical signal takes to reach the Orb. Should only take a matter of hours to find it."

Cissy bobs up and down on her heels. "That's awesome, guys!"

"Great work." I do my golfer's clap.

A silly-slash-pleading look crosses Erik's face. "Great Scala, I mean, Myla. Since you're so happy with my work, I was wondering if I might ask a favor."

"Sure. What is it?"

Erik gestures across the table. "Some of these things you clearly won't need, and I might have a use for them."

Lincoln's face warms with an indulgent smile. "More of your pranks, Erik?"

"You know me, Linc. Man's got to have a hobby."

"That's for Myla to decide." Lincoln turns to me. "What do you say?"

Have Erik clean out some of this magical garbage for me? That's a big yes.

"Sure, have your fun."

Erik pumps the air with his fist. "Yeah."

"Back to the warehouse, though." I pick up the tin bird from the tabletop. "When can we try out your idea?"

Erik glances up at the clock. "Not until tomorrow morning. We're due back in Antrum in a few minutes."

"Let me grab my stuff," says Walker. "I'll portal you." He steps out of the room.

I pull Lincoln aside. "Should we really have Walker portal these guys? I don't want his backdoors to get discovered. Don't you have some old transfer stations in Purgatory? Maybe Octavia could turn them back on for us. It's less obvious than using the official ones."

Lincoln shakes his head. "I don't want anyone knowing what we're up to. Adair is bad news and she has too many allies in Antrum. I'm already under a lot of scrutiny, but my parents have it much worse. We can't be too careful."

I rub my forehead, considering. "If you feel strongly about it."

"I do. And don't forget, Walker knows how to be stealthy."

"Good point, although he's not as stealthy as you are." Ever since I was nine, Walker's been trying to sneak up on me, but he never can manage it.

Lincoln's mouth rounds into a toe-curling smile. "Well, that goes without saying." He gently pulls my back against his chest, wrapping his long arms around my waist. It's a comforting position. I survey the kitchen, feeling some worry melt away. The Alchemists made huge progress today. Now, we have an actual plan to figure out how to find the Orb and restart Soul Processing.

Things are looking up.

The old rotary phone rings on my kitchen wall. Mom's working to upgrade technology in Purgatory, but we still don't have cellular service yet.

"I'll get it." I set the receiver to my ear. "Myla Lewis speaking."

The other end of the line is a cacophony of screams and crashing. "Great Scala, you're needed right away." It's Ramone, the Lead Warden for Ghost Tower One. "We've got a code-red failure."

"Be right there." I hang up the phone and frown.

Things may not be looking *that* up, after all.

7

Lincoln and I rush over to Ghost Tower One. After a great day with the Alchemists, we launch into a not-so-great all-nighter. It takes ages to pinpoint what's wrong with the Tower. At last, we figure out that the electricity levels in the containment fields were off kilter, zapping all the ghosts awake and angry. One spirit even broke out of the Carrier, but the Tower went on lock-down before he got too far.

Still, the whole thing was close. Too close.

It's late morning by the time Lincoln and I head over to the warehouse. The place is a huge long box made of corrugated metal and lined with shelves from floor-to-ceiling. The many aisles twist around in a way that reminds me of the hedgerow maze back at the Ryder mansion. Large wooden crates are stacked everywhere, all of them stuffed with magical junk. Like compasses that always point to Hell. Enchanted pens that'll only write praises about the ghouls. And my personal favorite, a box of old Scala robes that either belonged to Maxon Bane or were doused in 'eau de old guy'.

We find Cissy, Walker, and the Alchemists in a nearby aisle. Erik's the first guy I run into, which is cool since he's the head honcho of this mission. We say our hellos and chitchat for a minute before I realize there's something off about his face. His skin looks as white as Walker's.

"Erik, are you sick or something?"

"No, I'm not. Guess what's different." A mischievous gleam appears in his eyes.

Lincoln warned me about this. Erik and his pranks.

"Come on. What's the joke?"

Erik pulls on his ears, removing what ends up being a magical stone bust of himself. "Is this awesome or what? You wear it once, and then you have a living, talking statue of yourself forever. You can wear it as a mask, too. That's what I was doing. Cool, huh?"

The statue-Erik winks at the original. "Quite cool," it says. And dang, it even sounds like Erik.

"Put that thing away, now. We need to find the Orb."

"Fine, fine." Erik sets the bust onto the floor and then rests his hand atop the statue's head. "Sleep, friend." The fake-Erik closes its eyes and starts to snore. I'm beginning to understand why Lincoln stopped hanging out with these guys after age ten.

Lincoln approaches us, spies the statue on the floor, and half-rolls his eyes. "Let's get started."

"We were only waiting for you two," explains Erik. "We

can start any time." He pulls the small tin bluebird from the pocket of his white lab coat. "Who's got the rest of the stuff we need?"

Three other Alchemists step forward, each holding one item: the torquetum, the old-fashioned spectacles, and the Thigh Master. Lincoln and I share a sly look. The Thigh Master guy looks really embarrassed-slash-confused. Those things don't seem to be standard parts of the medieval lifestyle in Antrum.

Erik steps over to the torquetum. "This is the first link in the magical chain that leads to the Orb. We'll start off the bird here, and then it should follow the path of magic through all the warehouse until it reaches the Orb at the end." He twists the key in the bird's side and sets it free. The tiny tin creature hops onto the torquetum and pecks around its flat, circular surface. After that, it jumps onto the spectacles and flaps it wings. Finally, it paces along the Thigh Master before taking off in flight.

Erik bobs on the balls of his feet. "It worked!" He and Walker exchange a high-five.

"Looking good," I say. "How long before it finds the Orb?"

Walker purses his lips. "By my calculations, tomorrow morning at 6:17AM."

"Really?" My eyebrows rise with surprise. "How can you be so certain?"

Walker scratches his neck with his right hand. "Do you want a lesson on stuff like energy signatures and the laws of probability, or do you want to take my word for it?"

Walker can be such a smart-ass sometimes. "Your word is fine."

"How likely is it that you'll really find this thing tomorrow?" asks Lincoln. "Give me a percent chance."

Walker makes a great show of rubbing his sideburns as if he's lost in thought. "Oh, one hundred percent."

"Yeah, Walker!" My tail does a happy-dance over my shoulder. If Walker says one hundred percent, you can take that to the bank. The mood in the warehouse turns downright giddy.

"We should make this a diplomatic event," says Cissy cheerfully. "An inter-realm gala, even. Invite the press to the warehouse. The people will love it." She opens her arms like she's picturing a new sign above the warehouse door. "Lucifer's Orb, the Grand Unveiling."

I hate to burst her bubble, but that's so not-going-to-happen. "I like the way you think, Cis, but it's too risky. Let's just find the Orb and get that shizz out of here." Once we find it, Dad's agreed to transfer it personally to some super-safe vault in Heaven. "Sorry to ruin your fun."

"No worries, quasi girl. Once this is all over, I'll think of another Diplomatic-something to celebrate our victory."

Our group launches into excited chatter about finding the Orb, restarting Soul processing, and my first iconigration as the Great Scala. We're so loud, it's hard to hear someone pounding on the warehouse's back door. Erik and I don't miss it, though.

"I'll get it. We're expecting a delivery." Erik jogs away.

I watch him rush up to a door at the end of the aisle,

open it, and stare out into space. The skin on my arms prickles into gooseflesh. Something's wrong here.

Who opens a door and stands there like a statue?

I move closer to Erik. He looms in the doorway, blocking my view of the alley beyond. I can't see his face, but there's a crimson glow around his cheeks, almost like his eyes are glowing red. Erik's voice comes out in a strange monotone. "Please come in. I'll show you around."

I step closer. "Stop right there, buddy."

Erik flips around to face me. "Stop what?"

I do a double-take. Erik's eyes are the typical thrax mismatch of brown and blue. No sign of demonic red. Any trace of a monotone is gone from his speech, too. I shake my head. This morning has been a lot of excitement after an intense all-nighter. My mind must be playing tricks on me.

"Look, Erik. You were about to invite someone in and give a tour of the warehouse. Not acceptable. This place stays on lock-down until we find the Orb."

Erik looks at me like I'm nuts. "I wasn't talking to anyone. Look for yourself."

I pop my head through the opened doorway and into the alley beyond. It's empty. Huh.

"See?" asks Erik. "No one's there. The knocks were probably a prank from some kids."

I scan the alleyway again. Still empty.

"A prank, eh? One of yours, Erik?"

"Not this time."

I'm so sure.

Still, the situation with the mystery knock-and-run brings up a good question. This is a huge warehouse, and we definitely need to keep it secure between now and tomorrow at 6:17AM. As Minister of Infrastructure, Walker's in charge of providing guards for all government buildings. I seek him out and pull him aside.

"Hey, do you have enough security folks for this place?"

Walker tilts his head to one side, thinking. "Enough to cover through tomorrow, sure."

"Cool. And however many you'd normally put on a high-risk building, can you double it?"

"That won't be as easy, but I think I can manage it."

"Thanks." I watch the little tin bird flap around the warehouse, landing from box to box. "This is way too important to leave anything to chance."

"Agreed." Walker's mouth thins to a worried line. "I'll take care of all the plans personally."

8

Lincoln and I stand in the warehouse, alone. The Alchemists and Cissy are gone, having done an awesome day's work. Walker's waiting outside for us. Lincoln and I take a quick stroll around the warehouse interior, double-checking that all the new guards are in place. Tomorrow's a huge day, and we want everything to be secure.

As we make our rounds, some of the tightness and anxiety fades from my body. The warehouse looks good. Really good. Walker gave us some top-notch guards. I'd even like to fight a few in the Arena, just to see how they'd do.

After one last check, Lincoln and I step out the back. It's not even six o'clock yet, but since the alley's bordered by tall buildings, it gets pitch dark out here pretty quickly. A bare light bulb hangs above the warehouse door, casting a dim glow onto the cracked asphalt. I scan the darkened alley.

No guards are here, only Walker. That's odd. The building's exterior should be secured by now.

Walker leans against the opposite wall, his thumbs hooked into the belt loops of his jeans. A strange gleam dances in his eyes. "Are we all ready to go?"

I tilt my head to one side. "Mmmmmmmmaybe."

I've known Walker my whole life, so I can tell when he's up to something. And the way he looks now? It's the exact face he'd give me before sneaking my teenage tuchus into the Arena. He knew Mom hated the thought of me spending time watching demon battles, so he always played it cool. Even so, he could never hide the odd glimmer in his eyes from me.

Something is so up. "Where are all the guards, Walker?"

"I've asked them to hold off for a while." He rocks a bit on his heels. "Are you two ready or what?"

I glance over to Lincoln. He's got his Señor Sneaky face on, which means he's caught on to whatever's up with Walker, too.

"Almost, one last thing." Lincoln wraps me into a deep hug and whispers in my ear. "Adair's here. Walker held off his guard so we could do a little recon, find out what she's up to. Care you join us?"

"Oh, yes." One of the many advantages of being in a serious relationship with a demon hunter is that you never get surprised in a deserted alley.

"Excellent." Lincoln steps back from our embrace and

faces the darkest part of the alley. "Lady Adair, as your High Prince, I command you to halt and speak with me."

Three figures scramble in the darkness: Lady Adair and two huge ghouls, one of whom is taller and has a limp. I'd know that tall guy anywhere; he's the Ghoul Diplomat to Purgatory. What a creep. A low hum sounds, the unmistakable mark of a ghoul portal opening and closing.

After that, silence.

"They're gone." I say with a sigh. "We missed them."

"Not at all." Lincoln turns to me, his eyebrows bobbing up and down. "I'm sure that Adair *thinks* she's given us the slip, but few ghouls are so talented at reconstructing portals as Walker. How about we continue our recon mission? I for one, am still curious as to what she does in her spare time."

"Are you kidding? I'd love to find out where she goes when she's not stalking me. Sign me up."

Lincoln jogs towards the end of the alley; Walker and I are close behind. Within a few seconds, we've reached the spot where Adair and her ghouls were hiding.

"Need you, buddy," says Lincoln. "Where'd they go?"

Kneeling down, Walker touches the ground where the portal once stood. "Ghost Tower Four. Not the ideal place for a portal. What do you say, Myla?"

Walker's right to be cautious. Our Ghost Towers are jittery enough without people portalling in and out. Still, as long as we're careful, we should be fine. Besides, I really-really-really want to find out what Adair's up to.

"We'll be alright." I tap the baculum holster on Lincoln's

thigh. "Don't spark this baby up by the Carrier wall. It can break the containment field." I take Walker's hand in my left and Lincoln's in my right. When traveling by portal, you have to hold onto your ghoul or you'll fall through darkness forever. "Let's hit it."

A new black door forms on the same spot where Adair disappeared; only this time, the portal is Walker's handiwork.

Together, we all step into the black doorway, tumble through empty space, and then re-emerge in the middle of a heavy, ivory-colored mist. A loud droning-sound fills the air, like we're standing beside a huge waterfall or jet aircraft engine. Actually, we're standing near some of the most powerful power generators in the after-realms.

Ghostly shapes move through the mist. Men, women, old, young, human, quasi. These spirits should be sleeping peacefully, but instead, they're all meandering around, wide-eyed and agitated. Spectral whispers carry on the air.

Where am I?

Get me out of here.

Help me.

Each reedy voice sends a shudder through my stomach. I force myself not to meet their gaze, as that only freaks them out…And a freaked out ghost is a dangerous ghost.

I pause, the full impact of our location sinking in. The Lead Warden left a cloud on the Tower floor. Most likely, that means the entire Carrier's at risk. Long story short, we're surrounded by a bunch of quite-possibly-homicidal ghosts. My heart kicks harder in my chest.

I let go of Lincoln and Walker's hands. The din around us is so loud, I have to yell every word I say. "Can you portal us out of here, Walker?"

"I wouldn't risk another one," he replies. "The containment walls could have been weakened by my first portal. How about you use igni to lead us out?"

I shoot Walker a thumbs-up. "Will do."

With all my heart, I call out to the igni, asking them to lead me to Adair. The light igni respond to my summons, their twinkling and childlike voices echoing through my mind. I open my eyes to find their tiny silver bodies diving and spinning about my palms. I lower my hands, and the igni understand my wishes. They tumble down, creating a trail of lightning bolts that flash along the floor, creating a zigzag path over the spectral fields.

My gaze moves between Walker and Lincoln. "Okay, follow the igni. Keep staring at the ground and we'll all be fine. And, whatever you do, don't look in their eyes."

Lincoln still has to speak-shout to be heard. "What happens if we do that?"

"You'll wake them up. Ghosts get cranky in the Carriers. They don't like to see anything alive. If they get angry enough, they can tear you apart."

Lincoln lets out a high-pitched 'harrumph'. "So, if you look in their eyes, they'll wake up and kill you."

"Yup. That's pretty much what happens. Don't step on them, either."

A snarky grin rounds Lincoln's mouth. "Helpful safety tips. Thanks, Myla."

We march along, careful to keep our gazes fixed on the ground. Tension tightens up my legs and spine. One look from those ghosts and that could be it, not only for us, but for the containment wall, too. Our pace stays steady with the igni as their little bodies slowly form a winding path beneath our feet.

The ghosts start to get anxious. Spectral hands pull at my hair. Others tap my shoulder insistently. I've seen how quickly they can change from a sweet grandmotherly type into a bloodthirsty banshee. My palms turn slick with sweat. Step by step, we creep across the floor.

Although it's only a few minutes, it feels like hours pass before we emerge from the mist into the concrete Tower itself. I exhale a long sigh.

We made it.

On reflex, I set my palms against my ears. If anything, the background noise is louder here than in the Cloud Carrier itself. Beneath my feet, the igni flicker and disappear, their work now done.

I scan the containment wall behind us. It shifts oddly in some places. "Walker, can you talk to the engineers in the Control Room? Now that we moved through, they'll need to re-calibrate the containment field. Oh, and have them go on lock-down, too. Who knows what Adair's doing here? I don't want any escapees."

"Got it." Walker takes off at a run.

Lincoln points across the Tower floor. "And there she is."

Adair stands at the far wall of the Tower beside her two

ghouls, chatting up Frederick, our Lead Warden. Is this what Adair does when she's not stalking me…Work over my Tower Wardens for information?

Lincoln has to yell above the din, which is good, since we don't want you-know-who to hear a word. "You still practicing those igni cords?"

"Yup."

"How fast could you tie someone up?"

I can see where Lincoln's going with this, and I likes it. We can't use weapons in here, but I could restrain Adair with igni. That way, we can question her. "Fast."

"Good. Wait for my signal."

Up in the Control Room, Walker gets the Tower on lock-down. Instantly, the chamber goes from an overwhelming racket to creepily quiet.

The shut-down makes Adair jump, and she immediately scans the room. Once she spies Lincoln, her cheeks burn red with embarrassment. Evidently, she didn't count on us following her here. Good. Now, she has to deal with the fact that she ignored Lincoln in the alleyway.

A yummy sense of satisfaction warms me to the core. So nice to be on the stalker side of the stalker-stalkee equation, for once.

Lincoln and I walk slowly towards Adair, who slaps on an angelic face as we approach. Once again, Lincoln raises his arm, like he did in the alley. "Lady Adair, you defied a direct order from your High Prince. I asked you to halt and speak with me. If we were in Antrum, you'd be in irons by now."

Adair looks to Lincoln, her tiny eyes blinking innocently. "Did you speak to me before? I didn't hear anything." She turns to the Lead Warden. "That's so interesting about the Ghost Carriers, I mean, the Cloud Carriers."

I stifle the urge to roll my eyes. Nice. She knows I suck at my job, but she can't remember what to call the things I spend most of my day worrying about.

"Yes, Lady Adair." Frederick glares at me, something I've never seen from him before. "The Carriers can be incredibly dangerous when they aren't managed properly."

"Of course," says Adair. "We'll talk again soon."

Talk again soon? What the Hell?

"You got it," says Frederick. They share a knowing look, and then my soon-to-be-ex-Lead Warden returns to his post.

Adair twiddles her fingers in his direction. "Thanks, Freddie."

Freddie, not Frederick? Really? How long have these two been hanging out?

A nasty realization trickles into my mind. First Celia, now Frederick. In her spare time, Adair's been doing more than schmoozing my Wardens for information. She's been poisoning them against me. That's why Celia confronted me. Adair's been visiting the Towers, telling the Wardens what they want to hear: that I need to move souls, and that we all need to return to the ghoul-rules.

Unholy Hell.

Adair fiddles with her gown's long, loopy sleeves.

"Thank Heavens I became a Diplomat here. Poor workers like Freddie have no one to advocate for them." She offers a look of overblown sympathy to Lincoln. "And you? Our thrax warriors will be forced to murder all those ghosts once they break free and ravage Purgatory." She shakes her head sadly. "And all because the Great Scala is so incompetent."

Lincoln and I pause about five feet away from Adair and her pair of ghouls. We may be standing still, but my mind is whirling through her latest comments. Manipulating my people? Accusing me of not moving souls because I'm incompetent? Screw her. My fingers itch to have igni swirl around them. An igni-cord on her neck would be quite nice in particular.

Adair snaps her fingers. Her ghoul opens a portal behind her. "I'm afraid I must take my leave now. So much work to do. I'm sure you understand."

Without giving Lincoln a chance to reply, Adair quickly steps towards the open portal behind her.

Lincoln turns to me. "Now!"

Instantly, igni blast forward from my hands, creating two long silver ropes that whip across the Tower floor. In the blink of an eye, Adair and her two ghouls are all looped along like beads on a string. My igni-cord wraps tightly around their waists, holding their arms firmly to their sides. Adair's ghouls writhe frantically in my bonds as they try to escape. No dice.

All the blood drains from Adair's face. "I wasn't here

causing trouble," she says quickly. "I am not abusing my role as thrax Diplomat."

"No one said anything about abusing your post," says Lincoln coolly. "Although now that you bring it up, unscheduled visits to Ghost Towers should be investigated."

"You misunderstand, my love," coos Adair. "I work day and night for the good of all thrax."

She's so full of it. The good of all thrax is the absolute last thing on her to-do list.

Lincoln folds his arms over his chest. "Time to talk. You defied an official command from your High Prince. Twice. Any comment?"

"I am your loyal subject, Lincoln, first and always," whimpers Adair. "Especially in my role as Diplomat. You must believe me." Her eyes turn watery and pleading. Behind her, her ghouls still writhe in my bonds. Their portal wavers in and out of focus, but it doesn't disappear completely. Got to give them points for dedication.

"Excellent," says Lincoln. "In that case, you won't mind answering a few questions."

Adair stares at the igni cords around her waist. When she speaks, her voice comes out low and dreamy. All her attention is focused on her igni bindings. "What's your question about?"

Something about the way Adair is staring at my igni is wrong. Way wrong. My chest tightens with alarm. It becomes harder to breathe.

"I should think that would be obvious," says Lincoln. "I

want to discuss your behavior towards the Great Scala. Following her around. And now, visiting the Ghost Towers without Senator Frederickson. You know that breaks protocol."

A slow, evil smile rounds Adair's lips. "I didn't know igni could do this."

"Lady Adair," says Lincoln, his tone sharp. "Are you listening to me?"

Adair shifts her weight against my cords, testing them. Her poor-little-girl persona visibly melts away, replaced by something nasty, fierce and predatory. The sense of alarm inside my nervous system escalates into a downright panic. I fight the sudden urge to run.

"I won't ask this again," states Lincoln. "Why've you been following the Great Scala around for months? Why did you run away from my command?"

Adair looks up, her eyes bright. "Here's what I have to say. Myla Lewis is infected with the Bloodstone Curse. The igni have chosen me instead." With that, she raises her arms. My igni cords snap, setting her free.

The world around me freezes into one of those 'oh my freaking Hell' moments that stick in your mind forever. Adair just broke my igni cords. I outright gasp. There's no way she should be able to do that. Not unless Adair can control igni. But that would mean she's really the Scala Heir, which is impossible. Adair's only part human and angel. You must have demon blood, too.

At that moment, my igni cords reform, the ends looping around Adair's palms. This wasn't my wish. Adair made this alteration on her own. We stare at each other, each of us holding the end of two igni cords. It's like we're in some kind of supernatural tug of war. Adair's ghouls stand free beside her, satisfied looks on their faces, their escape portal standing wide open.

My igni-cord changed, and I didn't alter it. Now, Adair's free. Her ghouls are free. I try to make the igni-cord break or disappear. I can't.

Now, I'm the one who's trapped.

My mind goes blank with shock. How could Adair block my powers, let alone change what I've done? At any point in time, only two people can wield igni: the Scala and the Scala Heir. And both of those beings must have the blood of an angel, demon and human in them. Could Adair have gotten demon blood in her somehow?

The igni cord winds tightly around my hands, making my palms freeze over with an ethereal chill. A sickly feeling seeps into my belly. This is exactly what I experienced when Adair held my hands at the end of her so-called 'inspection' of Ghost Tower Six. Only this time, the sensation is far more intense. What is she doing, exactly? The answer to my question appears inside my mind, because the igni have started to scream. Both light and dark howl inside my head, their voices a mix of pain and terror.

This can't be happening. But it is.

Somehow, the igni cord between Adair and me has become a conduit. No matter how hard I try, I can't break the connection. I try to reverse the flow of power, pulling it from Adair to me instead. No go. All I can do is slow the transfer of my precious igni, but the effort makes every cell in my body hurt.

Light plays under my skin as igni are dragged from my soul, across the cord, and into Adair. Their tiny voices scream louder. My hands feel like blocks of ice. Adair's skin starts to glow with an otherworldly light.

Lincoln steps to my side. "Myla, what's going on?"

I speak through gritted teeth. "She's stealing my powers." I focus all my mental strength, slowing the loss of my igni. Pain spikes through my temples. "She needs to set me free. I can't break the connection from here. I can only slow the transfer."

Lincoln rounds on Adair. "Let her go."

"I can't," says Adair in a whining voice. "Lincoln, my love, you must see the truth. These are my igni powers, not hers. I'm the True Scala. I was the first one initiated by Verus. You were my Angelbound love before this demon whore came along. She stole my life and love, and now, I'm getting them both back. That's my right, don't you see?"

I may be in pain, but I'm not putting up with that crap. "Hey, nut job. I did not steal your so-called life and you know it."

Adair ignores me and keeps right on talking to Lincoln. "She's been tricking you all along." Her tone has turned pleading, desperate. "I'm trying to save you, and to do that, the demon whore must die."

"Damn it, Adair!" Lincoln stalks over towards her, igniting his baculum as a fiery broadsword. You go, honey.

The Ghoul Diplomat steps forward, blocking Lincoln's

path. In each hand, the ghoul holds a throwing dart. "Approach my Mistress and you'll have one of these in your gut." He grins, showing a mouth of blackened teeth. "Covered in sleeping serum."

Lincoln marches forward, his face set in determined lines. Fast as lightning, the ghoul launches his dart. It whizzes straight for Lincoln, only missing his neck by a fraction of an inch. Lincoln pauses.

"Come one step closer," snarls the ghoul. "I dare you. No matter how fast you move, I won't miss at this range."

Lincoln nods slowly. "You've thought this through rather carefully, I see."

Adair looks at him plaintively. "Only because I love you."

Lincoln glares at the ghouls. If he moves any closer to them, he'll end up with a sleeping dart in the gut...And all my igni stolen. Tiny voices scream in my mind as my powers are ripped from me. Pain sears behind my eyes, making it hard to focus.

We're at a stalemate. And with every second that passes, I lose more igni.

Turning on his heel, Lincoln runs over to the containment wall, well out of the ghoul's range.

"Here's one thing you haven't thought of." He raises broadsword high.

Unholy Moly. Lincoln's going to tear the containment wall open. And since I'm locked with Adair, I can't even send those escaped ghosts into Hell. I try to wrap my brain around what this means and come up with a plan, but all I can think about is the pain in my body and the howling cries of my igni.

Lincoln speaks in a creepy-low voice. "Join me in death, Adair."

What happens next takes seconds to complete, but my mind tracks each detail in ultra-slow motion. Lincoln brings his arm down, slicing straight through the containment wall. The entire Carrier shatters, sending spirits tumbling out onto the Tower floor. The sudden loss of mist wakes them up. Some cry, others laugh, more howl with rage.

Adair screams. Immediately, she releases the igni bond between us, grabs the hands of her ghouls, and jumps into her opened portal.

The world around me returns to normal speed. The pain slowly seeps from my limbs. The igni grow quiet. My mind clears. I'm aware of flashing red lights as the Control Room kicks on its emergency processes. A thick mist rolls across the Tower floor, making it hard to breathe. Lincoln races up behind me, wrapping his arm tightly around my waist. He pulls me back onto my feet, above the heaviest billows of mist.

"Stay up, Myla. Get above the mist."

My eyes widen with a realization. Breaking the containment wall floods the Tower with mist. It's standard protocol when a Carrier is breached. Lincoln would know that, too, after the night we spent in Ghost Tower One. But Adair's always been more interested in defeating me than learning how Soul Processing really works. She obviously thought we'd all end up dead, so she took off with her ghouls.

Way to think on your feet, babe.

The heavy mist rises higher and higher. Around us, all the spirits Lincoln released from their Carrier collapse into a deep sleep. My chest tightens as I gasp for air.

Walker's familiar hand slips into mine. The next thing I know, I'm tumbling through empty space as his portal transfers the three of us out of the Ghost Tower. It all happens so fast, I barely have time to register that I'm out of danger, let alone exhale a sigh of relief.

Walker, Lincoln, and I step out of the portal and into the main foyer of my house in Purgatory.

I cling tightly to Walker's hand. Somewhere in the back of my mind, I know I should be thanking him, but I have too many questions first. "What happened? Are the souls safe?"

"They're fine. None of them escaped. I need to go back, help them rebuild the containment wall."

"I'll go with you." For some reason, I'm having a really hard time letting go of Walker's hand.

"I'd rather you talked to Xavier right now. Whatever Adair did back there, I've never seen anything like it. If anyone knows what tricks she's pulling, it's your father."

I check my wristwatch. Almost 8PM. Dad doesn't need much sleep, so he's probably working out right now. "Alright." I finally release Walker. "Thank you."

"Anytime." A low hum sounds as Walker creates a new portal. He steps through it and disappears.

Lincoln enfolds me in a huge hug. "Are you okay?"

"I feel fine, now."

"Sorry I had to break the containment field, but I couldn't think of any other way to make her stop. She looked so scared when I held up the long-sword, I figured she'd panic and run."

"And you were right. It was a good plan."

I pause, rubbing my temples with my fingertips. All the events of the past two months swirl through my brain. Adair following me around…becoming Thrax Diplomat to Purgatory…causing trouble with my Tower Wardens…and now, stealing my igni. There's a pattern here, a systemized plan of attack. I need some battle strategy advice.

And Dad's the greatest General in the after-realms.

9

Lincoln and I turn down another creepy-dark hallway in my mega-mansion home, our footsteps echoing in weird ways on the black marble. After the Ghost Tower igni-steal with Adair, we're hitting the gymnasium to talk to my father.

As we close in on the gym, the corridor echoes with familiar noises: the unmistakable thwacks, rips, and slashes of a battle. Based on the way the punches sound when they connect, the opponent's one of the dummy demons that Dad brought in for battle practice.

Lincoln arches his right eyebrow. "Xavier has faux-demons in here?"

"Oh, sure. He brought in his best equipment from Heaven. You won't believe what he's done with our gym. Gutted a whole wing of the building to build it."

A sense of pride bubbles up through me. It's so cool to have a badass archangel demon-fighting Dad.

We reach the gymnasium's open door and stop. Inside, the place is huge, white and topped with a high ceiling. Padded mats cover the floor in four quadrants, each one holding different equipment. Every weapon imaginable lines the walls.

I scan the room, ready to say my hellos. What I see stops me cold. Dad spars against one of the dummy demons, which has seemingly come to life for the battle practice.

Only, it's not just any demon. It's Armageddon.

I grip Lincoln's palm more tightly. Part of me knows the King of Hell isn't really battling my father right now. Dad's fighting an enchanted mannequin that comes to life for practice only. But dang, whoever enchanted that thing did a good job. It's freaking terrifying. Armageddon stands seven feet tall with gangly thin limbs and black skin that's smooth as polished stone. His long face is divided by a blade-like nose and ends in a pointed chin. He moves with lightning speed, trying to place his hands anywhere on Dad's exposed flesh. Armageddon's preferred method of attack is to touch your skin and suck out your soul.

My attention turns to my father, and my jaw falls open with wonder. Dad's baculum are ignited as two short-swords. His movements are a blur as he blocks Armageddon's attacks. With each volley and thrust, intense emotions wrench across my father's face: rage, anguish, and fear.

A heavy sadness settles into my body. To save Mom's life, Dad spent twenty years in Hell, and Armageddon tortured him the entire time. Dad has the power to heal, so Armageddon tore off my father's wings off every day, a torment that only got worse when his wings regenerated.

Sensing our presence, Dad pauses in his volley. He calls out one word: "Halt!" The sparring dummy freezes, turning from a life-like version of Armageddon into a putty-colored model of the same shape and size. My father turns his attention to me, panting for breath. "Hello, there. I was wondering when you'd stop by. I suppose your mother told you about the Bloodstone Amulet."

My mind stalls out for a moment. In all the excitement of Adair in the Ghost Tower, I forgot all about the amulet. Dad was making an emergency trip to visit Emperor Tempest and try to borrow it.

"No, I haven't seen Mom all day. What's up?"

"I have the amulet with me. Would you like to try it on? See if it works?"

A chill of foreboding crawls up my back. This necklace will tell me if I've lost any of my igni. I steel myself, ready for anything. "Sure, let's have a look."

Dad walks over to a nearby cabinet and pulls out a small velvet box. "Here it is."

I turn the item over in my hands. It's a smooth disc of red stone, unmarked on either side, that's held on a long silver chain. I set it around my neck.

Instantly, the front of the amulet changes. The surface bubbles, turning into the image of two dragons facing each other, their claws extended and teeth bared. Their dragon-tails loop around to the backside of the disc, where they form a spiral that ends in the amulet's center. The roman numerals one to ten are marked along the length of the entwined tails, with ten at the outer edge and one at dead center.

"The back of the amulet shows the level of your powers," says Dad.

"Got it." I watch the entwined tails on the amulet's backside. Bit by bit, they turn black against the backdrop of red stone. The color reaches up to the numeral ten and pauses. "It looks like I have all my igni." I exhale a relieved breath. Maybe Adair has been playing some kind of elaborate mind game with me.

Whew. Mind games, I can handle. Losing my igni, not so much.

The color in the tails starts to disappear. Not a mind game, then. Adair really did steal my powers. My rib cage seems to squeeze in on me.

The level on the amulet slips past nine, then eight. My breath catches. How many igni did she take? I fought against her stealing every one of them. The readout finally comes to a stop at seven. I grip the amulet tightly, feeling my palms turn slick with sweat. "This says my powers are at seven out of ten." My throat constricts with grief and shock. "I've lost igni."

With that realization, my mind empties of everything but a single thought. It's one thing to suspect someone's stealing the little supernatural children that power your life. It's another to see evidence that it actually happened.

And they screamed so loudly as they were torn from me. Pain and terror.

My voice catches. "My igni." Their loss hits me like a punch to belly, the agony overwhelming and raw.

Lincoln steps up beside me, gently setting his hand on my shoulder. "Tell your father what happened tonight at the Ghost Tower."

I meet his gaze, my own eyes stinging with sorrow. "My igni."

"I know this is hard, Myla. But we don't have a lot of time. Tell your father what happened. Maybe he can help."

Little by little, I turn to face my father. "Just now, I got into a fight with Adair at Ghost Tower Four. I tied her up with an igni cord. It felt like she was using that cord as a connection. Taking my powers away from me." I run my fingers along the amulet. "And this confirms it. But how could that be possible? At any point in time, there can only be two beings with the blood of an angel, human, and demon. The Scala and the Scala Heir."

Dad keeps his voice soft and soothing. "That's correct."

"So how could she take my igni? Adair only has the blood of a human and angel in her."

Dad's mouth thins to a frown. "The trick isn't getting demon blood in you. That's pretty easy to do. And fatal, if that means you'll have all three blood types at once. If I injected Lincoln with demon blood right now, he'd die a long and painful death."

Lincoln nods sadly. "At some points in our history, it's been used as a form of execution. Excruciating way to go."

"In any case, getting demon blood isn't the problem," continues Dad. "The tough part is getting half-way through the Scala Heir initiation ceremony. After that, you can take all three blood types easily."

I let out a long groan. *That explains it.*

"Of course. Adair went through the Scala Heir initiation ceremony with me. She inhaled the special angel dust, got the sacred words said over her, and was proclaimed Angelbound by Verus. All she was missing was the demon blood."

Lincoln shakes his head. "But that ceremony was a sham. Verus only did that to actually initiate Myla on the sly. Adair had her igni powers faked with magic from Gianna of the House of Striga. It was never real."

"It wasn't real then," corrects Dad. "But that's only because Adair didn't have the blood of a demon in her. All she'd need is an injection, and then the ceremony would be complete. I'm sorry to tell you this, but right now, Adair is some kind of Scala."

The words keep echoing around my head, but they can't be right. *Adair is some kind of Scala.*

I'm vaguely aware that my father's still talking. "I wonder who would have had enough knowledge of Scala lore to have given her that advice?" Dad rubs his chin thoughtfully. "Injecting demon blood into a thrax is an extreme death. Normally, no one would even consider it. And it's not like there are many Scala books left around, even in Heaven. Interesting. Perhaps she wanted the powers badly enough to take a wild risk."

I appreciate that Dad is in thoughtful-mode and all, but I need more information, fast. "So, how is Adair getting my igni?"

Dad shrugs, his move when he's setting aside his thoughts for another time. "Normally, the Great Scala gives the Heir some igni. Or all of it, if they choose. The Old Scala gave you his willingly, am I right?"

"He was glowing blue and dead at the time, but yeah, it was willingly."

"Well, Adair knows you'd never do the same for her, so my guess is she got a spell somewhere on her body. Something to force the igni transfer."

A memory appears in my mind. I'm standing in Cloud Tower Six as Adair gives me a creepy handshake. She'd just announced her Official Investigation. "Would the spell be on her palms?"

"Surely," says Dad. "That'd be a great place to put it."

"Adair first grabbed my palms in Ghost Tower Six. At the time, it made me feel strangely cold and icky. She must have launched the spell with that handshake."

"Adair made the same physical connection with you tonight," adds Lincoln. "She made the igni cord wrap around your palms."

The full scope of Adair's scheme slams into me with a vengeance. My wrath demon awakens, heating my blood with rage. "Blazing Hell! She's really trying to replace me as the Great Scala. She wants to return to—"

I catch Lincoln's gaze, and deep sadness fills his eyes. No question what she wants to go back to. The time before he fell in love with me. When Adair was named the Scala Heir, and Lincoln was going to marry her. That's what she now sees as her birthright, and she's going to take it.

My warrior instinct kicks in as her full scheme becomes clear. The Great Scala can send any innocent soul to Hell, as well as any purely evil soul to Heaven. It's an outrageous amount of power. The igni chose me to wield it because they thought I'd use it wisely. Not fry up half the after-realms in a sick bid to reclaim my old fantasy-boyfriend. If Adair gets this power, she won't stop at anything until she gets what she wants. And I can't see anyone standing up to her, either.

More rage pumps through my bloodstream. I will not allow Adair to steal my powers so she can force Lincoln into marrying her. And I refuse to see her become another puppet-Scala like the last one, Maxon Bane.

My irises flash demon red. "This is not happening. We need to entrap Adair. Expose her. I want her in jail and out of my way."

Even as I say this, I know it means a lot of inter-realm falderal. Purgatory can't hold a thrax for more than twenty-four hours without essentially starting a war. Lincoln's parents would have to agree to lock her up, which won't be easy, especially considering how Lincoln's father kowtows to Acca like it's his job.

Lincoln rests both his hands on my shoulders, forcing our gazes to lock. "Look, I'm not any happier about the situation than you are, but Adair can't distract us right now. You still have most of your igni. That should be more than enough to move souls. And more importantly, you have the faith of your people. They like what Adair says about going back to the ghoul-rules, but they're still following you. We need to stay focused on that warehouse. Get Soul Processing started again. Solidify your role. As long as Adair can't touch you, she can't take any more of your powers. We'll put an extra guard on you, make sure she never gets near you again."

I tilt my head to one side, thinking through his words. My white-hot rage at Adair gradually cools into an icy resolve. "Yes, the real issue is getting rid of the Orb and moving souls again. We can easily ask Walker to find me some bodyguards."

"Be careful," warns Dad. "Make sure you have Striga guards in the mix. Your best magic casters. We don't know what we're dealing with here."

My heart sinks. I so don't like the sound of that.

"What do you mean, Dad?"

"You're a great fighter, Myla. In part, that's because you have wrath power coming from your demon blood. The same thing applies to Adair. Whatever demon blood she's taken in, she'll gain those same demonic powers. Could be fighting, magic, or something else. My advice is to stay away from her."

"I'll try," I say. "She follows me around, so it's not easy."

"Do what you can, I know she's a Diplomat." Dad slips on his post-workout hoodie. "Let me give you one last piece of advice. Take the rest of the night off. Clear your heads. Have some fun. You've a big day ahead of you tomorrow."

Good point. I can't remember the last time I took a night off.

"I like that advice, Dad."

Cissy appears in the doorway. "Hey, everyone." She holds up some small slips of pink paper. "Don't you check your messages, Xavier?"

Dad pats his pockets. "I never can remember those things."

"The President wants you at her office."

"I'll be over soon."

"She said you'd say that, and I'm supposed to accompany you. There's a car outside right now."

Dad chuckles. "Camilla was always the only one who could out-General me."

Cissy hitches her thumb towards the front door. "Ready to go? We can't keep the President waiting."

"Of course." Dad snaps his fingers. "Hey, will you two be alright on your own for a little while?"

The words 'on your own' reverberate through my mind in odd ways. As in Lincoln and I. Alone. In this house.

Ooooooh, yeah.

Suddenly, my recent igni-shock seems a million miles away. My lust demon awakens, filling my mind with all the yummy things Lincoln and I could be doing in a few minutes. When I speak again, my voice comes out as a high-pitched peep. "Sure."

"Bye, then." Dad and Cissy walk away.

For a while, Lincoln and I stand in a kind of suspended animation. At last, a click sounds as the front door closes. Dad and Cissy are gone. The two of us are alone. And we just got expert advice to take the night off.

But alone in a house with Lincoln? This brings up all the lust-demon-comfort-issues that I've been able to avoid over the last two months, mostly since Lincoln and I haven't been alone for more than five minutes.

Unlike what's happening now.

Suddenly, I realize that I've been standing around, saying nothing for quite a long time. I blurt out the first thing that comes into my head. "Hey."

Lincoln rocks back on his heels, a crafty light in his eyes. "So, what do you want to do?"

No question, I want to kiss his face off, but I'm still not sure about this whole lust-demon thing.

"How about a tour of the new house?"

"Sounds like a plan."

10

Lincoln and I stand by my bed, arms wrapped around each other, our mouths meeting in a gentle kiss. My tour of the house basically began and ended with my bedroom. No regrets, there.

Our kiss becomes slow and teasing. Every nerve ending in my body's attuned to Lincoln. The pressure of his hands. The sweet play of his tongue. The feel of his firm chest against my soft curves. It all feels real, intense, perfect. I can't help but moan.

Lincoln senses my rising desire, and it drives his heat as well. He lets out a yummy growl that makes my legs feel boneless beneath me.

Our kiss turns deep and fierce. We're together, we're alone, we're in love. Who knows what will happen next in our crazy lives? Why not take what pleasure we can, when we can? Closing my eyes, I soak in the sensation of

Lincoln's firm hands moving down my spine, the heat radiating from his palms. I suck in a shaky breath.

Warmth pools behind my eyes, which can only mean one thing: my lust demon's getting ready to take over. I'm seconds away from my irises flashing with demonic power.

Alarm bells go off in the logical part of my brain. The last time Lincoln and I hooked up, this is exactly what happened then, too. After my irises flashed red, I almost stripped down and did who-knows-what with him in a hedgerow maze.

You're heading into dangerous territory yet again, Myla.

I'm ready to put on the brakes when Lincoln nips my lower lip between his teeth. Suddenly, my inner alarm bells seem like so much nonsense. What harm can a few kisses really do? And while I'm at it, who cares if we happen to be horizontal while they happen? Balling my hands into Lincoln's white shirt, I guide him over to my bed. Sliding across the mattress, I settle onto my back and wait.

Lincoln stands at the foot of my bed, his mismatched eyes locked with mine. His face is the picture of power and control over mounting desire. Unholy Hell, that's hot. My heart kicks harder in my chest. I twine the comforter cover in my fingers.

Come on, Lincoln. Be with me.

Bit by bit, he crawls up the mattress, careful to keep his body inches above mine. I feel his warmth radiate over my legs, my belly, and finally, my mouth. My heart thuds so hard, I'm sure it'll burst from my rib cage. Lincoln lowers his hips; the firm muscles in his waist and thighs finally press against me. My inner lust demon starts to get rowdy, but I keep her in check. Our gazes meet, and I could drink in that look all day. Rock-solid control over raw desire.

Footsteps echo down the hallway outside my bedroom. I freeze.

Crap, someone's here.

With that realization, my logical self springs back into life with a loud 'told you so'. My lust demon fades. I lower my voice to a whisper. "Someone's outside."

"It's Cissy. I recognize the step." A conspiratorial gleam flickers in his mismatched eyes. "So, we'll be very quiet."

My breathing comes low and quick. "Quiet. I can do that." I close my eyes as he kisses my neck. "Maybe."

Another logical realization appears in my distracted mind. Quiet or not, there isn't much separating me from unwanted visitors. I shoot a worried glance at the door. "Is it…"

"Locked? Of course."

Heat, sense, and pleasure careen through me. My lust demon roars to life again, growling how there's way too much clothing here, and not nearly enough moaning. I grit my teeth, trying to get her under control.

"Full disclosure." I'm panting at this point. "I've never really let her out."

Lincoln leans in, nipping my earlobe in his teeth. That's so not-helping my lust-demon-control issues. "Her who?"

"You know. Her-her." Right now, eloquence isn't my strong suit.

Lincoln pauses, propping up his weight back onto his forearms. His gaze meets mine, his face doing that unreadable-thing. "Your lust demon?"

I nod. "Even when I'm alone, I kind of keep her on a leash. It's not easy. But with you, it'll be impossible. I think she might be really noisy and, uh, physical."

Lincoln's mouth slowly winds into a Cheshire-cat-style grin. "Oh, I can handle noisy and physical. Don't worry." He lowers his voice to a sexy whisper. "Do whatever you want to do. I'll follow your lead. No one will know a thing, Myla."

My tail hovers by his collar, ready to slice the shirt right off. Man, it would be so easy. Nakedness could be ours.

Lincoln leans in close, his mouth just above mine. "In case you're wondering, I hate this shirt." Translation: If you want to slice this off me, feel free.

The arrowhead end of my tail toys with his shirt-collar. Lincoln closes his eyes, soaking in the feel of my dragon-scale skin on the nape of his neck. Inside me, my lust demon instinct grows stronger. The drive to tear everything off him is almost irresistible.

And I can control my lust demon. Possibly.

My tail slides around to Lincoln's throat, tugging right below his chin. We're here. And all of this feels amazing. Plus, there are no guarantees about our crazy futures. Why wait? My eyes flicker red with lust.

Lincoln lowers himself on his forearms, stopping when his mouth's a breath above my own. "That's it, Myla. Set her loose."

All right, big fella. You asked for it.

A knock sounds on my bedroom door. We freeze.

The knock repeats. Someone's here.

Aw, fuck fuck fuckity FUCK fuck.

A muffled voice sounds through the thick wooden door. "Myla?"

No question who that is. "Hi, Cissy."

"Your Mom's been calling and calling. I have a limo waiting outside for you. We need to go to an emergency press conference. Guess who's gone public with her complaints about the Ghost Towers?"

Ugh. That would be Adair.

"Alright, Cis. Be right out."

Lincoln gives me one last kiss before rolling off the bed. "I'm afraid I must meet your lust demon another time."

I open my mouth, not sure what to say. On one hand, I'm colossally bummed out that Lincoln and I aren't kissing anymore. On the other hand, I can't say I'm too upset that I can keep right on avoiding my inner lust demon. Which hand is the right one?

Tough call, really.

I straighten my Scala robes and decide to worry about my lust demon later. Right now, it's time for my first serious press conference.

11

Cissy, Lincoln, and I sit in a limousine on our way to Adair's so-called emergency press conference. Lincoln's in a fine mood, especially since minutes ago, he almost met my inner lust demon again. He starts rolling the windows up and down, picking through the wet bar, and in general playing with every button, lever, and knob in the limo. He even rolls open the skylight and stands up through it as we drive along. I pull on his pant leg.

"Down here, honey."

He crouches over. "Wow. Not that I don't like riding Bastion, but limousines are phenomenal."

Cissy and I exchange a look of disbelief. Sure, Lincoln lives underground in a locked-down version of the Middle Ages, but I figured he'd ridden a limo at least once before. After all, he is royalty.

"Have you ever been in a limo before?" asks Cissy.

"No, why would I?" He stands back up in the skylight.

I tug on his pant leg again. "Down here, still."

Lincoln crouches once again. "Yeah?"

"Emergency press conference planning going on here. You need to participate."

"Right now?" He looks so disappointed; I hate to burst his bubble.

"How about this? One of these days, we'll ride around in a limo for as long as you want. How's that for a deal?"

"I like." Lincoln plunks back onto the seat beside me, a silly smile on his face. "Alright. Ready to focus on the emergency press conference."

Cissy hands us each manila folders. "It's being held at the Thrax Embassy."

Lincoln's grin melts away, along with any sense of playfulness. "I wasn't made aware of it." He flips through the pages inside the folder. "Acca informed Father, though." The muscles along his jawline tighten with rage.

I scan the documents myself. "Adair's formally announcing results from her investigation of the Ghost Towers tonight. What a very-very suspicious emergency, considering we're slated to find Lucifer's Orb tomorrow morning. Methinks she's trying to steal our thunder."

The limo turns off the back roads and heads into more populated areas. Almost immediately, quasis start to fill the roadsides, holding up signs that say 'quasi lives first' and 'iconigration now'. The crowd boos, shakes their signs, and screams obscenities as we drive by.

I point to the window. "What's up with this? I thought we were flying under the radar with the Ghost Tower risks."

Cissy shakes her head. "Adair's been giving speeches around the Thrax Embassy for days. Local schools, coffee houses, that kind of thing. Now, the quasi population around here is in a full-blown panic."

My hands ball with frustration. "So, we focus on the warehouse for two days and this is what happens. Adair takes to the streets."

"It totally sucks," says Cissy. "But, we hardly have enough staff to cover regular Diplomatic work, let alone following around Adair."

"I know, Cissy." I set my palms onto my eyes. This situation bites. So. Hard. "The biggest question is what to do now?"

Cissy's mouth thins into a determined line. "We have to nail this press conference, Myla. Otherwise, Adair will use the TV, radio and print coverage to spread that same panic all over Purgatory. Have either of you done damage control in a press conference before?"

"Antrum doesn't have an independent press," explains Lincoln. "At least, not when it comes to royalty."

"And I've only had Scala-love interviews. Everyone's been so thrilled that I'm from Purgatory, it's been one fluff piece after another." A pang of worry constricts my throat. How's this press conference going to work, exactly? I'm the girl who causes damage, not controls it.

We turn down onto a major street and the handful of quasis at the roadside turn into rowdy crowds. More signs. More screaming as my limo drives by. Some of my people actually hold clubs and guns above their heads. A new sign gets added into the mix: 'Cursed Scala, Cursed Purgatory'.

Hells Bells. For the first time, I'm very-very glad Purgatory doesn't have any cell service or Internet. Otherwise, we'd already be in full-blown riot stage by now.

The limo pulls up to the Thrax Embassy, a small stone castle whose even smaller front yard is crammed with people. I count three TV vans from Purgatory alone. Hundreds of reporters and photographers jostle for position. I see folks from Antrum, the Dark Lands and even Heaven. Thousands of protestors line the streets. My heart sinks to my toes. The situation's already veering dangerously out of control.

Cissy curls her fingers around the door handle. "Here's the drill. Adair will make her announcement. After that, Myla will say a few words. Lincoln, Xavier, Camilla and I will be on-stage for backup." She looks me over and frowns. "Maybe it's better if Camilla spoke, instead. You've never done anything like this before, Myla."

"True enough." I rub my chin, considering. Cissy's right. Mom does damage control all the time. She could easily take this press conference, too. I picture myself standing at the back of the stage, looking goddess-like while Mom works the crowd. Some of the anxiety eases from my neck and shoulders. That could totally work.

"You really think Mom can do it?"

"Oh yeah," replies Cissy. "I mean, she knows Soul Processing as well as you do, right?"

Wrong. The tension returneth.

"No, Mom's had enough to do without learning my job, too." Worry settles back onto my shoulders, heavy as stones. "No, Cis. I'm the Great Scala and this is my responsibility."

"Are you sure?"

"Sure, I'm sure." *Total lie.*

"Okay," says Cissy. "We're on." She pushes the door open and steps out first. The crowd on the Embassy lawn goes crazy. Two lines of Purgatory police in black riot gear hold back the mob on either side of us, creating a makeshift aisle to the front door. Dozens of flash bulbs go off in my face. Everyone yells questions at once. It's an assault without weapons, and that awakens my inner wrath demon. I snap into battle mode, my mind quickly running through strategies galore. My next step instantly becomes clear.

Get your goddess on, Myla.

Taking a deep breath, I step out into the fray. Lincoln walks beside me, taking my hand in his. Together, we stroll through the thin aisle made by the Purgatory police. I scan the crowd in a way that says: *I can send you to Hell in an instant, so back the fuck off.*

It works. The aisle becomes less crowded, fewer flash bulbs go off and the questions die down.

So far, so good.

Lincoln and I follow Cissy through the Thrax Embassy

until we reach a small auditorium in the back of the castle. Cissy's told me about this place. It's where Dignitaries run free seminars for quasis on topics like 'why the thrax are color coded', 'how to make sure we won't kill you on sight', that kind of thing.

Today, the small auditorium is crammed with reporters, all of them jostling for position. Up front, a tiny stage holds a podium decorated with the crest of Rixa, Lincoln's House. Along the back of the platform stand Mom, Dad and Adair. The crowd is a sea of strange faces, except for Walker. Seeing his encouraging smile makes me feel better. It means a lot that he hustled over here on short notice.

Cissy, Lincoln, and I press our way through the crowd. As we move along, Adair stares at Lincoln in a way that's somewhere between adoration and rage. She's so creepy, it isn't funny.

Once we step onto the stage, Lincoln turns to me. "Mind if I kick things off? The podium has my crest on it, after all." I glance over to Mom, quickly shifting my pointer finger between Lincoln and the podium. She nods quickly.

Excellent. That nod means that Lincoln's good to go.

"Mom says it's fine. Have fun." I kiss Lincoln on his cheek. Several lightning bolts worth of flash bulbs go off.

"Thank you." Lincoln steps up to the podium and taps on the microphone. An electronic thud-thud echoes through the auditorium. The crowd quiets.

Lincoln scans the room, his chin held high, and crown perfectly centered on his head. He looks very regal and badass. "Good evening, everyone. I am Lincoln Vidar Osric

Aquilus, High Prince of the House of Rixa. This is my Embassy and these are my Diplomats who run it. For the record, this emergency press conference was called without my approval. Anything said here tonight does not represent the full will and opinion of those who rule Antrum." He stalks to the back wall of the stage and glares at Adair, who quickly rushes up to the podium.

"Hello, I'm Adair, the Great Lady of the House of Acca, rulers of Antrum for countless millennia. I was also first to be initiated the Scala Heir after Maxon Bane."

Fresh anger pulses through me. The first to be initiated? What the what? Adair's entire initiation ceremony was a fake. She admitted so herself. And it was one thing when Adair spewed out this garbage to Lincoln and me. It's another thing to say it to the press.

Adair gestures to Lincoln. "I thank my esteemed colleague for his introduction, but I can assure you that the royal family was made perfectly aware of this emergency press conference. So, without further ado, I would like to officially announce the initial findings of my investigation into the dangers of the Ghost Towers."

The room goes quiet and Adair scans the room, prolonging the moment.

My rage level skyrockets. If there's one Adair-related thing I hate more than her lies, it's her drama. My tail arches over my shoulder, snapping into battle stance. I don't even bother to tell it to heel. At this rate, I may very well fight her on-stage in front of everyone, press be damned.

"Here's what I have to say," announces Adair. "You think those are Ghost Towers? They're pressure cookers, ready to explode any moment!" She does jazz hands. Actual jazz hands.

Every muscle in my body screams to take Adair down, right now. Lincoln senses my rage, and slips his hand into mine. I grip his fingers so tightly, I'm surprised he doesn't yelp with pain. Still, his touch centers me again. Somehow, I'm able to hold it together while the press reacts to Adair's show.

And react they do. The reporters go wild. More flashing. More shouting. The audience begins to move as an angry mob, pushing towards the stage in waves.

"We're on the brink of new Ghost Riots, my friends. I tell you, every quasi in Purgatory could be murdered at any moment. The bottom line is simple. You need someone to move those souls now. I am the Scala Heir." She raises her arms high and igni materialize around her palms. "Once I become the Great Scala, I'll move those souls for you, I promise. All I need is the opportunity."

Opportunity, my ass! What Adair's asking for is nothing less than my assassination. Once I'm dead, she'll get the rest of my igni, easy-peasy. The truth slams into me like a punch to the gut. Sneaking around…causing trouble… stealing my igni…all of Adair's actions have worked towards a single goal. Causing the mass riots, fear, and panic that end in my assassination and her ascension as the Great Scala. Bottom line: she thinks I stole her life, and now she's stealing it back. Unholy Hell.

"And if you don't believe me, I've brought Tower Warden Celia Graham to speak with you tonight. She's worked inside those ticking time bombs herself. She'll back up every word I have to say!"

Celia? Really?

That's it. Rage courses through every cell in my body. My eyes flare demon-bright. I march up to the podium and glare death at Adair. "Step aside." My tail arches menacingly over my shoulder. "And if you try to lay a finger on me, that's one less finger you'll have. Understand?"

The room falls eerily silent. Every eye becomes locked on Adair and me.

"I speak the truth," chirps Adair. But her voice comes out more as a question.

"Move it, Adair. Now." My eyes flare an even brighter shade of red, and Adair quickly returns to her place against the wall.

Nice.

Closing my eyes, I summon enough igni to pack every inch of airspace in the auditorium. Their little silver bodies whirl about, diving around the reporters' feet, spinning through their hair and equipment, and bursting fireworks-style above their heads.

Soft oohs and ahs fill the air, which I find most satisfying.

I'm careful to keep the igni well out of Adair's reach, however. I'm a theatrical leader, not a total dumbass.

I snap my fingers; all the igni disappear. Leaning forward, I speak into the microphone. "Hello, I'm Myla

Lewis, and I'm the Great Scala. For the record, the Ghost Towers are secure. No one in Purgatory is at risk." An idea appears in my mind. Well, it's Cissy's idea actually, but its time has come. "Tomorrow, my team will locate Lucifer's Orb and move it out of Purgatory. Within a few days, I'll hold my first iconigration. No more sending innocents to Hell. Come to the warehouse for a Grand Unveiling of the Orb tomorrow at 6:17AM. See it happen, live, with your own eyes."

Adair steps forward. You have to hand it to the girl; she does not give up. "What about the Bloodstone Curse? Isn't it true that you're stalling on moving souls because you no longer have enough power for an iconigration?" She wheels around to face the audience. "Myla's been lying to you for months! About her powers. About the Bloodstone Curse. This Grand Unveiling will be yet another lie, you'll see!"

I keep talking into the microphone as if Adair isn't behind me. "I know you've all heard rumors. About ghosts breaking free. About me having some kind of curse. The Diplomat's speech might lead some to think you'd be better off with another Scala."

I grip either side of the podium tightly. "I say this to you with all my heart. It would be easy for me to move those spirits. Too easy. And easy answers are not what Purgatory is about. We exist to give souls an even chance at the right afterlife. Trial by Jury. Trial by Combat. It's hard work. And it is only by your fair verdicts that souls should be judged and moved. No Orb should take that away from you."

Every eye is locked on me. The sensation reminds me of when I'm fighting a demon for ages without one of us getting any advantage. Then, at last, a killing blow becomes obvious. Only here, my Arena is this auditorium. The demon that I'm fighting is fear mongering from Adair. Now that I have the audience's focus, I know the exact verbal moves that will kill my people's terror.

I raise my fist to shoulder-height. "Right here, right now, this moment. We have a chance to change things. To take back what was stolen from us when Armageddon invaded twenty years ago. I need you to be strong with me. I need you to support these souls and have patience. And if you're in this room, I need you to have something more. Restraint. As members of the press, you have the ability to incite riots that could tear Purgatory apart."

I point towards the door. "You've all seen the angry mobs on the way here. I urge you to be responsible. Wait until tomorrow morning. I assure you, we will find that Orb. And finding it, we will fully return to the Purgatory that we once were." My eyes glow a bright shade of angelic blue. "I am the Great Scala, and that is my promise."

I quickly hustle over to Mom and speak in a low voice. "What should I do next?" Now that I'm away from the microphone, I'm starting to question my choice of holding a major press event in seven hours. "Do you think it was a good idea to have a Grand Unveiling? Should we cancel it or something?"

"Not at all. Opening up tomorrow's Unveiling to the press is a brilliant idea, Myla. You quieted the crowd and stopped any rioting tonight. Next, we need to get to the warehouse and plan the event at double-speed." She gestures towards the stairs leading off the stage. "You and Lincoln should leave now. I'll close things out here." Mom steps up to the podium and begins to speak, but I don't hear her words. Instead, I focus on grabbing Lincoln's hand and finding our way back to the limo. Once we're safely inside, he wraps me in a big hug.

"Excellent work. Octavia couldn't have done any better."

A happy blush crawls up my cheeks. Getting compared to Octavia? That's high praise, indeed. "Thanks."

He cups my face in his hands. "What a Queen you'll make one day."

For a few blissful seconds, all I can think about are Lincoln's gentle hands and kind words. After that, the adrenaline in my system goes haywire, focusing on all the things that could go wrong tomorrow. "I'm not so sure about that. We've only got seven hours left to plan this Grand Unveiling. And we must allow Adair to attend since she's our Thrax Diplomat. But what if she tries more sabotage? I hope I didn't trade one fiasco tonight for something worse in the morning."

"Hey, you made the perfect call tonight." He gestures to the tinted windows. Although an angry crowd still covers the sidewalk, the streets are now clear. "No riots, right?"

I nod slowly, forcing myself to take calming breaths. "True."

"The way I see it, we have seven whole hours left to plan. We'll miss some things, sure. But we'll get more right than we do wrong. I believe in you, Myla."

I wrap him in a tight hug. A feeling of love and warmth blooms through my chest. "Thank you."

"Any time. I'm well-known for a good pep talk before battle."

I gently kiss his cheek. "I can see why."

The limo driver rolls down the partition between the front seat and back. "Where to?"

Lincoln leans forward to chat up the driver. As we pull away from the curb, I'm feeling mighty pleased with my bad self. Opening up tomorrow's Grand Unveiling to the press really was a good call. The streets are indeed safe tonight.

That's when I see it. A thrax reporter with glowing-red eyes. Demon-bright.

I grab Lincoln's hand. "Come, look!"

He slips up beside me. "What's wrong?"

"The reporter in the purple tunic. Do you see his eyes?"

He leans closer to the window. "Yes. Is something wrong with them?"

"Of course, there is." I point at the window. "They're…"

But the eyes aren't red anymore. They're the mismatched hues of every thrax.

"They're what, Myla?"

I plunk back into my cushy seat and let out a long

groan. “It’s been a super long day. I might be seeing things.” I shake my head. “Mom said we should meet up at the warehouse. Let’s get over there.”

“How about we get you some java along the way?”

“I like that idea very much.” Once I start seeing things, it’s definitely time for extra coffee.

12

6:14AM.

I pace across the warehouse floor, anxious energy zinging through my limbs. Three minutes from now, our Grand Unveiling of Lucifer's Orb will begin. Yipes. Beside me, reporters from across the after-realms are packed along the back wall, seated on tiered risers that reach from floor to ceiling. All their gazes are glued onto the movement of a little tin bird.

At the far side of the warehouse, the enchanted bird in question flits above the aisles, landing one box, then another, continuing on in its mission to find Lucifer's Orb at precisely 6:17AM. All last night, Lincoln and I packed this warehouse with every security precaution we could think of: alarms, guns, secret agents, obvious guards, you name it. Once that Orb is found, it's staying in our control, end of story.

I quickly check the risers and my heart lightens. Two

minutes to go and still, no sign of Adair. Maybe the extra precautions weren't necessary, after all. The knots of worry in my neck loosen, making me feel more calm and optimistic. Not so chill that I stop pacing in front of the risers, though.

Lincoln waves me over. He stands on the left-side of the tiered seats, alongside my parents, Cissy, Walker, and the Alchemists. I'm feeling so good now; it takes an effort not to skip over to him.

"What's up?"

"You might want to stop pacing in front of the reporters."

"Why, I'm not bothering anyone, am I?"

"Far from it. The male members of the audience appreciate your parade in the extreme. I know I certainly am." A mischievous gleam dances in his eyes. "It's very-very cold in here, Myla."

"Ooooooh." I forgot that my Scala robes leave nothing to the imagination. "You know, that's a pretty pervy thing to notice."

He points to his face. "Uh, guy."

"Fine. I'll stand here by you, then."

"Thought you might want to."

Now that I can't pace anymore, I segue onto obsessively checking and re-checking the wall clock. 6:16AM on the nose. One more minute and we'll find that Orb and ship it out of Purgatory. Woo-freaking-hoo. My body fills with a mixture excitement and relief. We're about to do it, for real. Fix Soul Processing without sentencing millions of innocents to Hell...Or burning down Purgatory in a new round of Ghost Riots.

I'm feeling mighty awesome indeed when Adair steps through the warehouse door.

Boo.

Yeah, I knew she'd probably show, but I was really-really-really hoping she'd find someone else to stalk today. Adair stands on the right-hand side of the risers, directly across from my family and friends. She brought a guest with her, as well: Gianna, the very same Striga witch who faked Adair's igni powers at her pretend-initiation to become Scala Heir.

Anxiety corkscrews up my torso. Gianna is here? That is so not-good.

I turn to Lincoln. "Look who's arrived."

"I saw."

"Do the Alchemists practice witchcraft?"

"Not in the way Gianna does, if that's what you're thinking. They're more scientists than rapid-fire casters."

"Can we get our own witch in from Striga, then? Someone who can counteract Gianna?" I'm so hyped up, I could carry whoever-it-is back from the Pulpitum myself.

"Not in the next sixty seconds," explains Lincoln. "Which is undoubtedly why Adair arrived late."

"Crud." I'm so frustrated, want to face-palm myself or kill something. We put every security measure in the book into this dumb warehouse, except for an extra warlock or witch. Didn't Dad suggest that ages ago, too? How could I forget?

"I can't believe I missed this one. Gianna's helped Adair before."

"It's like I said last night, Myla. With seven hours to plan, we'll miss some things. Even big things. I'm sure I speak for all of us when I say that at this point, it's your decision what to do next. Do you want to move forward or call this off?"

I rub my neck, considering. Adair's a sneaky type of evil, which isn't necessarily my strong suit. I'm more of a straightforward fight-maim-kill kind of girl. I run through the implications of each decision, moving forward or calling it off. Both seem pretty sucky. Either I wait for Adair to show me up, or I retreat and look like a cursed liar. Either way, my people could still lose their freaking minds. Ghost Riots part two.

The crowd on the risers lets out a collective gasp, interrupting my thoughts. I scan the warehouse, finding that our tin bird has finally stopped flitting from box to box. Now, it's landed on a large crate marked Maxon Bane. There, it hops back and forth, stopping every so often to peck at the wood.

All eyes turn to me. The bird's stopped flying around. The Orb may have been discovered. I'm supposed to make a decision and do something. As in, right now. My heart pumps so hard, I hear blood whoosh in my ears.

The energy level in the room goes through the roof. Lucifer's Orb has been hidden for two millennia; seeing it unveiled is a once-in-a-lifetime thing. The crowd's excitement pulses through me and suddenly, I'm back in the

Arena, facing down my first demon at twelve years old. The sensations of that moment return to me, fierce and exciting. The dusty scent of the Arena air. Electric fear jangling my nerves. The crowd's energy, pulling me onward. My warrior sense, roaring through my brain.

This press event is the same thing. It has to be.

I didn't have any battle training when I was twelve, any more than I've done damage control in a press conference now. Still, I'm the kind of girl who runs into the Arena, kills now, asks questions later, and it all works out fine in the long run. A small voice in the back of my head says I'm far from the Arena these days, but I decide that voice is being a mega-wimp.

Time to turn off my brain and go into warrior mode. Forget Adair and her schemes. Screw whatever Gianna's going to do. I'm moving forward with our plan and, somehow, I'll make it work.

After taking a deep breath, I step in front of the risers and address the audience. Rapid-fire flash bulbs go off in my face. "Ladies and gentlemen, thank you for joining us today at the Grand Unveiling of Lucifer's Orb." The risers shake as reporters wave their arms, anxious to ask questions. I raise my hands to shoulder height, palms forward, which is the international sign for chill out. "Everyone, quiet down, now. I'll get to your questions after we show you the Orb." The press retake their seats.

With a dramatic flourish, I point to the final crate of the tin bird's journey. "As you know, the enchanted bird behind me has been following a series of linked magical objects. It's a treasure hunt, if you will. At the end of this search—the last link in the chain—is Lucifer's Orb." The crowd lets out a gratifying chorus of oohs and ahs. "Let's take a look."

I step halfway across the warehouse floor and pause. Something about this isn't right.

Then I realize what isn't right. Me.

I'm not in the Arena anymore. I'm the Great Scala. I can't fight first and think later. Turning around, I scan the faces of my friends and family. Mom, Dad, Lincoln, Walker, Cissy, and the Alchemists. All of them trust my call on this Grand Unveiling. I can't take that lightly. Turning on my heel, I walk back to the risers and press.

Barf. As much as I hate to do this, I'm calling it off.

I slap on my most confident demi-goddess face. "I appreciate your coming out today, and I'm sincerely sorry to have wasted your time. However—"

Adair rushes forward, pointing her arm at me while yelling to the risers. "See, I told you all. She's a liar. She doesn't have the Orb. All she has is the Bloodstone Curse. I'm the True Scala. I'm the only one who'll save you. Show them, Myla. Show them the Orb!"

"I was just about to say that we aren't showing anyone anything today."

"You promised. The box is right there." Her eyes flare red. "Show them the Orb. We'll go together."

I eye her carefully. She's pushing me too hard, and getting too emotional, too quickly. It's all quite fishy. "No, Adair."

Moving with almost supernatural speed, Adair races over to the crate and whips off the top. A huge puff of purple smoke rises from inside. Adair waves it away with her hands.

I call to Walker. "Have the Guards clear out the area. Starting with her."

On hearing those words, Adair reaches into the box, her hands flailing around in the smoke. The crate is shoulder height, so she's liable to fall inside if she isn't careful.

Adair's muffled voice sounds from within the wooden box. "It's not here. The Orb's not here. I'll prove it."

My mind freezes, capturing the moment. If she's so certain the Orb's not here, why make an ass out of herself? The girl's about to topple head-over-heels in front of every major reporter in the after-realms.

I step up behind Adair, grab her by the waist, and haul her out of the crate. Once she's vertical again, I take care to wrap my tail around her wrists, preventing any igni-thievery. "Calm down, Adair. You'll hurt yourself at this rate."

Her eyes turn wild with fear. "I have to show them. All of them. This crate is empty. Let me look around some more. I'll show you." She writhes under my tail.

"And why on Earth would I let you do that?" A trio of guards steal up behind Adair.

"Because I have to check. I have to show them all."

"Smoke clears on its own, Adair. They'll see soon enough if it's empty."

And watching her try to wriggle free of my tail and leap into the crate, Adair's scheme for today's event becomes crystal-clear. Gianna must've cloaked the Orb inside the box. Now, Adair wants to take it for herself. All she needs to do is hide the Orb for a few days and the Ghost Towers will blow. My people will panic. Adair will be proclaimed Great Scala. The quasis will force me to give her my igni, or even worse, take my life. She'll have won.

A guard sets his hand on Adair's arm, and she goes freaking berserk. "Unhand me! I'm a diplomat!"

Oh yeah, she wants that Orb, all right. Badly.

Hundreds of flashbulbs pop as three guards drag Adair off the warehouse floor. The whole time, she keeps yelling about inspecting the damn crate. "It's my right to show you! She's lying! There is no Orb!"

No Orb, my ass.

Once she's gone, the guards start evacuating the press. The reporters don't like being led away much better than Adair did. As they're walked to the door, they call out question after question, everything from 'when did you know you were cursed?' to 'why did you lie about the Orb?' and 'what will you do about the pending riots?'

I suppose all the nasty questions and blinding flash bulbs should leave me flipped out and-or pissed off. I'm neither. All I can think about is that Orb.

Please please pleeeeeeease let it be in the crate.

My heart hammers against my rib cage, its beat more powerful with every second. An idea has appeared in my mind and if the Orb is still here, I may actually have a chance at beating Adair.

I keep standing and looking goddess-like until they're all gone, Walker's guards included.

It's just my friends and family now. Time to check if my assumptions about Adair and the Orb are right.

I rush over to the wooden crate marked Maxon Bane. All the smoke's cleared away, so I can easily lean over and look inside.

Nothing. Nada. Empty.

My friends and family step up to the crate as well. Walker's the first to speak. "That can't be empty. I tell you, my calculations were correct. The Orb is in this warehouse. And the tin bird was enchanted perfectly. The Orb simply has to be in that crate."

"Then it is, Walker." I turn to the Alchemists. "Gianna cast some kind of cloaking spell on the Orb. Find it."

"Are you sure?" asks Erik. "She could have sent it somewhere else, too."

"No, did you see the way Adair fought to get something out of this crate? The Orb is in here, no question. Do your magic-thing and get it out."

"Yes, Great Scala." Erik and his buddies start pouring over the crate, discussing what kind of spell Gianna could have used. Minutes tick by while they try different counter-charms and enchantments. At last, a puff of red smoke rises from the crate's interior.

"Eureka!" Erik reaches into the crate, pulling out a small golden ball covered in a pattern of angel wings.

That's it. Lucifer's Orb.

I stare at the glittering surface. After so many days of

imagining finding this thing, I can't believe it's really in Erik's hands. Then again, Erik can be a tricky little bastard sometimes.

"This isn't one of your pranks, is it?"

"Nuh-uh." Erik offers me the Orb. "Do you want it?"

"No, give it to Walker. He needs to take some pictures and run some tests." We talked about this before; we'll eventually need proof for the papers that the Orb was found. And as for the tests? Walker tried to explain them to me, but my eyes glazed over after about ten seconds.

Erik hands the Orb to Walker, who turns it over in his palms. "The energy signature on this thing is unbelievable. I can even feel it against my skin. I won't know for certain until I run some tests, but it may take some time before the Orb's affect on Purgatory wears off."

I suck in a nervous breath. "Like, how long?" If he says he doesn't know, I'll have a coronary.

"No more than a few days, tops."

Relief washes through me. "That's fine. We'll need some time to set up the iconigration ceremony, anyway."

"I'll stay with Walker and the Orb," says Dad. "The second those tests are done, I'll run it up to Heaven. We've a special vault where the Orb will be safe."

Mom sets her hands in the pockets of her suit-jacket. She's all business now. "I'll call an emergency press conference immediately. Adair's accusations should be all over the news within an hour—Myla's supposed curse, Adair being the true Scala, the Ghost Towers ready to explode, and my people about to be murdered. I'll let everyone know the Orb's been recovered and within a few days, we can move souls safely. That should calm the worst of their fears."

Mom's words start the wheels of my mind a-turning. The Orb has been found…Or has it? The idea I'd started to form before now solidifies in my nasty little noggin. It's a totally kick-ass, awesome concept.

"Wait a second, everyone. I think we can use this situation to our advantage. Mom, can you do an emergency press conference to confirm that there was no Orb in the warehouse? You know, tell everyone that it's still okay and not to lose their minds."

"Surely," replies Mom. "But why would I ever do that? Our people will take it as a sign that Adair's right. They'll only get more agitated."

"I know, but I have a idea for defeating Adair. And for it to work, she needs to think we don't know the Orb is still in the warehouse."

Mom's eyes narrow. "I'm listening."

"For months, Adair's been one step ahead of me. But I believe that she screwed up tonight, trying to grab the Orb. Now, we can use that information to take the fight to her. I want to set up a sting operation right here, in this warehouse. Get her to admit what she's really done so we can slap her ass in jail. You know, before she causes even more trouble. But to do that, she has to think that we don't know the Orb is here. She'll come back to get it, I'll be here and—pow—that's when we get her confession."

"I don't know, honey," says Mom. "Even if you get the

evidence, we can't hold her in Purgatory for longer than twenty-four hours. That's inter-realm law. Lincoln's parents must agree to jailing her in Antrum."

"I can get their consent," says Lincoln quickly. "Call the press conference for two hours from now. Myla and I will go over to Arx Hall and get my parent's okay. If we get that to you before the press conference starts, will you say the Orb wasn't found today?"

Mom steeples her fingertips under her chin for what feels like a decade, minimum. "Alright, you've got it. Two hours only."

Lincoln kisses me gently on the cheek. "I like this, Myla. Taking the fight to her."

Something in Lincoln's words resonates through the deepest parts of me. This isn't the old Myla Lewis running headlong into danger without thinking. This is the Great Scala, using my warrior-brain to take the offensive in a smart way. And as Dad always says, 'when it comes to battle, take the offensive and never let go'.

13

Lincoln and I cross the enormous cobblestone yard that encompasses Pulpitum VII, Purgatory's official transfer station to Antrum. I've ridden a thrax transfer platform with Lincoln a few times before, and it's hella-fun. However, once we reach Antrum today, our fun-time will be over. We need to convince Lincoln's parents to help us take down Adair. Not a lock.

We close in on the Pulpitum, which is a temple-style structure built in Roman times. It's circular in shape and surrounded by tall stone columns. We locals call it 'the can' because the interior is tall, cylinder-like and made of solid rock. One small slit-like opening marks the only way in or out. An obnoxious amount of thrax guards surround the place, all of them wearing black body armor with the Rixa crest.

As we get closer, the guards recognize Lincoln and salute in sync. He waves at them in a friendly-yet-regal way. They're all supposed to stare straight forward, but most of them steal a look or two in my direction. As the Great Scala and Lincoln's Angelbound love, everyone's heard of me but few have actually met me. My tail alternates between waving at the guards and doing karate-style chops. That thing can be such a smart-ass sometimes.

Inside the Pulpitum, fire crackles in a series of bowl-like sconces set on tall metal braziers. At the center of the floor, there's a smooth metallic disc about ten feet wide. That's the transfer platform. Excitement thrums through my veins. Thrax transfer-travel is a blast.

Lincoln pauses just inside the entryway. "Activating standard station. Lincoln Vidar Osric Aquilus." A grid of white laser beams crosses the Pulpitum floor, performing a body scan on both of us. The one place thrax go high-tech is on anything to do with security or demon patrol. Pulpitum cover both areas.

A woman's voice echoes through the chamber. "Identity confirmed. Glad you're returning home, Your Highness."

"Appreciate the well wishes, Cassandra. How's the team at Transfer Central? I heard another Agent had an accident."

"Julian took a nasty fall. He's recovering in the infirmary."

"Another fall?" Lincoln frowns, considering. "Keep me informed."

"I will, Your Highness. We don't have you scheduled for transfer today. Is this for demon patrol?"

"We bring news of Lucifer's Orb, which is demon

magic, so it qualifies. Queen Octavia will have approved the rush transfer, as well as my guest."

A long pause follows. "Yes, both are approved. Destination?"

"Arx Hall Pulpitum."

"Confirmed and ready at your signal."

We step onto the metallic disc. On a thrax platform, the correct way to travel is in a huddle with your arms looped across the shoulders of the person next to you. Lincoln and I get into position.

Once we're settled, Lincoln speaks again. "Launch transfer on my mark. 3, 2, 1."

With a jolt of movement, the circular platform whips downwards, hurtling through the ground. The temple's circular walls are replaced by a blur of soil, water, and stone as we careen through the earth. From time to time, the disc lurches from one side to another as it avoids some obstacle, mostly seams of diamonds and lava flows. Their glittering presence flashes along one side of the platform as we pitch in a new direction, always keeping in a downward trajectory.

Another jolt hits, and then the platform comes to an abrupt halt. We've stopped at the end of a gilded corridor. The Arx Hall platform.

Octavia and Connor are already waiting for us.

"Myla, so good to see you." Octavia is petite with long brown hair that's wound into a neat chignon. She wears a simple medieval-style gown of Rixa black with a scoop neck and long, loopy sleeves.

"Lincoln, my boy!" Connor is barrel-chested and full of energy. He wraps Lincoln in a bear hug before nodding in my direction. "Myla."

"Connor."

Octavia clasps her hands together at her waist. "Why don't we visit the Feasting Hall?" Without waiting for a reply, she leads us all to a wooden chamber with plaster walls and an arched ceiling. Long feasting tables with matching benches fill up the floor.

Connor gestures to one of the benches. "Shall we sit?"

"I'd rather stand," says Lincoln coolly. It's his way of saying he's all business today.

"So, what are we here to discuss?" asks Octavia. "Your message was most cryptic."

I pull a document from my Scala robes and hand it to her. "Adair is using magic in a way that breaks inter-realm law. She's stealing my powers. This parchment outlines my charges."

Octavia purses her lips and scans the page quickly. "Has this been filed with the Thrax Embassy?"

"Not yet," I reply.

Connor leans against a nearby wall and kicks his left ankle over his right. "Well, how could you file? Powers. It's not like stealing real property."

Lincoln pulls out his own set of papers and hands them to Connor. "I thought there might be confusion on that point. Illegally taking powers is exactly like stealing any other kind of property. In fact, capital punishments are recommended for taking magic that ensures the after-realms run properly. Myla's igni certainly qualifies in that category."

The barest smile curls Octavia's lips. She's so loving this. Adair and the House of Acca have been on her hate-list for ages. "These charges require some proof," adds Octavia. "What do you have?"

I force on my confident demi-goddess face. I've only met Lincoln's parents a handful of times. Now, I'm about to ask them to imprison one of their so-called Great Ladies. Sure, she's a barking lunatic, but even I know this is a ballsy move for a new girlfriend.

"Here's the thing," I explain. "We're setting up a sting operation in Purgatory. I think Adair will confess before witnesses. If she doesn't, then I'll drop the entire matter."

Octavia returns my papers to me. "You seem rather confident in her guilt."

"Rock solid."

"Why come here, then?" asks Connor. "You don't need our permission for a sting operation."

"True," I reply. "We need you to jail her once we prove her guilt, however."

Connor's face takes on the look of a cornered animal. "That's assuming she's guilty anyway. And what's this I hear about a Curse? I've gotten reports that murderous ghosts are about to roam Purgatory, as well. That's one mess we thrax don't look forward to cleaning up."

Whoa. In a surprise move, Connor tries to steer the conversation away from Adair-slash-Acca's guilt and onto my problems. Note to self: one of these days, ream Connor out about his Acca-love program. It's ridiculous.

"I am perfectly healthy and our Ghost Towers are secure. All of that is Adair's cover story for stealing my igni. Until she's behind bars, she'll continue to cause us trouble. She's the one who's really placing Purgatory at risk."

"What are the specifics on this trap?" asks Connor. "Must be quite a scheme."

Riiiiiiight. It takes everything I have not to roll my eyes. Like we're telling Connor diddly.

"I'm sure the children wish to keep the details to themselves," says Octavia simply. A long pause follows as she glares at Connor. Whole conversations hide inside that glance.

While the stare-fest continues, I give Lincoln's parents a careful once-over. What is it between them and Acca, anyway? They seem super-close except for this one area. It's obvious that Octavia hates that House with a passion, while Connor doesn't necessarily like Acca, but he certainly gives in to them all the time.

At length, Connor looks away. "You don't need to go into specifics. We understand the gist of your operation."

"Excellent," says Lincoln. "So, what do you say?"

"I see no reason not to support you," declares Octavia. "If you get the proof, we will uphold inter-realm law and place Adair in our prisons. Don't you agree, Connor?"

"Yes, yes, of course. Inter-realm law and all that."

Okay, that's about the lamest endorsement I've ever heard.

I whip out my snarkiest tone. "Well, thanks for the support and all that."

Connor looks dumbfounded for a full minute.

Lincoln and I share a look, and I know he's fighting the urge to burst out laughing. Thrax are raised to never say 'boo' to their King. For me, mouthing off to power comes quite naturally.

Octavia quickly changes the subject. "I hope you'll get this nonsense fixed right away. We're holding Myla's Ball of Welcome tomorrow night. If Adair's sabotaging things, I certainly don't want my event affected."

Oh, crap. I totally forgot about that Ball of Welcome.

Images flash through my mind. Dresses. Shoes. Small-talk. Waltzing. *Arrrgh.* No question. I need to sweet-talk my way out of this.

"Come to think of it, there's a lot going on this week, what with the sting operation and all. Maybe we should put off the Ball for a while and—"

Octavia fixes me with a stare that could melt lead. I fight the overwhelming urge to cower and yell 'yipe-yipe-yipe' at the top of my lungs. Damn, but when she wants to, Octavia can be scary. And I know scary.

"Or, on second thought," I add quickly. "We could still have the Ball tomorrow night."

"As I'd hoped," replies Octavia. "My seamstresses are working on a lovely over-gown for your Scala robes. That way you can keep them on and still look thrax traditional."

"Thanks, Octavia, that sounds—" *What should I say about this over-gown thing?* I mean, if she's gotten me nun-chucks,

I'd have tons of comments. My mind becomes a total blank as a single word escapes my lips. "Nifty."

Nifty? Really, Myla? Yow, it's been a long day.

"You're most welcome," retorts Octavia. "I've made other interesting plans for the Ball as well." With that, she launches into a long explanation of all her Ball preparations. I do my best to listen, but I can't help noticing that Lincoln pulls his father aside for a heated discussion. I've never seen Lincoln so angry.

A chill of foreboding creeps up my skin, making me shiver. Based on the way my life is going lately, I'd bet a million dollars that their talk has something to do with Adair.

And something mighty unpleasant, too.

14

Lincoln and I rush onto the transfer platform in Arx Hall. All through the ride back, he doesn't say a word. Every time I try to look at him, he glances away. Whenever I ask a question, I get a one-word answer. If I take his hand in mine, he gives my palm a quick squeeze before letting go.

No question about it. Lincoln's fight with his father has him mega-bummed out.

Once we reach the Pulpitum in Purgatory, I find us a quiet bench on the nearby cobblestone yard. A few silent minutes pass while we soak in the gray Purgatory day. Finally, Lincoln meets my gaze. A sad smile rounds his lips.

That's my cue. He's ready to talk.

"What happened back there?" I ask.

He exhales a long breath. "What didn't happen back there?"

"I mean with your father. I saw you two chatting after

your parents agreed to jail Adair. You looked not-too-happy."

"Well, it's obvious where this is going, from Adair's point of view anyway. If her plan works, she'll take the rest of your powers. Become the Great Scala herself."

Every muscle in my body cringes with loathing. *Adair taking my place? No freaking way.* "You know I won't let her do that. Ever." Even as the words leave my mouth, a little voice in the back of my head says that I may be giving a knee-jerk answer.

I pause, grip the edge of the wooden bench, and force myself to think past my first reaction. If Adair gets my powers, she'll threaten every last thrax with Hell until she has what she wants, and what she wants is Lincoln.

Suddenly, I feel very small, alone and powerless, a tiny fly caught in a complex web of forces out to destroy everything I have and cherish. "What if Adair succeeds? I can't stand the thought of us being forced apart."

Lincoln shifts to face me, cupping my face in his hands. "Listen to me, Myla. You will be my Queen one day, mark my words. Adair will never come between us."

His eyes are fierce with resolve. However, I can't ignore the nagging doubts at the back of my mind. "I want to believe you, but let's be honest. Our sting operation has a fifty-fifty chance at best. Adair may not take the bait and go to the warehouse. And even if she does, she may not confess to her crimes."

"Then, if the sting operation fails, we'll try something

else." He rests his forehead against mine. "I'm never giving up on you. Believe that."

The force of his determination coils around me, warm and strong. I've never felt more loved and protected. "I believe you, Lincoln."

When he speaks again, his voice is rough with emotion. "Good."

Leaning back, I carefully inspect Lincoln's face. Something is definitely still bothering him. If Adair isn't the problem, then his father is. I'm certain of it.

"So, what did you talk to Connor about?"

"This is all wrong. I wanted this to be special, Myla."

"What?"

"I asked my father for the royal betrothal jewels." He takes my hands in his. "I want to make our engagement official."

My heart lightens. "That's awesome." I picture Lincoln and I married, spending all our time together. Killing demons, cuddling, fooling around, killing some more demons.

The idea is so amazing, I can't even think straight.

I bob a little on the park bench. "I mean, we talked about it the other day over pizza, but I didn't realize you were really going for the jewels." My tail musses Lincoln's hair. "Knowing this is something you're really thinking about? You've made me super-happy."

"Still, the first time we seriously discuss an engagement, it shouldn't be on a random park bench in Purgatory."

So, that's what he's worried about? I don't need champagne and roses to make the moment special. Okay, that honestly wouldn't suck, but hey. Getting married will be the bomb, and I'm happy to have it happen, end of story.

"Look, in my mind, our engagement happened when we fell in love and became Angelbound."

Lincoln keeps looking away, which is totally inconsistent with the typical upbeat 'we're getting engaged soon' vibe. I set my fingers on his cheek and slowly guide him to meet my gaze. His eyes are filled with grief and doubt. The lighthearted feeling that hit me at the start of our engagement-chat turns into something leaden.

"This is supposed to be awesome stuff and you look so sad. What's going on?"

"Father can't find the jewels. Lost in the Royal Vaults."

"Okay, that doesn't sound too believable. How do you lose betrothal jewels?"

"You don't. Father won't give me them until things are sorted out with Adair, one way or another."

My chest tightens. Now, I can see the problem. Betrothal jewels are a super-old thrax tradition, dating from their earliest times. Before there were written marriage contracts, there were betrothal jewels. There's only one set per House, no copies. Once you give them to another House, you marry someone from there, or else. But that tradition's thousands of years old. Certainly, they've moved on from it by now.

"Sure, I heard about betrothal jewels, but I figured you wouldn't really…"

"Oh, we really."

I tilt my head to one side, still trying to wrap my head around this. "So until you get the jewels, we can't get engaged."

"I will find them, Myla. Make no mistake." He rubs his neck with his hand. "This situation with my father and Acca is frustrating in the extreme, that's all."

A spark of inspiration appears in my mind. I know exactly what to do. Someone here needs a little pep talk, and I know just the one to give.

I pull Lincoln to his feet. "Remember when we were in the gym with my father, and I was all freaky because I'd just lost my igni?"

"Sure."

"You said I needed to tell Dad what happened. Keep things moving forward. Well, that's exactly what we need to do now. Focus on putting together the finest sting operation in the history of the after-realms. Let's take care of Adair, and I'm sure your father will find those jewels."

"This idea has some merit." He laces his fingers with mine, and swings our arms between us. "What do you suggest, then?"

"How about we go to my place, sync with Mom about the press conference, and then run through some scenarios for Operation Take Down Adair? I even have a few that involve killing her." I bob my eyebrows up and down. "That'll make you feel better."

He smiles, a genuine one at last. "And here, I thought I was the Master of Pep Talks."

"I've a feeling we'll be taking turns at pep talks for a long time to come. It's all part of being a team."

He wraps me in a deep hug. "With you, it is."

"Damn right." I nuzzle into his shoulder, my chest filling with warmth, love and, best of all, hope.

15

It's late at night when I approach the back door of the warehouse. Today's been one Hell of a long day, starting with the Grand Unveiling and continuing with a quick trip to Antrum.

And it's not over yet. The moment I walk through this door, Operation Take Down Adair begins.

I scan the darkened alley leading into the warehouse, nervous energy making me shift my weight from foot to foot. All of Walker's guards left a few minutes ago. The alleyway sure looks empty, but then again, I'm not a hunter like Lincoln. With any luck, Adair's still following me around, same as she's been doing for the last two months. I need her to enter the warehouse, say something incriminating, and end up in jail.

I twist the door's rusted handle; it opens with a long creak. I step inside, my footsteps echoing eerily through the darkened warehouse. Turning on the flashlight in my hand, I scan the empty aisles around me. Everything looks deserted although, in truth, that's far from the case. Lincoln and Company got into this place about an hour ago. Now, they're waiting in position in case Adair takes the bait.

And that bait would be the Orb and me. Alone. Unprotected.

Come and get us.

I navigate through the network of aisles and wooden crates until I reach a box labeled Maxon Bane. I slip off the wooden top; it lands with a thud on the concrete floor. The interior is empty. I pat around the crate's wooden walls, like I'm searching for the Orb. I want Adair to think that I'm coming back to check if the crate's really empty because, hey, it really wasn't. Now, all I need is for Adair to show.

My heart kicks faster in my chest. Come on, Adair. Show up, already.

Turns out, I don't have long to wait.

Suddenly, an igni cord wraps around my waist, lifting me from the ground. For a moment I'm held aloft, my legs dangling. After that, the cord slams me against the aisle behind my back. There, the twenty-foot-tall stack of boxes topples over, causing a domino effect on the rows nearby. With a deafening boom-boom-boom, three aisles tumble over in succession.

I lay on my back for a second, feeling the tug along the igni cord around my waist. It's Adair, trying to pull power from me through the cord. Now, I know how the transfer works. Our palms need to be connected. I'm careful to keep my hands far away from the cord. Still, the rope of igni winds up my chest, starting to crawl vine-like down my forearms.

The cord curls closer to my hands, and panic zooms up my spine. Once the cord hits my palms, it'll be the same deal as in the Ghost Tower. I can't block the transfer. Can't reverse it, either. My only option is to slow how quickly Adair can take my igni.

Not a great option.

I summon my own igni. They blast off my arms like piston rods, whipping across the toppled aisles. The igni-shafts slam into Adair's stomach, and then retract once again. Adair gets pummeled against the stacks of boxes behind her. With more ear-splitting booms, four more aisles topple over in domino-style.

Around me, Adair's cords stretch, flicker and loosen. This didn't happen at the Ghost Tower. What could be causing Adair's igni bindings to weaken now?

The answer appears in my mind, simple and perfect.

"You need to be connected to my palms to have a really strong grip, Adair." I conjure a huge pair of igni clippers and snap the ties between us. Adair's cord disappears. "So, guess who's never getting near my hands again?"

I hop onto my feet. Now that I'm in battle mode, my Scala robes have changed into armor. I brush my fingers across the baculum-holster on my thigh. I'd love to ignite these things, but angelfire isn't any good against igni. I'm better off keeping my hands free so I can counter Adair's next igni-fueled attack.

Across from me, Adair rises to her feet, unhurt. Whoa. She must've gotten some nasty demon blood in her. My last igni-punch should have at least taken her breath away. Adair straightens the skirt of her yellow gown. "Stop making it harder on yourself," she says primly. "I want my igni."

Meaning she wants to steal my Scala powers. If only she'd say that in plain English, I could use it as a confession.

"I owe you nothing. You're here to steal my powers." I'm tempted to add a 'riiiiiiight?' to the end of that sentence, but that falls into the 'not too subtle' category of sting operation. I'm already pushing the envelope as it is.

Adair raises her arms again. Another igni cord blasts at me, heading straight for my waist once more. I leap high into the air, do a somersault, and land safely out of harm's way. In response, I conjure an igni wrecking ball that swings across the warehouse floor, taking out Adair as well as five more aisles of crates.

This is fun and all, but neither of us is getting the upper hand. And at this rate, we're bound to knock over the aisle where Lincoln and everyone else are hiding. I need a new strategy and fast. My warrior sense kicks in, running through approaches and options. An idea appears in my mind. I nod once to myself. It's worth a try.

The next igni-cord that Adair sends my way, I dodge it

while making an offer. "How about a quick truce? Let's see if we can talk this out before we kill each other."

"Before I kill you, more like. Why don't you send me to Hell?"

"So you can steal my igni? Not going to happen." I lower my arms. "Let's discuss options. Short truce?"

She doesn't need to answer, really. I know I have my truce because she's stopped sending the same igni-cord attack at me for the umpteenth time.

I slowly walk towards Adair, my arms down and palms facing forward. "Here are my terms. Want my igni? Come and get them like a warrior. Let's fight one to one, not use igni as shields. You've got the blood of a demon in you now. Show me how strong you are. Take what's yours, if that's what you think my powers are."

We're a yard apart when I stop.

Adair's mismatched eyes narrow. "You're an Arena warrior."

"I thought you were the Great Lady of the greatest House, Acca. The first Scala heir. The first Angelbound to Lincoln. Are you telling me now that you're too frightened to fight?" I slap on the snarkiest grin I can manage. "Let me guess what kind of demon blood you have in you. Slug class? Insect, perhaps? No doubt, it's something small and slimy that hides in the shadows. Lowest of the low."

It's the 'lowest of the low' bit that gets her.

At those words, Adair's eyes flare demon-red. Pay dirt. It took me years to learn to control my inner wrath demon. As Adair's about to discover, that inner fighter will make you do all sorts of stupid stuff if you aren't careful. I don't want to be a premature gloater, but I can't help but smile, just a little.

Adair bends over at the waist and races towards me, ready to head-butt me in the stomach. As she rushes forward, I work hard not to roll my eyes. Here's exactly the kind of stupid move that I was hoping to goad her into. Head butting? Really?

Adair's skull rams into my belly, slamming me onto my back. I make a great show of pretending to pant for air, like the wind got knocked out of me. Adair straddles my rib cage and presses my hands against the floor, careful to keep our palms flush against one another.

The set-up is in place. Time to get a confession.

"What are you..." Pant, pant, pant. "Going to do now?"

"Steal your powers, of course."

Bingo. A massive jolt of happy runs right through me.

The ignited end of a baculum sword appears at Adair's cheek, the rest of it attached to a very pissed-off Lincoln. He speaks two words in his most menacing-yet-Princely-way: "Get up."

Adair looks into Lincoln's eyes. "No, my love. I have to take—" But then, her gaze rests on the array of folks standing behind Lincoln. "How are you all here?"

I hop back up to standing and I must admit, it's a pretty impressive group we pulled together at the last minute. There are my parents, Octavia, Connor, Cissy, and about a dozen Rixa knights in blood-red armor. These guys run the top-priority jail for especially bad thrax.

My tail and I exchange a high-five. We did it. We actually caught Adair.

Suddenly, my heart feels so light, I could float out of this warehouse. It's probably bad form to do a happy-dance right now, but that doesn't mean I don't want to. Badly.

Mom steps forward, pulls out a parchment, and reads the official charges against Adair. There's a lot of awesome stuff in there about why stealing igni power is one of the worst crimes in the after-realms. Dad suggested putting that in. Nice touch.

Once Mom's done, Octavia takes the sheet from her hand. "We accept the prisoner transfer." She motions to the Knights. "Take her to the dungeons."

It was Connor's idea to put Adair into the dungeons at Arx Hall. They aren't exactly a five-star hotel, but they're pretty close. I pushed for a more dungeon-y setting, but there's only so far I can push at this point.

All the blood drains from Adair's face. "You can't do this. Not after the price I paid."

That isn't the first time she said that particular phrase. "What price are you talking about, Adair?"

"You'd know nothing of such things," she snaps. "You're an imposter. I am the True Scala."

I'm tempted to say something snarky about what makes a True Scala, but I don't want to be a sore winner.

The Dungeon Knights end the moment by marching Adair towards the warehouse's back door. The heavy dread that's been weighing on me for weeks lightens to nothing. This is it; Adair is captured.

Oooooooh, yeah.

Adair tries to break away, babbling how she deserves to get her life back, but the Knights are a pretty agile bunch despite their armor. They easily recapture her and push her towards the door. It's such a pretty sight, I could cry.

What a day.

This morning, Adair sabotaged my Grand Unveiling. Twelve hours later, and she's heading off to jail, led by thrax guards, no less.

Octavia steps up to my side. "Job very well done, my dear."

"Thanks, Octavia. Couldn't have done it without your support. Now, I can really focus on getting ready for my first big iconigration." It's only forty-eight hours away. Yowza.

"Obviously, the iconigration is a top priority," answers Octavia smoothly. "But, don't forget. Your Ball of Welcome is tomorrow night."

Oh yeah, oops. "That, too."

Octavia tilts her head to one side. "I hope you're looking forward to it."

I brace myself, waiting for the typical sense of dress-up-party-yuck to settle into my belly. It doesn't. In fact, I feel downright pumped for the Ball. Getting rid of Adair makes everything seem that much better, I guess.

"You know what, Octavia? I am looking forward to it." I exhale a satisfied breath. "Most definitely."

16

I sit at a tiny make-up desk in my chamber at Arx Hall. My ladies' maid, Clover, stands behind me as she fiddles with my hair. Clover's on the short side with a rail-thin body topped by a large, moon-shaped face. Like all thrax, she has mismatched eyes of brown and blue. Her uniform's a simple peasant dress of black cotton with a long white apron.

"How would you like your hairstyle for tonight's Ball?" she asks.

"Down my back is fine. Just what you're doing."

"We could try something more formal, too. It is a Ball of Welcome in your honor, after all. I have some diamond hairclips around here. Let me show you." She steps away and starts scanning the nearby tables.

I frown. The Ball starts soon and I don't want to be late. This room's so cluttered, it could take hours to find anything in the piles of statues, vases, tea sets, and music boxes.

"Ah, here they are!" exclaims Clover.

"Great news." Looks like I won't be late, after all.

Clover steps up behind me, showing me some hair clips decorated with diamond eagle claws. I give them a quick once-over. The design is lovely but the execution is huge. I'd need a beehive hairdo to make them work, and that's just for starters.

"They're very pretty, Clover. But I don't think they're me. Thanks, anyway."

"As you wish." She takes a brush to the back of my head. "So excited to hear about the iconigration, if you don't mind my saying so."

I straighten in my chair, a sense of pride swelling within me. "No, I don't mind you saying that at all." The iconigration is all set for tomorrow morning. Inside my heart, my igni pulse with excitement at the very idea.

"Any luck getting Lady Adair to give you those..." She clicks her tongue. "What are they called again?"

"Igni."

"That's right." Her eyes grow large with alarm. "Or is it not proper to ask such a question?"

"No, you can ask. It's fine. Adair did take some of my igni. We've been trying to get them back, but no luck so far." I tried pushing, pulling, cajoling and bribing. Nothing. After that, the House of Striga has cast every spell, charm and enchantment in the book. My igni still won't budge. Whatever spell-n-demonic-blood combo Adair is working, it'll take some time to crack the code. I will crack it, though.

"That's a shame," says Clover.

"I've enough igni for my first iconigration, though. That's the big one."

"Well, that's good to hear, anyway."

A knock sounds at my door.

Clover inclines her head, making her long braid of brown hair swoosh to one side. "Who calls upon the Great Scala?"

"It's me, dear." That's Octavia's voice.

I fidget on my cushy little seat, nervous energy bounding through me. I hadn't expected Lincoln's Mom to stop by and I'm not ready yet. Normally, I'm not the kind of girl who worries if she looks perfect, but right now? I totally worry if I look perfect.

Clover turns to me. "Shall I bid her enter?" The thrax have all sorts of funny rituals; anything related to the King and Queen gets downright hilarious.

I almost say 'shall we stop talking like we're clones of Shakespeare?' But I stop myself. "One sec." I smooth out my Scala robes. "Okay, now I'm ready."

Clover pulls the hefty door open, revealing Lincoln's mother standing in the hallway beyond. Octavia looks gorgeous in a black velvet gown embroidered with silver thread.

I never can remember the thrax ritual for greeting royalty, so I do what I always do. Make it up. "Hey, Octavia. How's it going?"

Octavia makes shoo-fingers at Clover. "Go find somewhere to be useful."

"Yes, Your Highness." Clover curtsies. "I'll put fresh linens on the Great Scala's bed."

Octavia steps up behind me, setting her dainty hands firmly on my shoulders. She meets my gaze through the little mirror at my make-up desk. "I came by because I simply couldn't wait. I have excellent news for you."

My face brightens. "What's that?"

"I've made an inquiry into the status of the Royal Vaults."

Butterflies start doing their pitter-patter thing in my belly. Royal Vaults? She can only be talking about one thing. Lincoln's search for the Rixa betrothal jewels.

"I'm so sorry for the delay, my dear," says Octavia, shaking her head. "Not able to find the jewels? Ridiculous. Turns out, all the guards and staff at the Vaults were from the same House."

"Let me guess. Acca?" Anger winds through my arms; I so want to punch something. Instead, I grab a brush, ready to go to town on my hair. I barely raise the thing from the tabletop when I snap the handle in two.

"Oops." My cheeks flush with embarrassment. "Didn't realize that was so dainty."

"Don't worry about it, my dear. I have similar reactions to Acca all the time. To answer your previous question, yes, they were absolutely behind the troubles at the Vaults. I had them all thrown in the dungeons, but they left things in a terrible mess. Catalog cards wrong, safes moved around, that kind of thing. Clearly, it's some kind of ploy to stall out your betrothal. Now, my people are cleaning things up. They'll find the jewels soon." She gives my shoulders a squeeze. "I'm very excited for both of you."

Acca, at it again. Unbelievable. I flex my fingers, my hands itching to break something else on the table.

"Octavia, can I be honest with you?"

"Always, my dear."

"Why isn't there an inquiry into these things? Acca should be disbanded or something."

"I've been trying to do that for twenty years, but the King..." She exhales a long sigh. "He favors Acca, we'll leave it at that. Perhaps with you and Lincoln together, you can give him the strength to stand up to them. Maybe he'll become the man he once was when I married him."

An image flashes in my mind. The look on Octavia's face when she first spied me on the battle practice grounds in Purgatory. "Me and Lincoln teaming up against Acca. You've been planning this all along, haven't you?"

"Of course, child. I should've thought that obvious."

I let out a nervous laugh. "Not that obvious."

"Give it time, you'll learn the chess game that is statecraft in Antrum. Besides, the two of you are so well suited. I can't imagine a better match for my son."

"Wow. Thanks." My blush returns, a little deeper this time. Octavia's never said sweet stuff like this before. Makes me feel all squishy inside.

"By the way," adds Octavia. "Any luck getting your powers returned?"

"Not yet, but I'm not worried. It looks like Adair has to agree to give me my igni back, but I'll wheedle them out of her. I still have plenty left to do the iconigration tomorrow, and that's the important thing."

"As long as you're confident, then I'm pleased." She kisses my cheek. "See you in the ballroom."

A nervous twinge rolls up my belly. *That's right. The ballroom.* I need to finish getting ready and how.

"I'll see you there, Octavia. And thanks for throwing the Ball in the first place."

Laughter hides in her mismatched eyes. "Liar. You hate formal events. But I appreciate a well-intentioned fib, same as the next woman. You can come out now, Clover." Octavia whips through the door; it closes behind her with a soft click.

My ladies' maid peeps her head in from the bedroom. "Your Highness?"

"She's gone."

Clover lets out a visible sigh of relief. "Our Queen is not a little frightening."

"Oh, she's pretty cool when you get to know her."

"My, my. I've lost track of time. We don't want you to be late." Clover rushes to stand behind me again. "Where were we? I'm afraid the royal visit has me a little flustered."

"That's fine, Clover." I scan the dressing table in front of me and its overwhelming landscape of bottles. There can't be much left to do. I check off my beauty-accomplishments on my fingertips. "First, make-up's finished. Second, hair's done. Third, my Scala robes are on. All I need is my over-gown, am I right?"

More knocks sound. Clover frowns. "Now, who can that be?" She rushes over to the door. "Who calls upon the Great Scala?"

No answer.

"I said, who calls upon the Great Scala?"

Still, no reply.

A creepy feeling makes the hairs along my arms stand on end. Something about this feels off.

Clover pauses a moment longer, and then shrugs. "Ah, well. There's always a new servant getting lost in the Arx. Where were we?" Clover claps her hands together at her waist. "Ah, I have it now. Your over-gown. I'll fetch it." She disappears into the walk-in closet, followed by much rustling of fabric. "I know they delivered it earlier today. One minute, please."

"No worries."

To kill time, I step to the window and look out on the Rixa lands beyond. Nothing less than gorgeous. I pictured Antrum as a series of tiny and dark caves, but that's not true when it comes to Rixa territory. The caverns here are massive and filled with white light. Columns of opaque crystals scale up the walls at funky angles. The ceiling's lined with the hexagon-ends of those same glassy white stones, making an artsy, uneven pattern. A loose forest of white crystal trees extends below my window.

I watch the scenery another minute before I get bored. Looking out windows isn't my thing, really. Besides, I do need to get ready. I change my focus from the external Rixa lands, looking instead at the reflection of my room's interior.

What I find mirrored in the windowpane surprises me to the core.

There, reflected in the glass, I see Clover still standing by the closet door. But that's not what truly astounds me. It's her eyes. Moments ago, they were the classic-thrax mismatch of brown and blue. Now, they glow bright red. Demon eyes.

A mixture of terror and shock press in on my lungs, making it hard for me to breathe. This can't be happening. Impossible.

Clover speaks to me in a creepy, monotone voice. "Don't you look pretty?" With every lifeless word she speaks, a fresh chill rolls through my belly.

Spinning around, I face her once again, only to find that her irises have returned to their mismatched state. No demonic light at all. Shock squeezes the air from my chest once again.

I force myself to speak, despite my panting breaths. "What did you just say to me?"

"Did I say something?" Clover's face looks so round and innocent, it's hard to imagine the demon-red eyes I saw a moment ago. I wish I could find that comforting, but the realization only rockets my anxiety higher.

"So sorry," gushes Clover. "I must have daydreamed there for a moment. The Queen's visit has me all a-flutter. Where was I, again?"

Remember to breathe, Myla. Stay calm.

I watch her carefully, like she'll burst into demon-form at any second. "The over-gown."

"Right, right. Won't be a moment." She disappears into the closet.

I pace in front of the window, my mind trying to process this latest turn of events. Clover eyes turned red while she spoke in a strange monotone. That reminds me of something—maybe more than one thing—but with so much going on, I can't place the memory. My warrior sense rails through me, strong as an electric current.

Danger, Myla.

A fresh knock sounds from across the room, followed by a familiar-but-muffled voice. "You're late, my dear."

I rush over and open the door, finding a portly woman in a simple black gown. It's Bera, Octavia's handmaiden. I haven't seen her since the last thrax tournament, when she helped me with my armor.

"Bera. So nice to see you." Actually, it's not all that nice. I'd rather have a few minutes of quiet to sort things out, but the look in Bera's mismatched eyes says that won't happen. My hands ball into frustrated fists. After what I just saw, I can't rush off to the Ball. "I need a few minutes."

"You need to leave. Queen's orders. Can't be late." Bera pats her gray hair, checking that it's all in place. "They only play the fanfare once, and tonight, it's for you. If you miss that trumpet music, I'll never hear the end of it."

"Right." Octavia's only warned me about the fanfare a

hundred times. I rise to my feet and head towards the door. "We better go."

"You wearing them robes tonight? I thought the Queen made you an over-gown."

A queasy feeling settles into my stomach. Clover's eyes plus the missing betrothal jewels add up to trouble. Somehow, Antrum is unsafe. And if I have to face trouble, then I don't want to do it in a fancy over-gown. No, I want my Scala robes only, so I'm ready to transform them into armor at a moment's notice. Resolve steels through me, straightening my back and shoulders.

"No, I'm going Scala traditional tonight."

Bera eyes me for a long moment. "Fair enough. They'll be plenty of other Balls for you." She reaches her plump hand towards me. "Let's go."

I take her hand and smile, but inside, my warrior sense still screams.

Danger, Myla. Danger, Danger.

17

I stand on a high platform, staring down into the Crystal Ballroom of Arx Hall. A thousand thrax partygoers fill the floor below me. And the rest of the chamber? When they say crystal, they aren't kidding. This ballroom is one giant geode made of luminous white stone. Crystal clusters jut down from the ceiling, serving as chandeliers. Subtle beams of light dance through everything.

I shift my weight from foot to foot, anxiety zooming through me. Any second now, I'll be announced as the guest of honor for tonight's Ball of Welcome. Unfortunately, thoughts other than the Ball keep popping into my head. Like the weirdness back in my chambers with Clover. What was that, anyway? Why do her red eyes and strange voice keep triggering something in my mind?

Searching for a distraction, I scan the thrax below me. The men are in velvet tunics and their ladies wear long matching gowns. They're all so prim, proper, and color-coded by House. If I were about to fight them, I'd be totally calm. But coming here to dance and make small talk? It's way overwhelming.

I come to a quick decision. I'm having a mega case of the jitters, which is why I keep thinking about Clover. Mystery solved.

A blare of trumpet music interrupts my thoughts. A few yards away, a Herald in a black Rixa tunic plays on his silver instrument. No question what that means. The Ball has officially begun.

Hells Bells.

My stomach and heart decide that now's a great time to swap places. As a result, I can't decide if I want to puke or have a coronary.

The Herald lowers his trumpet and launches into a lot of ceremonial blah-blah-blah before ending with: "Please join me in welcoming our guest of Honor, Myla Lewis, the Greatest Warrior in Antrum, and the Great Scala of Purgatory."

I carefully pick my way down the slippery crystal steps, trying to look regal and cool. A chorus of whispers sound from the ballroom floor. I hear the words Soul Processing, Purgatory, High Prince and Angelbound. There's also a lot of repetition in there, namely Demon, Demon, Demon, and Demon.

Not a shocker.

When we first met, Lincoln had some serious issues about my quasi-demon heritage. Most thrax are trained to kill anyone with a drop of demonic blood on sight. It took a while for us to move past my quasi side. Looks like his people still have a lot of moving left to go.

The staircase isn't nearly as tricky as it looks, and I make it to the floor without tumbling. There, Lincoln stands, wearing his traditional Rixa tunic, chain mail, and crown. For a moment, and I soak in every aspect of his face. Strong bone structure, full mouth, firm jawline, and mismatched eyes that glisten with excitement. No one's ever looked at me the way Lincoln does. Like I'm the most beautiful, intelligent, sexy, kick-ass warrior chick in the after-realms. My tummy gets all fluttery.

I cross my fingers on my right hand. Demon-phobes or not, I can't help but hope that his people like me, just a little.

"Shall we say our hellos?" asks Lincoln. It's so obvious that he can't wait to introduce me around. My tummy-flutters grow more intense.

"Sure thing."

He wraps my hand around his forearm. "The Earls and Duchesses are anxious to meet you."

I vaguely remember that I was worried about something before, but for the life of me, I can't remember what it was.

As we walk along, I inspect the audience for any sign of Mom and Dad. Nothing. Octavia's been hounding them about when to show up and what to wear. Actually, I was pretty surprised when they weren't standing at the bottom of the staircase, snapping pictures while telling embarrassing stories about me to random passers-by.

Where are my parents, anyway? They live for crap like this.

I keep watching the crowds, hoping to pick out Mom and Dad. They keep not being here at all. A gloomy weight settles into my bones. Maybe they aren't coming.

"Have you seen my parents?"

"Not yet. They might have gotten held up."

"Could be." Knowing my parents are MIA, I scan for the other key members of my personal life. "I don't see Cissy or Walker, either."

There's the slightest catch in Lincoln's stride. I know my guy well enough to realize that means he's concerned. "Neither do I."

A group of ghouls step by, all of them wearing long black robes, the cowls drawn low over their faces. I can tell that one of them is Adair's Diplomat buddy because of his pronounced limp. I so wish that creep had been at the warehouse when we arrested Adair. Would've been great to lock him up, too.

One of the ghouls steps off in our direction. Judging by the height and frame, it could be Walker, only he never wears his cowl down.

The mystery ghoul steps up to our side. "Glad I could catch you two."

I exhale a sigh of relief. That particular voice is unmistakable. "Walker, it's you. Why don't you pull up your cowl?"

"Don't say my name, no one knows I'm here." Walker

speaks in an urgent whisper. "Listen closely, we don't have much time. The transfer stations are on lock-down."

All the oxygen seems to get sucked out of the ballroom. Transfer stations on lock-down? That means no going in and out of Antrum.

"How did the stations go on lock-down?" Lincoln's careful to keep his voice low. "I didn't approve that."

"I thought as much," says Walker.

"Did Mother or Father sign off on this?"

"No, I don't know how it happened," explains Walker. "That's the problem. The ghouls that I'm following around, they keep babbling on about a secret scheme that launches tonight. I'm trying to find out what it is. As long as they think I'm an average ghoul, they may open up."

Everyone knows Walker and Lincoln are friends. He can't keep talking to us, or the ghouls will get suspicious... And we'll miss any chance to learn about this secret scheme.

"Are Mom, Dad, and Cissy alright?"

"They're fine, but they're getting the runaround at the Purgatory transfer station. Camilla's about to call in the military. I snuck off and got in through my back doors."

Bit by bit, Walker's news seeps into my brain. My parents and Cissy really aren't coming, and it's all part of some secret plan to ruin my big night. My gloomy mood deepens.

Lincoln lightly touches Walker's arm. "You better go."

Walker steps away and merges into the crowd.

"Well, that news is a whole lot of awful," I say. "Some scheme to keep my family away. Nice."

"I suspected something was off when we transferred into Arx Hall yesterday. All the non-Acca agents at Transfer Central seem to keep falling ill. No doubt, they're trying to ruin tonight for you. My apologies, Myla."

"Hey, it's not your fault." I decide that now is a really good time to stare at my sandals.

Suddenly, I feel very alone, lost in a sea of faces that don't want me here. Sadness presses in around me. I hope the transfer stations open up soon, because at this point, I'd really like to go home.

"What's wrong?" asks Lincoln.

"Nothing."

"It's a big something, your nothing." He runs his thumb along my jawline. "Transfer stations got you down?"

"Maybe."

"Come here, you." Lincoln wraps me in his arms, kissing me in a way that's slow, gentle, and all-around perfect. I open my eyes, feeling a blush crawl up my cheeks. Half the ballroom is staring at us.

"What was that for?"

"For you're wonderful." He cups my face in his hands, and all the love in the world rests in his eyes. "I don't care what anyone else thinks or does. You're meeting my nobility tonight and one day, I'm making you my Queen. Believe that, Myla."

"You know what? You said that once before and yes, I totally believe it." A tingly sense of joy shifts across my skin. What do I care about the rest of the world? Screw Acca. There's Lincoln. He's what's important about tonight, and he's right beside me.

"Hey, I've got an idea." Lincoln leans in close and whispers in my ear. "How about we start working the ballroom like we're having the time of our lives? That'll really frustrate Acca."

"Oooooooh, I like this concept. A lot."

At that moment, the Rixa Herald plays another tune from his post atop the stairs. Lincoln and I share a confused glance. As the guest of honor, I'm the only one who should get a fanfare. Octavia only drilled it into my head a thousand times.

The Herald lowers his trumpet, and for a second I see his irises glow red. I suck in a shocked breath. *This can't be happening.* I grip Lincoln's arm more tightly. "Did you see that?"

His voice takes on a menacing edge. "Yes, I did."

Up on the platform, the Herald's eyes return to a mismatch of brown and blue. He gazes at the trumpet by his lips, the lines of his face slack with confusion. For a full minute, he stares at the instrument as if he isn't sure how it got by his mouth.

Unholy Hell. That's the same thing that happened with Clover. Red eyes, weird behavior, and finally, confusion.

Seconds tick by as everyone stares at the top platform, waiting for someone or something to appear.

Before, I struggled to find the pattern in Clover's red eyes and strange actions. Now, those mental connections quickly snap into place. There's the thrax reporter whose eyes flashed demon red…Erik speaking in a creepy monotone at the warehouse…the Durus getting red eyes and turning from a killing machine into a lumbering dodo…and both Clover and the Herald having red eyes, creepy voices, and later, no memory of either happening.

Each time these odd things took place, Adair was either there or could easily have been lurking nearby. Plus, Dad once said that demon blood gives extra abilities. What if Adair has gained the demonic power of possession? If so, she must only possess demons and thrax. Otherwise, she could've walked away from our sting.

A chilly realization seeps into my stomach. Supposing all this is true, what's keeping Adair in prison now? She could easily possess her thrax jailers.

My hands tremble as I grip Lincoln's arm more tightly. "I know who's behind all this. It's—"

"Adair," finishes Lincoln. He gestures towards the top of the staircase. What I see makes my jaw fall open with shock.

At the top platform stands Adair, wearing a smug grin and fake Scala robes. Two prison guards flank either side of her, the visors on their crimson armor pulled down to hide their faces. No doubt, under those helmets, the guards' eyes are bright red. Possessed. Afterwards, the poor suckers don't remember a thing that Adair made them do.

Wish I could say the same for me.

No question. This is the secret mission that Adair's

ghoul buddies were talking about before. She's crashing my Ball of Welcome in order to...Do what, exactly?

I automatically go into battle stance. Feet set wide apart, tail arched high. Whatever's coming, it can't be good.

Adair raises her arms high above her head. "My people! I've been cleared of all charges!" She parades slowly down the staircase. "I come to you today as the True Scala."

A collective gasp rises from the crowd. I let out a low groan. How can I wonder what she's up to? It's the same thing she's wanted all along: to be the Great Scala, Lincoln's bride and Queen of the thrax. I square my shoulders, ready to march over and kick her ass. After all, that's what I do best.

Octavia beats me to it. Fast as a heartbeat, she pushes through the crowd to stand at the base of the stairs. "Knights! Take her back to jail, immediately."

The red-armored Knights don't even flinch.

My upper lip curls with a mix of disgust and dread. The Knights not acknowledging Octavia? That's so not-good for our side.

Undeterred, Octavia steps closer to Adair. "What's the meaning of this? You should be in prison, not breaking into someone else's Ball of Welcome."

Got to hand it to Octavia. She doesn't miss a beat.

I speak to Lincoln in a low voice. "Should I go over there?"

"No, give Mother a chance. This is better coming from one of our own."

"Understood." If anyone commands respect in Antrum, it's Octavia.

"My poor, sweet Queen," coos Adair. "My confession was forced by demon magic. That's why the Dungeon Knights have set me free. Please, don't believe what that demon girl has told you. I am the True Scala. I can prove it." With a snap of her fingers, Adair makes a handful of igni appear, their tiny bodies hovering about like fireflies. The crowd gasps again, but this time with awe.

Octavia quickly scans the audience, the wheels of her mind turning at super-speed. The slightest droop sets into her stance, and I know she's come to the same conclusion that I have. It isn't going to be easy to get rid of Adair. I may be the Great Scala, but I'm also a quasi-demon. Adair's thrax. The people want to believe her.

Frustration makes me clench my fists so hard, my fingernails bite into my palms. I shouldn't let it bother me that the thrax judge me based on my tail, but damn it, it totally does bother me.

Adair walks across the ballroom floor, making a beeline for Lincoln and me. The Dungeon Knights march stiffly on either side of her. I remember how badass and agile the Knights were when we captured Adair. Now, they move with the same clunky movements as the Durus.

Huh.

Adair must be puppeteering folks, but it looks like her control skills are rather clumsy. A happy-sneaky feeling lightens my tummy, like the day I snagged two of my ghoul-teachers making out on the sly and thought…This little bit of info may come in handy one day.

As Adair saunters closer, more and more thrax part before her. Some even bow. Others whisper True Scala in reverent tones.

My sense of frustration boils over into outright anger. Heat pools behind my eyes; my irises flare demon red. There's only one True Scala, folks, and she has a tail. Get over it.

Adair pauses before me, a smarmy look on her face. "I am the True Scala. You've stolen my love, power, and throne. I want them all back."

Comments sound from the nearby crowd. I hear words like gracious, regal, lady-like, and thrax. I notice that most of those talking are wearing yellow, the color of the House of Acca.

Note to self: if you get out of this alive, make them pay. Lots.

Adair's gaze shifts to Lincoln. "You must see that this is over. I'm the True Scala. She's nothing."

"No," says Lincoln coolly. "She's everything." Fast as lightning, he whips a helmet off the nearest Knight's head. The man's features are blank and empty, except for his eyes, which glow demon-red.

Fresh gasps sound from the audience. This time, the inflection is not of awe, but of stomach-churning horror.

My heart kicks harder, all kinds of happy pumping through my bloodstream. The thrax hatred of demon kind has been working against me all night. Now, it's playing in my favor. Seems there isn't much that demon fighters fear more than being turned into demons themselves. The partygoers start to quiver in their collective boots.

Across the ballroom floor, Octavia slices through the crowd, heading in our direction. Things are looking up. My tail gives Lincoln a congratulatory pat on the arm. That was a pretty sharp move on the part of my honey, there.

Lincoln tosses the helmet to the floor; it lands with an angry clang. "You're a liar, Adair. Always have been. And now, you bring demonic powers into my lands? Possess my people and force them to act as puppets to your will? Stop this, now." He raises his hand, motioning to a cluster of men in black body armor. "Guards! Take her."

Now, awesome-sounding murmurs run through the crowd. I hear new words that are music to my ear, stuff like traitor, liar, and fraud. Some of the Acca folks start to not-so-subtly sashay towards the exits. Like I won't remember all of their faces and arrest them later on. You are so going down, my friends.

As the guards close in on Adair, Octavia bursts through the crowd to stand at our side.

"Clap her irons," commands Octavia. "And then—"

The Queen stops halfway through her sentence. Her body freezes in place. All across the ballroom, the same thing happens. The thrax become immobile, stopped mid-motion, like a living photograph. My chest aches with grief to see the reason why.

Virtually all of them have demon-red eyes. Adair has

taken over their minds. Only a small number of thrax stand at the top of the crystal staircase, their eyes still mismatched. These outliers must be beyond Adair's range of power. The faraway thrax race from the ballroom, with all of Adair's ghouls following close behind. A yucky feeling sinks through me. I doubt they'll get far.

I turn to Lincoln, my heart kicking hard in my chest. Framing his face with my fingertips, I scan his eyes. The irises are still mismatched. He's not possessed. I don't know whether to laugh or cry, so I think I end up doing a bit of both. "You're alright."

"I'm fine, Myla."

We both scan the crowd, and I know we're looking for the same person. Walker.

I spy him standing a few yards away, his cowl still pulled low.

Excellent. Our secret weapon is still in place. Lincoln and I share a nod. No question what we'll do next.

I go into battle stance, my tail arched over my shoulder. "Let's get her."

"Right." Lincoln whips his baculum out of his tunic, igniting it into a long-sword. Quick as lightning, he brings the blade down towards Adair's neck. The angelfire blade comes within inches of her throat.

And then, it stops.

Lincoln's eyes burn demon bright. He extinguishes his baculum, resets it into the folds of his tunic and stands still as a statue.

Possessing Lincoln? Now, she's done it.

In my heart, I unleash my inner wrath monster. A jolt of adrenaline courses through me; my mind snaps into battle mode. I see heads and bodies, attack vectors and weapon options.

I leap high into the air, somersault, and land in a crouch by Adair's feet. By the time I've touched down, my Scala robes have turned into awesome white battle armor. Moving my leg in a sweeping motion across the ground, I take Adair down at the ankles. Her skull smacks onto the crystal floor with a satisfying thwack.

Dozens of hands pull at me at once, dragging me away from Adair. Fortunately, all my attackers are clumsy thrax puppets under Adair's control. They grasp and claw at my limbs, trying to hold me down.

Not going to happen.

My tail punches one in the gut. After that, it topples another over by pulling the feet out from under him. I don't want to kill any of Lincoln's people, but I certainly won't mind if they wake up tomorrow with a headache, especially if they're wearing Acca yellow. Within seconds, the hands that were holding me back are now a dozen bodies lying prone on the ground.

Adair rises to her feet, her face the definition of smug. "And what was that little display about, Myla? Do you really think you can defeat all these thrax single-handedly? Even you aren't that good."

At those words, the entire thrax audience, all thousand-or-so of them, turn to face me, their eyes flaring demon bright. Moving as a single unit, the possessed start to lumber in my direction.

Typically, this kind of situation would spell disaster, but I know something Adair doesn't, and that knowledge makes me all kinds of happy.

Walker's standing right behind her.

"Hey, Adair!" I wave my arms wildly, trying to pull her attention to me and away from Walker.

"What?" she snarls.

With a series of swift kicks, Walker takes Adair out behind the knees. Oh, I wish I had a camera. Adair topples over.

"That."

Adair leaps back to her feet and instantly, a horde of possessed thrax descend on Walker. They have crap for reflexes and strategy, but what they all lack in brains, they more than make up for in numbers.

I rush to help Walker break free when I get stuck under my own pile of the possessed.

I make some quick calculations, and it isn't looking good for us. So far, Walker and I have taken down about four dozen thrax. That leaves 950 or so to go.

All this adds up to one conclusion. We need to grab Lincoln and get the Hell out of here, fast.

I down the latest pile of thrax attackers and come up for air. Adair stands across the dance floor, her eyes blazing bright red as she scans the scene, her lips whispering commands to her possessed minions. Walker and I battle it out on opposite ends of the room. We keep on fighting, but fresh attackers lumber in our direction.

We can't keep this up forever.

Walker calls to me from across the ballroom. "Lincoln, now!"

I take down another Acca thrax with a combination upper-cut and kick to the gut. "Got it."

Knowing Walker my whole life, I understand what those two words mean. He wants to form a portal behind Lincoln, which the three of us will then run into and escape.

Fortunately, Adair doesn't catch on to Walker's meaning. She starts whispering in Lincoln's direction, and he shuffles off to a deserted corner of the dance floor. Most likely, she doesn't want him to get hurt in the battle. I exhale a relieved breath. Finally, something is going my way tonight.

Walker breaks free from his latest horde and yells out one word. "Go!"

Behind Lincoln, the dark form of a ghoul portal appears. From opposite ends of the room, Walker and I race towards Lincoln and escape. All we have to do is hold his hand, jump into that opened portal, and our troubles are over.

Adair sees what's happening and starts whispering at double-speed. Lincoln begins to lumber off in a new direction, but I expected this might happen.

"Walker! Move the portal behind him!"

I race towards Lincoln's new trajectory. Walker does

the same. The moment the three of us meet, Walker opens a fresh portal directly into our path. Walker grabs Lincoln's right hand; I wrap my tail around Walker's left wrist. Together, the three of us slide into the portal. Darkness starts to close in around us. My rush of battle adrenaline turns from wrath to joy.

We did it. We rescued Lincoln and got out alive.

Suddenly, a burst of light explodes into the darkened portal. Something holds me back; I'm no longer falling through empty space. I look up, seeing Adair at the portal's edge. She's created an igni cord from her hands to mine, and she's not letting go. Even worse, the cords are already wound tightly around my palms, making an unbreakable connection between us.

Unholy Hell.

Behind Adair, the demon-eyed thrax line up, helping her haul the three of us out of the portal. Adair doesn't so much pull on my weight—she leaves that work to her thrax helpers—but she drags something else from me.

Igni.

Panic shoots through every nerve ending I've got. This is just like at the Ghost Tower. I can't break the connection. I can't use the link to pull my igni back. I can only slow the transfer as she steals my powers.

Tiny voices begin to howl in my mind. It's the igni. She's taking them again.

Adair leans into the opened portal, her eyes red with rage. "None of you are getting away. Not after the price I paid."

More about the price? This bitch be cray-cray.

All the more reason I can't let her take us.

In a flash, I know the only way to escape. It's simple, perfect, terrible. I have to push all the igni I can at Adair. That's how the Old Scala gave me his powers, and it knocked me for a loop. It's the only thing Adair won't expect, but even thinking about it tears at my soul.

Still, I have no choice.

I command the igni to leave my body, move across the cord, and enter Adair in a great burst of energy. Issuing the command rips at my heart; pain and loss wrench through my rib cage.

You must go. I'm so sorry, my little ones.

They understand my request and instantly do as I ask. A great wave of light crashes down my arms, moves across the igni cord, and slams into Adair. She falls back, shocked. The portal closes, and we tumble through empty space once again.

Moments later, the three of us step out of Walker's portal and into my gymnasium back home. I grasp Lincoln's forearms and look into his eyes. Mismatched. No sign of demon-light. It's as I'd suspected. Adair needs to be close to her victims in order to take over their minds.

Lincoln shakes his head, his eyes unfocused. "What happened?"

Fresh panic jangles through my nervous system. How many igni did I lose? "I'll explain in a minute." I rush over to my father's cabinet, the one where he stores the Bloodstone Amulet. I open the drawer, pull out the red disc, and set the chain around my neck.

Bit by bit, the front of the amulet transforms into the image of two dragons, just like it had before. I turn the disc over and watch the back. Again, the entwined tails form a spiral accented with numerals, from one to ten. The level starts at ten, pauses for a moment, and then starts to fall. Nine, eight, seven, six…

Please let some of them have stayed.

Five, four, three, two. The level finally becomes steady. One.

I'm torn between wanting to cheer and weep. I have hardly any igni left. Certainly not enough to perform an iconigration. But a new plan has begun forming in my mind. This amount of igni may not be much, but they may get the job done. Still, it's a last-ditch option, only if all else fails.

Although, with the way my luck has been going, all else will fail.

18

Connor, Octavia, Lincoln, my parents, and I all sit around my kitchen table. Walker and Cissy are off planning the big iconigration tomorrow, assuming I can get my powers back to do it. After my battle with Adair, I don't have nearly enough igni. I tried, too. I can barely get a few dozen to appear around my arms.

I try to wrap my head around this turn of events, but my mind's numb with shock. Only two hours ago, I was the Great Scala at my very own Ball of Welcome in Arx Hall. Lincoln was about to introduce me to his nobility as their future Queen. Now, one hundred and twenty minutes later, I've hardly any powers left.

It's a flat-out disaster.

I inspect the faces around the kitchen table, and a spark of hope lights up in my chest. My parents, Lincoln, and I have spent the last two hours coming up with a kick-ass plan for a special ops mission into Antrum where we'll take down Adair and get my powers returned. Hopefully, we can use this time with Lincoln's parents to convince them into helping us make it work. A shiver rolls up my back. I don't want to think about what happens if the special ops idea hits the dust. My secret back-up plan is wicked unpleasant.

Lincoln eyes his father carefully for a time. "How did the pair of you get to Purgatory so quickly?"

Connor smiles as if Adair possessing his subjects happens every week. "Oh, Adair calmed down once you left. She's a high-spirited girl."

What the what? High-spirited? How about insane? I ball my hands into angry fists and thunk them onto the tabletop, ready to tell Connor exactly what I think of his casual take on Adair.

"Myla." Mom shoots me a warning look. She and I talked about this before. Until we know if Lincoln's parents can help us, I need to keep a lid on my temper, especially where Connor is concerned. Still, it's everything I can do not to punch him in the head.

If Connor notices my rage, he doesn't show it. "Adair's fine. We had no problem getting a transfer platform."

"And what of our nobility?" asks Lincoln.

I know what he's worried about. Two hours ago, Adair possessed the minds of all the thrax at the Ball of Welcome, turning them demon-eyed. Assuming she's released them, they shouldn't remember a thing about what happened.

But before that? Not so much.

"Lincoln whipped the helmet off a Dungeon Knight," I explain. "The whole crowd saw the guy's demon eyes, and they were freaked out with a capital F. How are the people handling that fact?" By this point, there could be mass panic in Antrum.

"The people remember the Knight's eyes turning demon-red, surely enough," says Octavia. "But I'm afraid Adair's saying that was your handiwork, Myla. The people seem to believe her explanation."

I punch my leg in frustration. Stupid thrax. "Why am I not surprised?"

Connor laughs a little too loudly at my sarcasm. "True, true. Adair's a slippery one."

Lincoln fixes him with an icy stare. "This isn't a laughing matter, Father. What Adair did tonight is treason of the highest order. And the insult to Myla? Outrageous."

"Yes, my son," says Connor quickly. "Most serious." He turns his attention to me. "Heartfelt apologies for how things went this evening. The House of Acca makes fearsome enemies."

I choose my words carefully. "I'm not afraid of them." *Unlike some people I know.*

"You've every right to be upset," says Octavia. "We ended up canceling your Ball of Welcome, much to my chagrin. Everyone went home, safe and sound, which is the *only* happy side in this sorry turn of events." Her words are clearly pointed at Connor. As in, stop pretending this is no big deal.

"What about the thrax who ran away?" asks Lincoln. "They were at the top of the stairs when Adair possessed the rest of the Ballroom. Ghouls chased after them. What happened next?"

I grab Lincoln's hand and give it a squeeze. *Nice thinking, babe.* Everyone else may buy a story that I possessed the Knights, but the thrax who escaped the Ballroom would've seen the full truth. Maybe they're in Antrum right now, clearing my name.

"I know all about those thrax from the staircase," says Connor. "Unfortunately, it seems they had bad falls once they left the Crystal Ballroom. They're all safe now, recovering in the palace infirmary."

Lincoln's eyes narrow. "So they were attacked by the ghouls, but now they say they all fell on their own?"

"That's their story," says Connor. "A pack of lies, of course. They're afraid of Acca's wrath. I'm so sorry, my boy."

My jaw clenches with held-in rage. Maybe they're clearing my name? Maybe they're in Antrum acting like a bunch of pussies. My inner wrath demon flares to life inside me. I slap my palms onto the tabletop.

"So, how much longer will we pretend this isn't a catastrophe?" I ask. "Some psycho's gotten my igni. I want all of my powers back, pronto. We have souls to move in less than twenty-four hours."

"You've not enough igni for an iconigration, then?" asks Connor.

How I hate admitting this. "No, I don't."

"We've news on that front," says Octavia. "The Earl of Acca visited after you left. He says he speaks for Adair."

"And you believe him?" Adair doesn't seem like the type to let anyone speak for her.

"Never," retorts Octavia. "But in this case, I see no reason why Adair wouldn't use her father as a go-between. The Earl has a message for you. He says Adair can move all your souls tomorrow."

"Hey, hey, hey," I caution. "Let's not get hysterical. Sure, I can't perform an iconigration right this second. But if I can sneak into Antrum, drag Adair out, and get my powers back, then everything will be fine."

"I've some crack angelic troops we can send in as well," adds Dad. "They're experts at extracting criminals from sticky situations. We still need to figure out how to restore Myla's igni, but that's something we can focus on once we have Adair back in custody."

My tail gives Dad a high-five. *Way to back up your daughter!*

For the last two hours, Dad's been leading the planning side of our special ops mission. At this point, all we really need is some intel on Adair's location. That's where Lincoln's parents come in. If they can say where Miss PsychoPants is hiding out, we can take the rest from there.

"It's a rock-solid plan," I declare. "I'd be happy to walk you through it."

Octavia's face melts with sympathy. "Whatever operation you have in mind, I see four issues with it. One, Acca has control over every Pulpitum, so we can't get you into Antrum without their knowledge. Two, even if we could, we've no idea where Adair is. Antrum's huge; it could take weeks to track Adair down, and that's assuming she didn't escape into another realm."

I frown. Okay, the lack of Adair intel is a huge bummer. That definitely throws a monkey wrench into our special ops mission.

"Three," continues Octavia. "Supposing you do find her and take her back to Purgatory, you didn't have much luck getting your powers out of Adair when she was in prison before. What makes you think you'll succeed now? And four, if your mission is discovered, the Earl will back down from his offer to have Adair do the iconigration."

"Assuming that offer is genuine," I caution.

"I give it a fifty-fifty chance. Still, those are the best odds you have to move souls in the morning. I don't see the benefit in jeopardizing that opportunity until we know if they'll keep their word."

The tiny hairs on the back of my neck prickle. I can see where Octavia is going with this, and it's not a nice place. "What are you saying, then? We shouldn't even try?"

Connor starts to speak, but Octavia raises her hand. "No, I think it's better if this comes from me."

"If what comes from you?" asks Lincoln slowly.

Octavia folds her hand neatly on the tabletop. "Trust me, I have no joy in sharing this message, but the Earl of Acca is willing to guarantee that Adair will be compliant, in writing if you like. She'll move the souls you want, when and where you want them, for as long as she lives. But there's a price."

Suddenly, it's very clear why Connor and Octavia were allowed to come to Purgatory so quickly. Lincoln. My stomach twists with disgust. I didn't just free Lincoln from Adair's mind control only to have this happen.

Dad leans back in his chair. "Does this compliance include protection for Myla and Camilla? I'd assumed Adair held nothing but ill will towards my daughter."

"They're both explicitly covered," replies Octavia. "And Myla's here right now, isn't she? If Adair wanted to, she could have sent her to Hell already."

Dad rubs his chin with his right hand. "Quite true."

Quite false, actually. If they think Adair's holding off on sending me to Hell because of some agreement with her father, they're nuts. Not that I'm sharing that fact at this point. That particular assumption is a key part of my secret back-up plan. I cross my fingers under the table. Let's hope I don't have to use the secret back-up plan. It's a little crazy.

Come oooooooooon, special ops mission.

Connor shakes his head. "I hate being the bearer of bad tidings, here. I know how attached you two are."

Lincoln's face is stone. "But the Earl has demands."

"Yes, he does," says Connor. "They aren't anything we haven't discussed before."

My chest tightens with a sense of fear and dread. I

know what those demands are. Marriage contract. My Lincoln stuck with that psycho.

Hell, no.

"Please, my boy," says Connor. "I'm no King without my best soldier at my side. We need you back in Antrum. Alone. And by first thing tomorrow morning." He pats Octavia's hand. "You can thank your mother for that. She fought hard to give the pair of you time to say good-bye."

Lincoln pins his father with a look that could freeze lava. "And what about the betrothal jewels? At least, grant me that."

Connor scratches his neck in a nervous rhythm. "Still missing, my lad. We'll find them. When you come to Antrum, we'll hunt them down together."

Meaning that he'll only get them if he goes to Antrum and does what Adair wants. My mind fogs over as rage, frustration and despair ricochet through my thoughts. I force myself to focus and slowly, my internal haze clears. A dark determination settles into my soul.

I don't care what the consequences, this isn't happening.

"So this is it?" I ask. "We sell out Lincoln to Adair. I refuse to believe this is our only option."

"It's the only option right now, my dear," says Octavia gently. "A war is battles. We lost this one, I'm afraid. I assure you, I'll do everything in my power to avoid actual nuptials with Adair."

"Then give Lincoln the betrothal jewels. Now."

"What if Adair hears of it?" asks Octavia. "There

wouldn't be an iconigration tomorrow. You must see reason."

I focus on my parents. "And what do you two think?"

"The Earl of Acca's offer changes things," says Dad. "At least, for the next twenty-four hours."

Mom's been quiet this entire time, watching the scene with a diplomatic eye. Now, she rises to her feet. "Thank you, Octavia and Connor. We'll take it from here."

There's no question what 'taking it from here' means in Mom-speak. She agrees with Dad, too. I know they're both only doing what they think is best for everyone—me included—but I still can't help feeling betrayed and hurt. A crushing sense of sadness weighs down on me, making every word I say a chore.

"You don't have to shoo them away, Mom. I know what you'll tell me when they go. You agree with them. We need to let Adair move the souls and think she gets Lincoln, at least until the crisis is over."

"I'm with your mother on this one, Myla," adds Dad. "Adair's too powerful. Gaining back your Scala abilities isn't worth losing your life in a last minute attack with no intel. And it seems like the girl's willing to be reasonable, do the work of a Scala, at least for now. It's the most we can do for the next twenty-four hours. There's no advantage in antagonizing her until this crisis in Purgatory is over."

I shift my gaze between Octavia and Connor. "So this may be the last time I ever see you two."

Octavia's eyes widen with surprise. "I certainly hope not."

"Of course, we'll cross paths again," adds Connor with an easy grin.

The way Connor talks, it's like Lincoln's only going on vacation. His casual attitude really ticks me off. Before our talk, I promised Mom that I'd keep my mouth shut around Connor, but now? If there's one advantage to this crap situation, it's that I can finally speak my mind.

I steel my shoulders. "Connor, I've something to say before you go."

"What is it, child?"

I turn to Lincoln. "You mind if I?"

"Be my guest." He sets his hand in mine. "I've got your back."

Some of my sadness lightens. Lincoln and I really do have each other's backs.

Octavia fidgets in her seat. "I appreciate that this situation is trying for you, my dear. However, you must understand. It isn't the thrax way to criticize—"

"Well, it's my way." I focus all my attention on Connor. "From the first time I met you back in Purgatory, you've been concerned about one thing. The House of Acca. Never about your son's feelings. Or what's best for him and his life."

All the blood drains from Connor's face. They weren't lying; no one gives this guy the truth. Well, he's about to get an earful now.

"Over and over, you tell Lincoln how he's your best soldier, how he has to do things for you. Even the first time I saw you at the Ryder mansion, you told him to approach the quasi girls because it was his duty to the angels. How about thinking about your duty to him as a father, for once? Maybe put Lincoln's needs above Acca or even Antrum? If you'd have given Lincoln the betrothal jewels when he asked for them, we wouldn't be in this situation right now."

Connor shakes his head. "It isn't that simple."

I rise to my feet; I'm on a roll. "I disagree. It's absolutely that simple. You're so stuck in your precious thrax traditions and House politics, you can forget what it means to be a good person. Or in your case, Connor, a good parent. Maybe yes, we must give in to Adair for the next twenty-four hours, but you're totally outrageous to play it off like she's just high-spirited...Or that the Earl isn't asking for anything new. Adair is part demon now. She possesses people. At least, do Lincoln the courtesy of admitting that we're locking him into a living Hell, and not pretending that everything's alright."

I glare at Connor, my eyes flaring demon red. His features turn slack with shock. A long silence follows.

Finally, I retake my seat. "That's all I have to say."

Mom straightens in her chair; she's in official President Lewis mode, now. "I think our meeting is over, then." She scans the table. "Unless anyone can think of other plans or options?"

"No, I can't think of anything." I reset my hand into Lincoln's. "I'd like our time alone now."

But that last part is a huge lie. I do have one idea on how to get my powers back. It's the last-ditch crazy option I thought of before, but was hoping I'd have better luck and wouldn't need to go there. Now, it seems that my luck has run out entirely, because as much as I hate this concept, I know that my parents will hate it more. So, I'm keeping it a secret.

I'm confronting Adair alone, tonight.

19

The Ryder mansion isn't far from my new home, so Lincoln and I decide to walk through their hedgerow maze. Here's where Lincoln and I shared some of our first kisses, so the place has lots of good mojo.

And with the stuff I have to discuss, I need all the positive mojo I can get.

It's a pleasant night, Purgatory-wise. The sky is gray, as always, but it hasn't rained in a few days, so the ground of the maze is dry and soft. We hold hands and stroll through the familiar paths. Funny how our feet take a direct route to the fountain at the maze's center. I suppose our kiss there is one of those things that stick with you.

We step along quietly for a time, and then Lincoln breaks the silence. "Thank you."

"For what?"

"Saying those things to Father. It means a lot to me,

Myla. I suppose in some ways, I'm very thrax traditional. No one questions the King."

"Well, you've got me to bring a little innovation into your life."

He chuckles softly. "So, what's your plan?"

"Who says I have a plan?"

"I do. Back in the kitchen, we were discussing the situation with Adair. Your mother asked you if anyone could think of other options. You said you couldn't think of one. You threw in the towel, just like that. I don't believe it for a second. You have another idea, only you don't think your parents will like it."

For the first time in what feels like forever, I get all warm and fuzzy inside. Lincoln knows me too well, and that's a wonderful thing. "Did you take a Myla 101 Class or something? Because I don't think I'm that easy to read."

"I study up in my spare time." He purses his lips. "So, what's this plan that your parents won't like?"

"You might not like it, either."

"Try me."

"I don't trust Adair as the Great Scala. Not even to move a single soul. And I don't believe she'll stick to some plan of compliance. The igni chose me. Scala powers are my responsibility, and I'm going to see it through. I have to get my igni back, no matter what. Even if it costs me my life."

"Go on."

"Now that Lucifer's Orb is safely out of Purgatory,

almost everyone thinks that Adair should do at least one iconigration. My parents. Your parents. All of Purgatory. There isn't a lot in my corner right now."

"Except me." He rubs his thumb along the back of my hand.

"That, and the fact that I'm here. Don't you see?"

"Not exactly."

"If Adair could move souls like she says, then why am I standing here? I don't buy that baloney about respecting some kind of offer from her father. She hates me. Plus, it's not like igni have a limited radius or something, like Adair's ability to possess demons and thrax. I zapped demons to Hell from halfway across Purgatory. I know Adair could do the same to me right now, even from Antrum. So, why am I here, holding your hand, still alive?"

Lincoln nods slowly. "Good point."

"There's more, too. I think Adair possessed the Durus. Now, imagine you've got a badass Durus under your control. You can make it do anything. But what's the first thing Adair forces it to do? Ask me to move the demon's soul to Hell."

"That is rather odd."

"And later, she sneaks up on me at the warehouse. She could take my igni or could grab the Orb. But what does she do? Dare me to try sending to her Hell. It all adds up to one thing."

A slow smile rounds Lincoln's mouth. "Adair doesn't know how to use your powers."

"Bingo. Hey, it took me forever to move my first soul. And I'd seen the Old Scala do a ton of iconigrations."

"I remember. You struggled for a while."

"Right. Adair's never seen igni in action. That's why she's keeps asking me for a demonstration."

"So, what are you thinking?"

"I bluff it out. Lie my ass off to Adair. Tell her I'll give her the inside scoop on how to move souls in exchange for a guarantee that she'll send mine to Heaven. After that, I meet up with her one-to-one for the trade."

Lincoln lifts his brows with interest. "And then, what?"

A grim chill crawls up my arms and legs. "Here's where things get ugly. Adair has to agree to give me my igni back. If she doesn't," I inhale a rattling breath. "Then, I'll have to kill her. It's the only way I can be sure they'll return to me."

"And you're not sure if you can kill her."

"Oh, I'll do it if I have to. It's just that I've only ever destroyed evil souls and demons." A bitter taste enters the back of my throat. Even thinking about this subject is disgusting. "Taking a mortal life is different, that's all."

"I know." Lincoln's eyes take on a steely look.

"Have you ever killed another mortal?"

"Yes. I've had warriors get possessed on demon patrol." A pained look crosses his face. "It's never easy." He shakes his head, as if dismissing a memory from his mind. "Still, Adair's committed more than a dozen acts of treason. Any one of them could be punishable by death. You'd be saving the executioner some effort."

I laugh, but there's no humor in it. "Glad to help."

"And you don't want to consult with your parents on this?"

"No way. They won't want me risking my life when Adair says she'll play nicely with others." I take a deep breath. Here comes the big reveal. "This is the thing. I know we had until tomorrow morning to say our good-byes. But if my plan's going to work, I need to leave tonight." My voice breaks as I say these last two words. "I'm sorry."

Lincoln stops, his mismatched eyes searching my face. This time, his unreadable face truly deserves the name. I have no idea what he's thinking.

"Is something wrong?" I ask quickly. "Don't bother trying to talk me out of this. My mind's made up."

"No, it's not that. Not at all. I'm going with you."

My brows lift with surprise. "I can't ask you to do that."

"You're not. And it's not a request. It's a statement of fact. I am going with you." He takes both my hands in his. "I don't want to be King without you as my Queen. The chances you'll win against Adair by yourself are slim. If this is going to work, you need some back-up."

My pulse kicks faster. With a warrior like Lincoln along, my chances would get a shit-ton better.

"And you're absolutely sure about this?"

He looks at me out of his right eye. "Keep asking me that and I'm liable to get insulted."

I can't help but smile. I'm so used to fighting in the

Arena solo. No coach. No back-up. No friendly faces cheering from the stands. Having Lincoln in my life makes me realize how alone I once was. A happy, summer-warm feeling spreads through my heart. "Okay, you're coming along."

He winks. "How very big of you."

"Also, there may be a way I can protect you from her. You know, so she doesn't turn you all demon-eyed. It's a lot more bluffing and lies, but there's a chance she'll buy it."

"What can I say? I love this plan."

"You know we'll have to hide this from your parents, too?"

"Clearly."

"So, how do we sneak into Antrum? It's always locked down super-tight. Right now, your parents are probably keeping an extra-close eye on who comes and goes."

Lincoln rubs his chin as he walks along. "Let me guess. You don't want to ask Walker."

"He's used his back-doors too much already. And he's needed here, in Purgatory. You know, if the plan goes wrong." *And we end up dead.*

"I may have an option there. You once mentioned an old inactivated Pulpitum in Purgatory. Since Acca has control over all the transfer stations, we could enter Antrum that way. My parents don't monitor it, but they do keep tabs on it at Transfer Central. And since the Pulpitum are under Acca's control, Adair should find out about our request right away. It could give us a way to contact her as well. Let her know we want to talk." His mouth rounds into winning smile. "When do we leave?"

"Right now. Adair could figure out how to use my powers at any time."

"Works for me. We're off."

20

Lincoln and I step towards Pulpitum X, ready for anything. He wears black body armor; I'm in my Scala robes. We both carry our baculum.

Pulpitum X is a decommissioned transfer station in Lower Purgatory. No one was using the place, so we shut it down a century ago. I doubt anyone's entered it in fifty years. Even so, Lincoln says it can be reactivated for emergency traffic. I suppose the situation with Adair more than counts as an emergency.

Once inside the Pulpitum, it looks like all the other transfer stations, a dark and empty cylinder. Only here, there are no guards, and a light coating of dead leaves and garbage covers the floor. If I didn't know for a fact this place could work, I'd think it was busted.

Lincoln speaks in a whisper. "Ready?"

"As I'll ever be."

I link my fingers with Lincoln's. Both our hands tremble slightly, which I find oddly comforting. We both know this plan is a series of educated-but-risky guesses.

Our first big guess is coming up, right now.

Lincoln's father admitted that Acca had taken over Transfer Central, the headquarters of all platform requests and routing. With any luck, Acca and Adair will intercept our message before anyone reports our request to Lincoln's parents. If Connor and Octavia realize that Lincoln is in Antrum, they'll bundle him off to the Earl of Acca in a heartbeat. Maybe less. We need to sneak in without them knowing.

"Activating emergency station. Lincoln Vidar Osric Aquilus." A grid of white lasers shoot across the room, doing a quick body scan.

The same smooth female voice echoes through the station. "Identity confirmed." Angelfire lights up the bowl-like sconces that encircle the room. Brightness reflects off the metal disc in the center of the floor.

A long pause follows. Lincoln and I share a nervous glance. Will our plan get stopped before it even begins?

The woman's voice speaks again. "What's your destination?"

"The Great Scala and I wish to talk to Lady Adair, wherever she is. Alone. There must be no records of our visit. No alerts to anyone but Adair. We want this done quietly."

"One moment, please." Another pause follows as

someone goes to check with Lady Adair. "Prince Lincoln is approved for transfer."

A familiar voice crackles on the line. "Tell him that I'm glad that he's come to his senses, at last."

No question who that is. Adair.

The Transfer Agent speaks again. "I'm instructed to congratulate you on coming to your senses."

I exhale a breath I didn't know I was holding. The Transfer Station has Adair on the line, alone. That means she's in Antrum. Whew. Even better, she's running her own show, separately from her father. I straighten my shoulders and get ready for the next phase of our operation.

Here it comes. Guess number two. The crux of my plan. My tail taps nervously on my thigh.

I stroll around the Pulpitum, careful to keep my voice casual and confident. "King Connor told me that Lady Adair can move souls. And sure, igni will appear pretty easily. You can even get them to visit Heaven and Hell on their own." So far, all of this is true. "But you can't move a soul unless you have every last one of them."

Bombs away. That was a nasty, mega lie. Adair has plenty of igni, only I'm gambling she doesn't know how to use them.

Another long pause follows. The wind moans through the entry slit of the Pulpitum. My heart beats so hard, I can hear the whoosh of my pulse. Lincoln and I stand motionless.

Some garbled chatter sounds on the line. Adair's talking again, but I can't understand her words.

The female Transfer Agent speaks once more. "What would be the purpose of your visit?"

Woo-freaking-hoo. Relief and excitement course through me. Adair's buying into my lie. She really believes that she needs all of my igni. And asking for the purpose of my visit? That means she wants to know what I'm willing to trade for them. Even though I realize Adair's listening in, I keep up the pretense that I can't hear her. Who knows? If she doesn't know her voice is live, she might blab something useful in the background.

"Please tell Adair that we can play cat-and-mouse for years, with her trying to get the last of my powers. But there are millions of souls that need to be moved in the next twenty-four hours. I want to make a trade. I give Adair my igni, and she promises to move all of Purgatory's spirits as their trial verdicts dictate, including me, when I'm ready."

There's a burst of static on the line, followed by a quick answer from the Agent. "You are both accepted for transfer. Step onto the platform."

My heart lightens. Adair gave in mighty quickly on that last request. She must be freaking out by now. Most likely, she's been trying to move souls for hours without any success. I'm sure she's gotten pretty sick of the screechy rock concert going on inside her head, too. My educated guesses are falling into place.

Here comes the last one.

I fold my arms over my chest. "Not so fast. I have a final condition. Adair cannot possess Lincoln during our visit. If

I so much as see a flicker of demon-red in Lincoln's eyes, then I'm zapping the rest of my igni to Heaven, where she'll never get them back. My father will store them right beside Lucifer's Orb for all eternity, or at least until Adair is stone dead. Do we understand each other?"

What an outrageous pack of lies. I'm guessing that Adair doesn't know enough about igni to realize what a load of crap I just shoveled her way. I can send my igni on a visit to Heaven or Hell, sure. But no one can actually contain them other than the Scala.

The quiet gets downright annoying. "I said, do we have a deal?"

"Yes. Get on the platform."

"Excellent." I try my best to sound confident, but I won't really know if my bluff worked until we reach our destination. Once we hit the Antrum transfer station, Lincoln should be close enough to Adair that she would make him demon-eyed, if she chose.

A fresh round of adrenaline hits me. This is happening, really happening.

Lincoln and I cross the room, stand on the metallic disc, and rest our arms on each other's shoulders.

Time to go.

Like before, Lincoln states his command to the navigational system. "Launch transfer on my mark. 3, 2, 1."

With a roar, the platform hurtles through the ceiling on a roller-coaster ride to the earth's surface. We speed through rock, water, and soil, lurching as our platform avoids immoveable objects. A short time later, we emerge in another deserted Pulpitum. This one's in a blackened cave with a few measly gray ceiling-crystals to serve as light. The transfer station is half rubble, covered in lichen, and marked with signs saying 'Mercor Temple'.

We're here.

21

Lincoln and I step off the Pulpitum platform in Antrum. A massive cave surrounds us; it's made entirely of dark stone. The ground is filled with ancient-looking trees and a half-ruined temple. Now that we've arrived, one thought consumes me.

My last big lie to Adair was that I could zap my igni to Heaven if she overtook Lincoln's mind. Did she buy it? Or, did she only say 'yes' to get Lincoln closer to her powers?

I turn to face Lincoln, cup his face in my hands, and exhale a sigh of relief. His eyes are still mismatched. No demon-red glow. Adair totally bought my story. I've never appreciated the ghouls, but man, do I ever at this moment.

Thank you, oh Ghouls, for so thoroughly destroying every last scrap of information about the Great Scala. You've made it possible for me to lie my ass off today.

A dozen Acca guards stand around us in a semi-circle. None of their eyes are red, so they're helping Adair of their own free will. Traitors. More faces for my to-destroy list when and if we get out of this.

The Acca Captain grunts the word 'go' at Lincoln and me, so we follow him away from the transfer platform to a long, jagged ledge of rock. There, the Captain raises his arm. Our group pauses.

All the guards stare at Lincoln and me, their eyes filled with an eager loathing. The air hangs heavy with anticipation. Like smoke, it constricts my lungs, making it hard to breathe. My tail coils behind me, cobra-like, waiting to strike.

I hate moments like this. We're trapped in the great pause before a greater battle. Bring it on, already.

Leaning forward, I scope out the grounds beyond the stone ledge. A steep incline rolls down below us. At the base of this slope, a wide valley opens up. The shadowy space is filled with a huge, broken-down ruin.

I picture the sign from the Pulpitum. Mercor Temple. This is the place. Here things will end with Adair, one way or another.

The Captain holds out his hands. "Baculum."

Okay, I totally knew it was a long shot that they'd let us keep our weapons, but I still hate handing over my baculum to this dip. Lincoln gave me these, and I'm very protective of them. I make a quick mental note of where the Captain stashes our stuff, namely the left-hand side of his tunic. Based on Lincoln's gaze, I can tell that he's doing the same thing.

"Let's move out." The Captain marches down the incline to the valley below. Lincoln and I follow.

In the dim light, the temple looks like a square framework of broken gray stone. In some places, great trees have grown up through the smashed rock. The ground is damp and foul-smelling.

Across the scene, Adair stands atop a wooden stage set against the temple's far wall. I roll my eyes. Great, more dramatics. She's wearing her fake Scala robes for the occasion, which pisses me off. The Acca guard march us until we stand right before the stage. The angle forces me to stare up at her. Not my favorite view.

Up close, the stage is broken and putrid, like everything else around here. Black paint has long since chipped away, showing underlying wood that's yellow with mold.

Adair surveys us each in turn, smiling. "Greetings."

Father always says that in battle, you have to take the initiative and never let go. So, here comes my initiative.

I jump onto the stage. "Let's skip the pleasantries," I say. "Do we have a deal, Adair? You move the souls the way Purgatory sorts them—including me—and I give you the rest of my igni."

Adair looks anxiously to her guard. She doesn't like being so close to me while the soldiers are outside of easy fighting range. She's right to worry, too. I went super-easy on her in the warehouse. She's no idea what I'm capable of.

"Well, Adair?"

"Agreed."

"Good. Want the rest of my igni?" I turn my palms to

face her directly. "Come and get them. I said I'd give them to you. I didn't say I'd make it easy."

Adair looks unsure.

"Come on," I continue. "You did it before, at the warehouse. You've got demonic blood in you now. Surely, you're not afraid of me." I gesture towards Lincoln. "And as an extra bonus, you could claim the last of my igni right in front of you-know-who. Now, that's got to make your inner psycho happy. It's a very good deal."

Adair still hesitates. Time to bring out the big guns.

I turn to Lincoln and roll my eyes. "I told you. She doesn't have what it takes to walk across a stage, let alone be Queen of the thrax or the Great Scala. I'm the one you should choose."

With that, Adair finally takes the bait. Her eyes flare demon-bright as she races towards me, her shoulder aiming straight for my gut, same as she did in the warehouse. Only back then, I took a fall so we could get a confession out of her. This time, I have other plans.

Lincoln sees his chance and springs into action. Gripping the Acca Captain's head, he twists it until the neck snaps. As the man falls, Lincoln reaches into the Captain's tunic and grabs his baculum.

Meanwhile, I allow Adair to ram her shoulder into my gut and slam me onto the floor, just as she did in the warehouse. New warriors always use the same attacks over and over, as long as they worked in the past. Total rookie mistake.

I let my head slam into the floor and then, I lie still. I've never been knocked out before, but I've done it to other people a ton of times, so I've a pretty good idea what it looks like.

Adair paces back and forth before my prone body, an evil smile on her mouth.

Out of my half-closed eyes, I see Lincoln battling it out before the stage, his baculum ignited into two short-swords as he goes to town on the Acca guards. They've got him surrounded, but their approach is perfectly suited for a short-sword counter-attack. It doesn't look like it right now, but I give all those warriors about two minutes to live.

Adair flaps her hands at the guards. "Be careful, now! Don't hurt him. I want him brought back to Acca, safe and alive." She chuckles softly. "I promised I wouldn't possess him, but I never said capture was off the menu."

I blink my eyes wildly, as if I'm just coming to. Adair sees the movement and pounces on my torso. While straddling my rib cage, Adair presses her palms against mine, holding my hands flush against the ground. I make a great show of writhing under her like I can't get up.

The next time Adair speaks, her mouth is only inches above my own. "Now, you'll see what death looks like."

I don't think so.

I command my tail to move. It arcs high, the arrowhead end flexed into a fist. Quick as lightning, it swoops low, pounding Adair right in the gut. The force of my blow sends her flying across the stage. Adair's head slams onto the wooden floor with such force, the planks splinter and snap. She lies on her back, unmoving. I hop up onto my feet and size up Adair.

"Now, that's what a concussion looks like."

I race over to Adair's body. Meanwhile, Lincoln's finished off the guards, so he leaps up onto the stage to do the same. Kneeling by Adair's side, Lincoln sets his fingers against her neck. "She's alive but unconscious." He tosses me my baculum.

I kneel down beside Adair as well. "Now, we wait for her to wake up and see reason."

Lincoln raises his right eyebrow. "You really think that'll happen?"

"Not a chance. We'll ask her for my igni back, she'll say no, and then—" I don't want to talk about the killing part, but we both know that's the most likely end game.

Lincoln rubs his chin thoughtfully. "I don't think she'll see reason, but she may follow tradition."

"I'm listening." No one knows better than me the power of tradition, rules, and brainwashing. I see it every day.

"Ever since our encounter at the Ghost Towers, I've been considering the best way to approach Adair. Last time, I ordered her to speak to me. But I think there's a higher ritual that I can invoke."

"You mean, like a thrax ceremony or something?"

"Precisely. She and her House have given oaths of fealty to Rixa. If I ask her something in the names of those oaths, she can't turn me down. In theory, anyway."

My tail makes a stabbing motion at Adair's chest. I smack the arrowhead end. "Down, boy. We're talking to her first." I shift my attention to Lincoln. "Go ahead. Give it a try."

Lincoln gently sets his hand on her upper arm. "Adair?"

Her eyes flutter open. "Lincoln."

"Am I your Prince?"

"Yes."

"Will you honor your oath to my House and title, as you and your ancestors have done before you?"

Adair stares into his face for a moment. "I don't know."

My breath catches with a mixture of surprise and joy. She's thinking about it. Actually considering sticking to her oaths. I take back all the nasty stuff I said about thrax worshipping ceremony. Go tradition!

Lincoln's voice takes on a steely tone. "I am your Prince. You made these vows knowing their import. Now, will you honor them?"

"I…I…" Adair hunches over, her body curling forward in pain.

Lincoln leans in closer to her. "You can keep your title. Stay Great Lady of your House. All will be forgiven if you give Myla back her powers."

"No, no, no." Adair curls her body into a tighter ball. "Too soon to pay."

I remember Adair saying the same thing at the warehouse when we captured her, and then later, at the Ball of Welcome. "She's talked about this before. Something about paying a price for everything."

Lincoln speaks louder. "What's happening, Adair? Maybe I can help."

With a wild groan, Adair flings back her arms and head, her spine twisting in a painful arc behind her. "Too soon to pay!" Fast as lightning, her body twists and elongates before us. Her limbs turn gangly; her fingers stretch until they have three fat knuckles. I outright gasp.

Unholy Hell. Adair is turning into Armageddon.

Only, while the King of Hell's flesh is black and smooth as stone, this merged version has human-like skin that's colored gray. Adair's Scala robes reform into a charcoal-colored tuxedo, as well. It's almost identical to the one always worn by the King of Hell.

This must be the payment Adair mentioned before. She made a deal with Armageddon. It makes perfect sense. If you want to gain demonic powers, there's no one stronger than the King of Hell. And Armageddon isn't the type to do something out of the kindness of his heart. There would certainly be a price.

The reformed Armageddon pokes at his stomach. "I'll have you know I was quite busy torturing some Seraphim when you decided to get all wobbly about our deal. Actually contemplating giving back your igni, after all we've been through? Sad little thrax." He frowns. "The very thought made me call in my debt early, and I never like changing my timelines. I wasn't planning on taking this odious form until you'd moved a soul or two."

Armageddon looks up. The lines of his face freeze with shock, as if he's noticing Lincoln and me for the first time. "Although, seeing the situation, I'll change my mind. Nice work, Adair."

I ignite my baculum. "You can't be here. I locked you into Hell."

"Well, I'm not here, technically. I'm still in Hell. The little thrax sold her soul to me for a vial of my blood." He cups his hands and looks at his nails. "I'm just taking possession of her spirit early, so to speak."

"Possessed." The word echoes through my mind. "So once Adair moved some souls, then you'd move into Adair."

"Now you're getting the idea. Never occurred to you, did it?" He steeples his three-knuckled fingers under his chin. "I love it when I'm brilliant. With Scala power, I can take over the after-realms. Now, what were the three of you discussing?"

"Adair needs the rest of my igni. All of them are required in order to perform an iconigration."

"Really? And I thought she was exceptionally gullible to sell her soul to me so quickly. No, my sweet ex-Scala, I know how igni work. I've seen enough iconigrations with my son to last a lifetime." A too-wide smile stretches across his long, thin face. "Now, I'd like to introduce you to your new accommodations in Hell. Hope you hate them." Armageddon closes his eyes and igni appear around his hands.

Hells Bells. Armageddon is about to move us to Hell with my igni. With control of my Scala powers, he'll easily have all the after-realms at his feet.

Think, Myla, think, think.

Seconds crawl by until the realization finally appears.

This isn't Armageddon, really. The King of Hell is an immortal greater demon who's locked away forever. This is Adair. And she's as mortal as you can get.

My mouth twists with disgust. But destroying the King of Hell means killing Adair. More igni swirl up Armageddon's arms, preparing to form a Soul Column. A sad fact seeps through my mind.

This isn't Adair anymore. She's long gone. It's Armageddon.

I turn to Lincoln. "This ends, now."

"Agreed."

Moving in sync, we ignite our baculum as broadswords and charge at the merged form of Armageddon and Adair. Bringing down our weapons in a coordinated arc, we slice off Armageddon's altered head, our movements smooth as scissors. The possessed body falls forward onto the ground, lifeless. Still in its Armageddon-like shape, the cadaver lies on its belly, the severed head resting just above its shoulders.

I stare at the prone body, an awful chill crawling across my skin. I killed Adair. Not another evil soul or foul demon. A mortal. Sure, she was merged with Armageddon and about to take over the after-realms, but still. It's an awful thing to destroy life.

I kneel beside her, folding my hands in my lap. A prickly feeling of guilt slowly winds up my throat. Bit by bit, it climbs until it contorts my mouth with pain and stings my eyes with tears. I never meant to fall in love with

Lincoln or become the Great Scala, and it's all Adair ever wanted. Now, I've killed her. How did it come to this?

Lincoln wraps his arm around me, pulling me back up onto my feet. "You need to turn away, Myla."

"I can't. Not yet."

He stands in front of me, blocking my view of Adair. "Whatever happened with you, Adair and your igni, it's never taken place before in the history of the after-realms. There are no rules or guarantees here, Myla. You need to get your powers back, now."

My eyes open wide with shock. I always assumed that with Adair gone, my igni would return. The surprised feeling turns into jolts of adrenaline and panic. It's true. My powers could easily go to a new Scala Heir instead. And I have an iconigration to do first thing tomorrow morning.

I walk away from Adair and find a quiet spot by an old, arching tree. Closing my eyes, I reach out to my igni. "Hey, guys."

I pause, waiting for the sweet music or cacophonous chatter that means they hear my summons.

There's nothing. Only silence.

Fresh pangs of panic run through me. Every muscle in my body seems to constrict with worry.

Come on. I still have some igni left. Not many, but enough to give some kind of answer to my call. By now, at least a few igni voices should be echoing inside my head. My stomach twists with anxiety. Unholy Hell, what if when Adair took my igni, she parted them from me forever?

I set my palms onto my eyes and press hard. "Where are you?"

Still, no reply.

I focus deep within me, finding the emptiness and grief where power once saturated my soul. I sense a handful of igni hiding there. Frightened. Lost. Hurt. They're rarely separated from each other, let alone from their chosen Scala. I'd never thought about it before, but it was a brave and terrible thing for them to leave me for Adair.

The few igni I have left now sing a reedy song to me, telling me how their brothers and sisters are lost in the darkness. Abandoned. Afraid. Separated.

I raise my arms, close my eyes, and begin to speak to them all. "I'm here, my little ones. Find me. My soul is your home."

The music in my mind grows louder. An electric charge fills the air. My powers are getting closer now, gathering invisibly in the cavern around me. Excitement makes my heart drum faster.

I reach out to my igni with all the love in my heart. "Come back to me and I'll never let you go again, not while I've breath in my body. You are my children. I am your Scala. Hear me."

This time, they hear my call and how. Both light and dark igni instantly appear, the powers that draw souls to both Heaven and Hell. The dark cavern becomes blindingly bright as millions of tiny lightning bolts hover in the air. Joy pulses through my bloodstream.

That's it. Come home.

With an ear-splitting crack, the igni move toward me in a web of lighting, all aiming for my hands, the point where they were pulled to Adair in the first place. As the igni reenter through my palms, every cell in my body becomes flooded with strength and power. My skin glows with their energy. A sense of bliss and peace overtakes me. My returned power pulls me upwards, rising my body a few feet off the floor. Beams of light shoot out from my fingertips, eyes, and legs, sending another flash of brightness throughout the cave.

I land back on my feet, feeling awesome. The power has returned to its nesting-spot inside my soul. I wrap my arms around Lincoln's neck; he spins us about and laughs.

I lean my head back and watch the gray ceiling whirl overhead. A mix of emotions spin through me as well. There's the elation of victory, the delightful fire of shared love, and the soul-calming serenity of having my igni returned. It's a moment some part of me will cherish and relive forever.

"What a team." Lincoln resets me onto my feet, smiling in a way that warms me through and through. "And now, comes the fun part."

22

I pace inside a long stone corridor that opens onto the Arena floor. Pacing is definitely my thing when I'm nervous, and today, I'm pretty anxious. It's not a bad sort of worry, though. My first iconigration will begin in a few minutes and man, am I pumped.

Nearby, all of Purgatory's Senators wait in neat rows, ready to process out onto the stadium floor. Inside the Arena, the stands are packed for the ceremony. The low, happy roar of the crowd reminds me of my old battling days. So great to be back in the Arena again.

My friends and family stand close by as well. There's Mom in her purple suit and sash of office, Xavier in his dress armor with wings on display, Walker in his long black ghoul-robes, Cissy in her Senator's get-up, and Lincoln in his classic Princely ensemble. As for me, I'm wearing my Scala robes and an ear-to-ear grin.

First iconigration. Can't wait.

Cissy rushes towards me, her purple Senatorial robes swaying with her quick steps. She wraps me in a huge hug. "I'm so proud of you, quasi girl." She waves to the Alchemists, who return the gesture. "They're super-excited to be part of the ceremony, by the way."

"Of course. We couldn't have done it without them. Or you." I kiss her on the cheek.

"Any time, quasi girl." She steps back and straightens her robes. "Can you be ready in two minutes?"

"Surely."

Cissy runs off as Lincoln slips up behind me. He sets his long arms around my waist and speaks low into my ear. "You look gorgeous."

"Thanks." I rub my palms together greedily. "I can't believe it's here. My first iconigration." Most of the souls in storage had already been through Trial by Jury or Trial by Combat. Now that the Orb's gone, I can move them to wherever their verdict had placed them, which is mostly Heaven. There's one exception, however.

Adair.

Although she sold her soul to Armageddon, I can still try to send her to Heaven. It's not an easy thing to do, but a strong Scala can override certain kinds of magical bindings on a soul. Few things are as powerful as Lucifer's Orb, and I've bested Armageddon in the past, so there's a good chance I could break his hold on Adair.

Lincoln gently kisses my head. "Still want to hold back Adair for questioning?"

"Are you kidding? Absolutely."

I'm willing to bet that Adair will trade an eternity in Heaven for help with our investigation of Acca. Taking over the transport platforms, losing the betrothal jewels, providing guards at Mercor Temple...Adair didn't act alone. Now, Lincoln and I want information.

Out in the stadium, the orchestra strikes up the processional. Inside our hallway, all of Purgatory's dignitaries start marching out onto the Arena floor: Senators, Alchemists, Cissy, my parents, Walker, Lincoln, and me. Keeping in formation, we cross the grounds, ending in a long semicircle that stretches across the stadium floor.

My tail bounces happily behind me. It likes iconigrations almost as much as I do.

Once we're all in place, Mom steps into the empty center of our semicircle and tosses her head. Suddenly, she's no longer my mother, but President Lewis extraordinaire. She raises her right hand; the stadium falls silent. "Tonight, it is my honor to introduce my daughter, Myla Lewis, the Great Scala. You all know her as the supernatural warrior who fought off Armageddon and his ghouls from our lands. More recently, you know how tirelessly she's battled to keep innocent souls from being sent to Hell. And I'm sure you've all seen this morning's headlines. My daughter saved us from Armageddon, once again!" She claps in my direction and the crowd goes wild, tails wagging everywhere. Adair's possession has been all over the news. I am the undisputed Great Scala once again.

Signs appear in the crowd, and unlike my ride to the press conference at the Thrax Embassy, this time they're all pretty sweet. My favorites say 'No curse, all awesome,' 'quasi Scala=best Scala' and 'Myla Lewis, protector of souls'.

Mom circles her hands towards her chest, encouraging the crowd to continue cheering. I take a moment to allow their roar to wash over me. Mom always says that when it comes to ruling, the happy moments are always far shorter than the ones filled with fright, worry, and despair. So, you must take time to really enjoy the cheers. Thanks to my mother, the applause goes on and on. In short order, my face actually hurts from smiling.

At length, Mom raises her hand, signaling for silence. The crowd quiets down. "So, without further ado, we'll begin the first-ever iconigration from our new Great Scala."

I step over to my parents, give them both big hugs, and take my place in the center of semi-circle as the ceremony's main attraction. The spotlight hits me, making me wince. The audience falls absolutely silent. Excitement and adrenaline zing through my bloodstream.

I so love this.

Raising my arms, I summon the igni with my mind. At my call, black clouds roll across the horizon. The Arena darkens. An odd mist coats the stadium floor. Blasts of childlike laughter and metallic discord take over my mind.

Okay, this is different from anything I saw the Old Scala do before. But the Old Scala never moved this many souls at once, so I suppose there should be a few surprises.

I sense light and dark igni materializing, but not around

my hands, like the usually do. So, where have those little buggers gotten to now?

Looking up, I see the igni's tiny bodies spinning inside the rolling storm clouds overhead. Within seconds, they've formed a great whirlpool of light that stretches across the darkened sky. Bit by bit, the center of this igni-whorl lowers towards the stadium's ground. I stare in awe at my creation, finding it hard to breathe.

This is some kind of igni-tornado. Who even knew this was possible?

The igni speed faster inside, their lights flashing within a cone of dark cloud. As the tornado's peak touches the Arena floor, it pauses, shivers, and then keeps moving downwards. An inverted tornado forms under the stadium's grounds, a perfect match to the one reaching up into the sky. Soon, its depths sparkle with red flickering light.

I've seen that glow before: it's the fires of Hell.

I watch these twin tornadoes of light, my skin prickling with shock. Normally, the igni create one soul column for every spirit. But this time, the igni have formed the Mother of all soul columns, a giant hourglass-shape that reaches from Hell right to Heaven. The thin neck between these two extremes is a small circle of earth on the Arena floor that's directly in front of me. A strange electric charge fills the air. The growing speed of the igni sends wind whipping through my hair and Scala robes.

I nip my lower lip with worry, wondering if I should pull up stakes and try again. Whatever this shape is, I've never heard of a Scala summoning it before. However, the igni could care less about my concerns. They were trapped with some wacko, and now the little critters are on a roll, so happy to be back with their proper Scala, doing their proper work. In the neck of the hourglass—the eye of the dual-tornado—an image starts to appear. It's an old man, bent with age whose long white beard falls to his toes.

My mouth falls open with shock and recognition. I'd know that guy anywhere. It's Maxon Bane, the Old Scala. I haven't seen him since he gave me his powers and the igni sent him to Heaven. Who knew he'd show up today? His mismatched eyes meet mine and the old scoundrel winks. He mouths two words: good work. Pride swells inside me. The Old Scala zapping back here for a complement? Now, that's cool stuff.

I close my eyes and my mind flickers through images of thousands of men, women and children…Quasi, thrax and human alike. These are the souls to be moved. My consciousness reaches into their spirits, sensing their lives and history. Millions of moments flow through me, all the courageous, lovely and terrible episodes that make up a life. Every timeline converges at a single point: Purgatory. Trial by Jury or Trial by Combat caps all their lives, and my mind flows through millions of verdicts. Most I agree with, and I move the soul accordingly.

However, I do override one verdict. Adair's. I make sure to set her aside for later. She was awarded Hell, but I won't send her there. At least, not yet.

I reopen my eyes, and see my handiwork come to life inside the Soul Column. Where Maxon Bane once stood, now there is a morphing image of millions of different bodies. All of them appear and disappear within milliseconds, creating a single morphing figure, the soul icon, which holds every spirit that needs to be moved. With another flash of light, the icon splits into two, just as I'd divided them. One version rises up towards Heaven; the other tumbles down into Hell.

Above us, the clouds flare with white light as Heaven accepts its icon of souls. In the stadium's floor, red light blazes as Hell receives its spirits. The lightning-tornadoes let off similar blasts of brilliant light, white above and red below. Both swirling forms deliver a fireworks-style explosion that leaves us all seeing spots.

In between these two brightly-lit tornadoes, at ground zero, one soul remains, waiting to be moved. My heart leaps into my throat.

Before me stands Adair.

Lincoln speeds to my side, his unreadable-face firmly on. "Hello, Adair."

Her body appears misty in form. Other than that, she looks as I last saw her: long blonde hair, pretty face, and Scala robes. Her face twists into a scowl as she recognizes Lincoln and me.

"Come to gloat?" asks Adair. "What a shock."

"Actually, we've come with an offer," I explain. "Above you is Heaven, below you is Hell. I have the power to send you to either."

"No, you can't. I sold my soul to Armageddon."

"Last time I checked, I can kick his ass pretty easily. I'm

willing to bet that I can move you wherever I want. Only one way to find out, Adair."

"And what do you want in exchange?"

"Information," says Lincoln. "Who's been supporting you? What are their plans? How did you get Armageddon's blood? I want names, places, anything you can remember."

"Never. I'll take Hell."

The memory of Adair's broken body appears in my mind. I didn't want to kill her mortal self; I certainly don't want to sentence her soul to an eternity of pain and torture.

I raise my right hand, ready to command the igni to cast her down. I can feel the dark ones chafing to send her into Armageddon's tender mercies; they really hate her guts.

"Think carefully, Adair. Give us information or get Hell."

She looks down, seeing the fires of damnation lick up beneath her feet. Little by little, raw fear twists across her pretty features.

A pang of hope brightens my heart. Maybe she'll see reason, at last.

Adair looks up, opens her mouth, and then, her gaze runs across Lincoln and me, hand in hand. The look on her face changes from terror to a mixture white-hot rage and jealousy.

"I said Hell," she cries. "Send me!"

I remember when I last hoped for Adair to see reason. It

ended with her dead. This time, I really thought that the threat of Hell would change things.

A heavy sense of sadness settles onto my skin. She has no idea what she's asking for. I fought so hard to keep anyone I could out of Hell. For all Adair's faults, I hate to send her there.

I begin to issue the command to move her, but stop one last time. "I wish I didn't have to do this."

"That's why the igni chose me as the True Scala," says Adair with a sneer. "If I had to send a soul to Hell, I'd never hesitate."

"Actually, they chose me because that's what I'll always do. Goodbye, Adair."

Lowering my hand, I send her spirit through the Arena floor and into Armageddon's realm. A small flash of red light flares as Hell accepts its latest resident.

With Adair gone, there are no more souls to move. The two tornadoes recede into their original places, one rising into the clouds while the other collapses into the Arena floor. The stadium falls quiet. Thick mist still hangs heavily on the ground; the sky remains black with storm clouds. As I survey the filled stadium, one thought echoes through my mind…

The iconigration may be over, but with that little chat, our investigation of Acca has officially begun.

23

Once again, I stand on a high platform made of pale rock, staring down into a massive geode crammed with thrax partygoers. The Rixa Herald waits nearby, ready with a silver trumpet and pre-set speech about yours truly.

I scrunch and un-scrunch my fingers, trying to release some anxious energy. It doesn't work in the slightest. Long story short, there's no way to avoid high levels of adrenaline and excitement tonight.

This is my Ball of Welcome, Part Deux. Only this time around, the audience won't get puppeteered by a semi-demonic Adair. So, I've got that going for me.

The Herald plays a regal tune, makes my intro, and it's go-time.

I start the long trek down the crystal staircase to the ballroom floor below. Tonight, I'm wearing the golden over-gown that Octavia made for me. I'm not a dressy-dress girl, but this thing's sweeeeeet. The fabric's woven through with little dragons, the symbol of the House of Gurith. The front is cut wide open, showing my white Scala robes beneath, and I even have matching stilettos. Unfortunately, I'm not too confident walking on them. With every step down the stairs, I'm sure I'll slip on my ass and-or break my neck. But once I hit the base of the staircase, the risk of sudden death soon becomes worth it. A look of 'gee wiz' awe crosses Lincoln's face.

A soft blush colors my cheek. Now's when all the girly-girl effort pays off. This moment, that look, right here. I feel like the most beautiful woman in the after-realms.

Lincoln has gotten dressy, too. He wears a new flavor of royal get-up, namely a long, fitted coat of black velvet with a high collar and cool golden buttons that cross his chest at a funky angle. The coattails fall well below his knees, showing a hint of his black leather pants and tall matching boots. Delish. His golden crown mixes the Rixa eagle and Gurith dragon motifs, making me want to run my fingers through his wavy brown hair.

Lincoln offers me his hand. "Shall we greet your guests?"

I'm careful to keep my face calm and gracious. "Do we have to? There's plenty of booze and shrimp to keep them happy for ages." I set my hand in his, feeling the warmth of his firm skin under mine. "Really, I only want to hang with you."

Lincoln wraps my hand around his forearm. "We'll say our quick hellos and get right to the dancing-part of the evening. Soon after that, we can get to the sneaking-out-early part of the evening. How does that sound?"

I subtly hip-check him as we walk along. "Deal."

He grins. "Those of us in stilettos shouldn't be pushing other people around."

"Good point." I click my tongue. "And look at you, knowing all about girly shoes."

"Appreciating a beautiful woman in stilettos is common guy territory, Myla. We'll have a talk about that later." He slides his hand to the base of my back, guiding me to talk to some Earl or other who I couldn't care less about. We yammer on for ages about nothing. Every so often, I jump in with non-committal comments like 'surely' and 'you don't say'. Lincoln keeps rubbing the base of my spine with his very warm and firm hand, which is super-distracting.

This goes for an eternity: Lincoln introducing me to important thrax, me smiling, him rubbing the very top of my butt in a way that makes my lust demon get rowdy. After a while, my tail takes matters into its own hands and sneaks under Lincoln's coat, doing who-knows-what under the long velvet. The Prince doesn't send my tail packing, or show any reaction, really. Except every so often, he'll answer a question with a 'yes' where his voice turns a little too husky while his hand slides a little too low on my butt.

All in all, I'm having a grand time.

After the greeting-and-groping part of the evening is over, we decide to take a break before dancing. I head over to my parent's table at the feasting side of the ballroom.

This'll be fun. Not only haven't I seen them yet tonight, but they also got clutch seating right by the roast beast and dessert display. Yummy. I don't get within a yard of their long, mead-hall style table when Mom hops to her feet.

"Don't move a muscle!" She whips her camera out of her bag. "I want a picture." She takes about twenty shots until we pass the line from Cute-Mom-Land into Awkwardville. I reach for the camera.

"Hey, I should take some pictures of you and Dad." The pair of them look awesome. Mom's in a black sheath dress accented by her purple sash of office; Xavier wears silver dress armor with his golden wings on display. I reach for the camera. "Get up and pose already."

Sliding the camera out of my grasp, Mom steals closer. She makes a great show of whispering in my ear. "Your father doesn't like having his picture taken when he's in archangel-form."

"Why? He looks great."

She's careful to keep her voice low. "He says archangel-form brings out the wing-nuts, as he calls them. He doesn't want pictures to get around and make things worse."

I peep over at their table. Sure enough, every seat's filled with a pie-eyed thrax, breathless to be sitting next to a real-life archangel. "Oh, I can see what he means. No wonder he liked you from the get-go. Everyone else kisses his butt."

A satisfied gleam appears in Mom's brown eyes. "As he puts it, I out-Generaled him."

Dad steps up and pops his head between us. "What are we whispering about?"

"You." I stick out my tongue and make a silly-face. "And all the angel-loving wing-nuts."

"Please, don't remind me. The next time you have one of these thrax galas, I'm wearing my gray suit."

Mom lets out a long sigh. "That's so drab, Xav."

"For a reason." Dad raises his pointer finger, pauses, and looks over his shoulder. "Please stop petting my wings, ma'am."

A crinkly woman who's about a thousand years old lifts her papery hand from Dad's feathers. "Sorry, your worshipfulness." She stares at his back, mesmerized. "You're so very-very sparkly."

Dad rolls his eyes. "What did I tell you?"

"Myla agrees with me." Mom wags the camera before resetting it into her purse. "We should have at least one picture of you looking so handsome."

My father bows slightly at the waist. "All the more reason to enjoy my handsome-ness live and in person." He pauses, pressing his lips together. "Is she touching me again?"

I lean back and take a quick look. "Oooooooooh, yeah." I wince at the weirdness. "It's really nasty."

Across the ballroom floor, the orchestra strikes up a slow tune.

Mom takes Xavier's hands in hers. "How about we dance?"

"Love to."

I watch them step away and feel the comforting awwwwww that only happy parents can deliver. My Mom and Dad, two crazy-cute lovebirds off for a waltz. It's a mighty cool thing.

Out of the corner of my eye, I see Walker steal up beside me. It takes a supreme act of control not to jump up and down and scream 'Waaaaaaalker!' at the top of my lungs. After all, I haven't seen him all night.

But Walker's been trying to sneak up on me since I was nine, and he sucks at it in a big way. It would be breaking with our tradition for me not to call him out at the last second.

Walker tiptoes up behind my left shoulder and raises his hand to tap me on the back. When I speak, I make a point of not looking at him. "Only Lincoln can do that, you know."

I can hear the grin in Walker's voice. "Do what?"

"Sneak up on me. You're way too loud." I turn to face him, encasing him in a big hug. "So good to have you here. I can't thank you enough for everything you've done."

Walker purses his lips. "Actually, there is one way you could thank me."

"Name it."

"The Ghost Towers are running fine, but I think we can do better. New buildings for a new regime, that kind of thing. I have some engineering ideas that—"

"Say no more. Go for it."

"Thanks, Myla." He rubs his palms together. "This will be fun."

A new voice sounds behind me. "Excuse me." Turning around, I find Connor standing there. He wears a traditional thrax black tunic with chain mail and a silver crown. "Would you like to dance?"

This is the first time I've seen Connor since I read him the riot act back in my kitchen. "Are you sure you want to?"

Connor fixes me with an earnest and open look. "Very much, if you'll allow it."

Okay, I haven't exactly been the leader of the King Connor Fan Club, but right now he's being very sweet, sad and honest. Plus, as Lincoln's father, I'll need to get along with him sooner or later.

"A dance would be nice, thank you." I give my honorary brother a quick peck on the cheek. "Catch you later, Walker."

Connor and I step onto the dance floor and begin a very slow, quiet and awkward dance. His mismatched eyes scan my face carefully. "I heard you're thinking of starting an investigation of Acca."

Great. More Acca-love is coming from the Connor-quarter. What a shocker. I should've known better than to agree to dance with this guy. My tone turns to ice. "Word travels fast in Antrum."

"I've thought a lot about what you said back in the kitchen." He steels his shoulders. "You were absolutely right."

I can't believe my ears. "I was?"

"People have been letting me get away with unacceptable behavior for far too long, even Octavia. I want to apologize to you for my actions. Sincerely."

"I'm not the one you should apologize to."

"I already spoke to Lincoln."

"And?" I scan the dance floor, seeing Lincoln dancing with Octavia. He's smiling from ear to ear. My heart lightens. That's a good thing.

"My son seemed very pleased. I made a vow to him that I'd like to repeat to you, if that's acceptable."

"Sure."

"In this Acca investigation, I want to do whatever I can to help. I've spent far too long under their thumb. My heart's wish is for you and my son to have a strong rule, whatever that takes. Your happiness is what's really important to me. I see that now."

My breath catches with surprise. Is this the same guy I yelled at before the showdown with Adair? I soak the open and earnest look in Connor's eyes. It's true. He's really changed. "Wow. I don't know what to say."

"Say I can help you. That's all I ask."

"Yes, we'd love the help. Thank you, Connor." And I mean it.

Lincoln and Octavia waltz up to our side. "How's the world's slowest dancer treating you?" asks Octavia.

Connor eyes her from head to toe. A slight blush crawls into Octavia's cheeks. "You look lovely tonight, my Queen."

Octavia steps aside from Lincoln, straightening the folds of her black velvet gown with silver silk overlay. With a simple, bell-shaped skirt and long loopy sleeves, her dress perfectly frames her lovely face and figure. "Wait until you see the bill from the royal tailor."

"However much we paid, it's gold well spent." Connor stops dancing with me and offers his hands to Octavia. "Still the loveliest girl in the room."

"Flatterer," she replies.

He tilts his head to one side. "Ah, but is it working?"

"Always." Octavia wraps her arm around his. Together, they dance off.

Lincoln offers me his hands as well; I slide my palms against his. We stand a few feet apart, looking gawky and definitely not moving. I keep thinking about earlier tonight, when all we were supposed to do was meet some Earls and make small talk. Instead, Lincoln finds a way to get my lust demon all lusty. I don't even want to know what he'll do on the dance floor.

Well, I do want to know. I just don't want an audience of thrax to know, too. I'm not ready for their nobility to see my eyes red with demonic lust.

The Prince raises his brows. "What's with all the space between us?" His full mouth rounds into a sly grin. "Can I come closer by two inches?"

"Absolutely not. You stay over there."

"You didn't mind me touching you when I introduced you to the Earls."

"That was before."

"Before what?"

"Before, well…" I want to say, before I knew you could get my lust demon all riled up simply by standing around making small talk. But I don't. "Look, I don't want my eyes to flash in front of your people."

"That is an inevitability." He slides his palms up my arms, and then over to my waist. I contemplate batting his hands away, but decide against it. His touch is very yummy, after all. It doesn't hurt to enjoy it a little bit.

We stand on the ballroom floor, closer now, but not moving. Lincoln's eyes sparkle with held-in laughter. "This is the part where you put your hands on my shoulders and we dance."

He has a point. Standing on the dance floor like two statues is mighty odd.

"Fine. No funny business."

"Never."

I slowly wrap my arms around his neck, and we start to sway to the mellow tune. Without consciously willing it, my fingers play in his silky hair. My body moves even closer to his. Warmth spreads through my veins. The music hits a slow crescendo, and I move nearer until my breasts barely brush his chest. Okay, that's reeeeeeeeeally nice. Suddenly, touching the bare skin at the Prince's neck isn't enough. Like the day in my room, I can't wait until there's far less clothing between us. As in, none at all. Fire begins to build up behind my eyes.

I quickly pull back, careful to ensure there's at least two inches of airspace between us at all times. Note to self: keep hormones in check.

Lincoln keeps his grip on my waist, his thumbs arcing up and down my belly. "You're doing it again."

"What?"

"Stopping her."

I'm so snagged. "Her who?"

"Your lust demon. Ever since the hedgerow maze, you've been holding back. I like her, you know."

I up the air-space quota between us to four inches. "We shouldn't talk about that here."

"If you say so." But he says that in a growly-sexy voice that makes the extra airspace between us totally useless. Grrrrr.

Once again, Octavia and Connor dance up to our side, their faces the definition of 'up to something'. The Queen scrunches up her features in mock-confusion. "What did you say, my son?"

"I said not a word and you know it, Mother."

"You didn't?"

"Nope."

Octavia turns to Connor. "I heard something."

"I did, too." Connor loops his arm through Octavia's. "Let's help the kids get started."

Lincoln sets his palms onto his eyes. "I don't know why I tell you two anything."

Octavia speeds to the edge of the dance floor and claps her hands in a rapid rhythm. "Everyone! Quiet now." The crowd instantly turns silent. Octavia gestures to Lincoln. "My son has an important announcement to make."

The air couldn't have gotten knocked out of me faster if I'd been hit with a choke-slam. With Adair gone, the Rixa betrothal jewels must finally have resurfaced. Happiness percolates through me. Betrothal time, yeah!

Octavia launches into a cute speech about how much she loves her son. I use the opportunity to whisper to Lincoln.

"Found the jewels, did they?"

He leans in close, looking at me out of his left eye. "Maybe."

"Cool." I watch Octavia finish up her speech. She's getting misty remembering how the toddler-Lincoln tried skewering the cat with a wooden sword. It gets a big laugh. After that, she asks her son to say a few words.

Lincoln turns to address the crowd. "My people. A few days ago, the Great Scala once again saved all of Antrum and the after-realms. Two times she has triumphed over the King of Hell. She's long ago won my heart." Lincoln gets down on one knee and holds up a large velvet box that holds a diamond necklace, ring, and tiara. "Myla Lewis, the Great Scala, champion of the House of Gurith, Greatest Warrior in Antrum, will you marry me?"

My eyes bead with tears as I meet his gaze. "Lincoln Vidar Osric Aquilus, High Prince of the House of Rixa, yes, I will marry you." I scan the audience filled with hundreds of thrax. Sure, I'm the Great Scala and I saved all their sorry hides, but these are demon hunters. Can they really be happy with a quasi-demon as their future Queen?

A long pause follows where I'm sure a bunch of thrax have ran off to boil tar and pluck feathers. At last, one reedy voice starts to chant 'Scala, Lincoln. Scala, Lincoln'.

My face breaks out into a huge grin, all kinds of happy pumping through my body.

More voices join in. Soon, the words 'Scala, Lincoln, Scala, Lincoln' echo through the entire room. I wag my head in disbelief, the movement sending my gaze to the edge of the dance floor. There I see my parents, Lincoln's parents, and the ever-present Walker standing in a neat row, all misty-eyed with joy. I get a little more sniffly myself.

Lincoln gives my hands a squeeze, making me return my attention to him. Rising to his feet, he speaks in a loud voice that carries over the din of his people's chanting. "Therefore, I offer you the mark of our betrothal." Raising his hands, he sets all the jewels in place. "There." His voice breaks with emotion. "That's perfect." Cupping the back of my head, he slowly guides our lips together. The crowd breaks out into a wild cheer.

Once our sweet kiss is over, I whisper softly in his ear.

"No, together's perfect."

24

My back presses against the thick mahogany door to my suite in Arx Hall. Lincoln's chest moves against me, pushing me a little too roughly as his mouth grazes up the most sensitive part of my neck. Unholy Hell, that's good. I pant for breath, heat pooling in my veins.

Lincoln's lips brush the shell of my ear. "What to show me your rooms?"

Panic zooms through my nervous system, short-circuiting my brain. I'm sooooo not at peace with the super-special relationship Lincoln has with my inner lust demon. Twice now, Madame du Lust has almost taken over, getting the rest of us into situations we absolutely aren't ready for. And being that Lincoln's my first boyfriend—and as of fifteen minutes ago, fiancée—I don't have a lot of experience chatting about this stuff. I brainstorm different ways to raise the topic and yet remain cool-looking at the same time. I got nothing.

Eventually, I do what I do best under stress, and say the first thing that comes into my head.

"Shouldn't we go back to the party?"

"No, everyone's drunk or dancing by now. We won't be missed." Pulling away from me, Lincoln carefully scans my face with his mismatched eyes. "Is everything alright?"

"Yeah. Fine. Tired." Why can I only speak in single syllables? "Night."

I wrap my fingers around the handle and slip past, quickly closing the door behind me. I really hope I didn't bop Lincoln in the nose, there.

Inside, the room looks the same as when I changed for tonight's Ball of Welcome. Lots of space, lots of bric-a-brac. Now that Clover's gone for the night, it's awfully quiet-slash-creepy in here, too. Not sure I'm psyched to be alone in the same room where I saw Clover turn all demon-eyed. Plus, Lincoln was definitely in for a visit. So why did I slam the door in his face again?

Oh, yeah. My lust demon issues.

Damn, I keep panicking every time she shows up. And now, it's got me hanging out by myself on the night of my own engagement. Smooth, Myla. I kick off one of my stilettos and sigh.

A voice sounds behind me.

"Wait a moment. Weren't we planning a discussion about stilettos?"

I look over my shoulder and dang. The Sultan of Stealth has opened some kind of door hidden in my wall. Lincoln now leans in the doorjamb, wearing his leather pants and a white high-necked shirt.

"Lincoln!" I shift my weight onto my shoe-free foot. "How'd you get in here?"

"I had my things moved in next door. Didn't I mention that?"

"No." I kick my second shoe aside. "You're a downright Peeping Tom."

"Only on nights when I get betrothed."

Crap, we're totally engaged. He's totally hot. And I'm still totally panicking. Ugh.

Lincoln grips his fist behind his back and rocks on his heels. Long minutes tick by while I stare at him, scrunching my toes into the carpet, and feeling awkward as Hell. Every so often, I open my mouth, ready to finally start some kind of conversation. Each time I start to speak, Lincoln looks at me, an expectant gleam in his eyes. After that, I chicken out, close my yap, and go back to scrunching my toes.

This is the pits.

Lincoln scratches his neck with his hand. "I'll leave you to it, then." Turning on his heel, he starts to leave. The sight snaps me out of whatever communicative funk I've been stuck in.

"Wait." My hands ball and un-ball with nervous energy. "Here's the thing. It all started when I was twelve." I stare at him like that will make sense.

Lincoln leans against the doorjamb once again. "Go on."

"The ghouls sent me to fight in the Arena. The first evil soul came for me and whoa, my wrath demon had to rip loose or I would've died. I've spent years getting to know my battle side. But my lust demon? I didn't even know she existed until I met you." My face burns with embarrassment. "I can't even imagine how that must sound."

Wow. Could I be a bigger loser? This whole experience is so cringe-worthy, it isn't funny.

Lincoln steps closer. "I'm honored. Really."

I set my betrothal jewels onto a nearby table and try to think of something cool—or at least not humiliating—to say in reply. Nothing comes to mind.

Lincoln takes another cautious step closer, like I'm a wild animal that could bolt any second. "What are you worried about?"

"Honestly, I have zero self control around you. First, I almost tackled you in the hedgerow maze. After that, it happened a second time, the other day in my room. Don't get me wrong; I want to do things with you. Really. But I have no idea what'll happen." I wince. "My inner lust demon."

Lincoln's voice is gentle. "It's like I told you before. I'm not worried. I don't think she'll be as crazy as you think. And if she is, I can handle it."

"I don't know. In my room, you got pretty carried away, too."

Lincoln's brows lift with surprise. "Did you ever see me lose control?"

"No." And I liked that, too.

"Is my experience the problem? Does that upset you somehow?"

"Not at all. It's good that one of us knows what they're doing. You're the first guy I ever..." I search his eyes, but he's doing that unreadable-thing again with his face. Worry rises up inside me. Does he expect me to be experienced, too? "Don't get me wrong. It's not like I don't know anything. I think about stuff a lot, when I'm alone. Well, I think about you, if you know what I mean." I press my lips together, beyond embarrassed. That was the worst speech about sex and masturbation from someone who's part lust demon, ever.

I straighten my spine. I'm the Great Scala; I can say this. "Here's the thing. I don't want to go too far. But I don't think she feels the same way."

Lincoln takes another step closer. "Leave her to me. How far do you want to go?"

"Not sex, but, you know, anything up to that."

"All right." He offers me a knee-melting smile. "But we don't have to go that far, either. We'll be together for a long time, Myla. I'd like to take things slowly. Is that okay with you?"

I exhale a shaky breath. "Sure."

Another long pause follows, which I decide to fill with a too-fast laugh. "Why is this so weird all of a sudden?"

"May I make a suggestion?"

"Please."

"You said that you thought about me when you're alone."

A blush crawls up my cheek. "Yeah."

"What do you picture?"

"Us." I look his way, catch his eyes, and look away again just as quickly. "In the stables."

"After the Winter Tournament."

"Yes, when you…" I mime-pinch my fingers like I'm giving a massage.

"Got it. Let's start there."

"What do you mean?"

"I never did finish that massage. Would you like me to now?"

I nod so fast, I'm shocked I don't get whiplash. *Yes, yes, yes.*

Lincoln gestures to his room. "Perhaps we should move in here."

More fast nodding.

I step past Lincoln and into his room. It's a nice mix of modern and medieval with lots of brown and gray tones, accented by comfy leather chairs. "I like your place."

"Thank you." He gestures to the oriental carpet at the floor of his bed. "Why don't you sit here?"

"Right, like I was at the stables."

"Yes." He hands me a blanket. "You'll need to cover up again, like you did back then."

Stripping down in front of Lincoln feels a bit advanced for me. A more intense blush crawls up my cheeks.

He covers his eyes with his hands. "I promise not to peek."

I quickly slip off my Scala-robes-plus-over-gown combo, and then wrap the blanket around me. I tap his arm. "Okay, you can look now."

Lincoln opens his eyes, watching me with a coiled interest, like he's sizing up an opponent before a fight. My lust and wrath demons agree; that's a crazy-hot look on his face, right there.

"Excellent. Sit down." The way he says those last two words—a little bossy and husky—starts my pulse pattering away at double-speed. After making sure my blanket isn't tangled up, I sit down on the oriental carpet, carefully folding my legs beneath me, exactly as I did in the stables so long ago. Excitement pours through my veins.

Lincoln sits directly behind me, the body heat from his chest radiating along my back. He runs his finger along the line of fabric behind my shoulders. "As I recall, you weren't wearing anything from the waist up. This blanket does limit my massage moves."

My voice comes out breathy. "All right." I loosen the blanket, holding it to my chest and leaving my back bare. "How's that?"

"Perfect." Lincoln goes to work on my shoulders, his nimble fingers alternating between rough pressure and feather-soft brushes. My body warms, my muscles loosen. Exhaling, I lean forward, bracing my arms on my knees. Lincoln slides his fingers up to massage my scalp. Every so often, his nails gently scratch my skin. I like that part, a lot.

Lincoln leans in. "I remember when I first sensed her."

Without meaning to, I let out a long 'mmm' noise. "My lust demon?"

"Oh, yes. I was right here." His hands press down on my lower back and knead along my hip-line, hard and rough. His warm breath cascades down my neck as he speaks. "And you shivered."

I tremble once again. "That's right."

"At that moment, I thought we might have a real spark, other than wanting to kill each other."

I laugh, the sound low, husky and real. Behind me, Lincoln takes off his shirt.

This is getting good.

Lincoln leans in again. His bare skin brushes against mine. "You tried to get away." He sets his hands on either side of my waist. "And then, I held you down." His grip turns hard and tight as he presses my hips against the floor. His voice sounds low in my ear. "Like this."

My breath catches. Every cell in my body is on alert, waiting for his next touch or word.

"And I knew you liked that even more." Lincoln's fingertips glide around my upper arms until his touch traces the line of my collarbones. "You did, didn't you?"

I look over my shoulder and meet his gaze. "Yes." His face radiates raw passion under airtight control. Damn, that gets me. My eyes burn bright red with lust.

Lincoln's mouth winds into a knowing grin. "Why, hello, there."

"Hi, yourself."

Lincoln slowly pulls my hair to one side and starts kissing a soft line along my neck. I close my eyes and revel in every sensation.

And just like that, it's official. Having an inner lust demon might actually be pretty awesome, after all.

25

I don't like going anywhere blindfolded, but then again, Walker insisted. And after everything that guy's done for me, who am I to deny him anything? Right now, Lincoln holds my right hand and Walker holds my left while our little trio marches across a cobblestone yard. Our destination? An excellent view of the prototype building for our new Ghost Towers. After six months of fast construction, the structure is ready for a first look.

As we step along, my heart pounds at double-speed. I approved the plans for the new Tower, of course, but after that, Walker's been super-secretive. He even built covered scaffolding around the construction site, all the better to keep away prying eyes and cameras.

I stop moving. "Can I peek now?"

"No." Walker chuckles; he knows I have zero patience. "You'll have to wait a little longer. I want you to have the perfect view when you first see it."

We march a little father along. My tail pokes Walker on the shoulder the entire way, a movement that asks 'are we there yet?' over and over. Finally, we come to a full stop.

"You ready?" asks Walker.

"So ready."

I pull the blindfold down from my eyes and gasp. This is probably the most gorgeous building in the history of ever. I look at it again. No, it's definitely the most gorgeous building, period.

The new Ghost Tower is made of clear and super-strong glass, so you can see the lovely clouds floating inside. On the exterior, etched words appear on its surface. Some stuff scrolls up and down. Other things start off small and grow huge, only to disappear. The text is all statistics about the Tower in question. How many souls are in there and how many we've moved, that kind of thing. 'Information as decoration' is what Walker calls it. Since sorting and processing souls is what Purgatory does, I call it beautiful.

"Wow, Walker. It's gorgeous."

"Wait until you see it at night. The words will light up at different levels of brightness." Walker hitches his thumb towards Lincoln. "That was the big guy's idea."

"It's all a team effort," says Lincoln. He and Walker exchange a fist-bump in celebration. The two of them have been working together on building the Tower prototype, and having a blast doing it. Plus, it's helped my people get used to seeing Lincoln around Purgatory and being involved in stuff. They now call us The Great Scala and

Companion. I think it's a crappy title compared to Princess-In-Waiting, which is what I get in Antrum, but Lincoln says he likes it just fine.

My tail bounces anxiously behind me. "Can I go inside and take a look?"

"Not yet," says Walker. "There's still a lot left to do."

"Besides, we're due in Antrum soon," adds Lincoln. "Our transfer platform leaves within the hour."

"Oh, that's right. I almost forgot."

Since our engagement, we've been spending six months in Purgatory followed by six months in Antrum. Wherever we are, I'll always pop back to the Arena for my monthly iconigrations. Tonight, seeing this Tower prototype officially marks the end of our first six-month stint in Purgatory. To celebrate our return to Antrum, Octavia's holding another royal Ball tonight. Lincoln says that after the first dozen or so, they won't bother me so much. I say that as long as we get to sneak out early, I don't mind them at all. We're still taking it slow with my lust demon, and having a damn good time, too.

Lincoln and I say our goodbyes to Walker and walk away from the Tower, hand in hand.

"After the Ball, how about joining me on demon patrol?" asks Lincoln. This is where thrax sneak onto Earth's surface and kill some baddies. It's their whole raison d'etre, and it can be a kick-ass experience, depending on the demon in question.

"Anything good?"

"The House of Kamal reported some trouble in Bali. The weather there's supposed to be really nice."

Mister Sly. He knows I could care less about the weather.

"You know what I mean."

"Oh, are the demons any good?"

"Yes, are the demons any good. Bali happens to be home to the very rare and interesting Blue Simia." This variety of baddie is a monkey-giant hybrid that spits purple poison. I've been dying to fight one for ages.

"You know." Lincoln taps his chin, as if the thought were just appearing in his mind. "I think they may have reported seeing a Blue Simia or two."

I exhale a bliss-filled sigh. "Oh, Lincoln. You say the sweetest things."

"So, is it a plan?"

"Absolutely. Formal Ball followed by killing Blue Simia. Sold."

As we finish our walk to the Pulpitum, I come to a very important conclusion.

Life for Lincoln and me may not always be easy, but all in all, it doesn't get any better than this.

EPILOGUE

1

TWO MONTHS LATER

Lincoln and I stroll up the round drive to the Ryder mansion. Most of the time, my guy and I are either fighting *big bads,* kissing like crazy, or stuck spending time apart. Sharing a quiet walk like this one? Major treat.

I soak in the moment.

Grey skies arch overhead. Early morning dew glistens on the mansion's white wooden exterior. More condensation drips off the emerald shrubs encircling the building's base. The scent of cut grass fills the air.

Life is good.

We pause before the front door. Normally, my guy and by now, mostly from quasis who want me to bless their goldfish or something. But it's early a.m. and the mansion grounds are deserted. I give my guy the once-over, simply because I can. Lincoln's in casual mode today, meaning he sports a black t-shirt, jeans and hefty boots. Meanwhile, I wear my white Scala robes and carry a leather satchel.

Key fact: Time was, you could never get decent handbags in Purgatory. Then I kicked the ghouls out and local shopping got crazy-better. Total victory bonus.

I ring the doorbell. Recently, the Ryders installed a fancy number that bongs to the tune of *Some Enchanted Evening.* It's an odd choice, but the Ryders are all part lust demon. To them, using a hookup song as a doorbell makes sense. Seconds pass before a muffled voice sounds behind the wooden panel.

"Who goes there?"

Lincoln gives me the side-eye. "Is that … Zeke?"

"Yup." On reflex, I pop the P-sound on the word's end.

This sucks.

Here's the deal. Cissy promised Zeke wouldn't be around this morning. Sure, Lincoln is my fiancée, but it's not like we've known each other for years. Plus, there's already plenty of weirdness in my life: I'm a demi-goddess, Dad's an archangel, and Mom's President of Purgatory. And that list doesn't even leave my immediate family. I'm in no rush to introduce my guy into my larger circle of strangeness.

Which mostly includes Zeke.

"Answer my question. Who goes there? I'm the Captain of the President's Guard."

"Maybe," I correct. "Mom's *considering* it."

Which is true. That said, Mom will probably give Zeke the gig. Two reasons. First, Zeke stood by my mother when she faced Armageddon. Loyalty like that gets rewarded. Second, my bestie Cissy is killing it in the diplomacy department. That's a huge help to the government in general, and to my mother in particular. There's a catch, though. Cissy's dating Zeke, who wants in on the military. Hence the guard thing.

I jingle the handle. "Open the door. We're late for Cissy."

"I need proof of identity," states Zeke. "Give me the password."

"Are you serious?" I throw up my hands. "No one told me you were guarding the door, let alone asking for passwords."

Beside me, Lincoln toys with the hilt of his baculum. "Shall I ignite my long sword?" His eyes light up with a sly gleam. "It would slice through this wood like butter."

"I heard that!" calls Zeke. "You didn't say anyone was with you, Myla."

I look to Lincoln. "Please don't ruin the door. Zeke's mom will call my mother in a nanosecond. Nothing but hideousness will result, trust me." I jiggle the handle harder while yelling at the door. "Listen to yourself, Captain Man Candy! You just called me Myla. You know who I am. And I distinctly used the word 'we' when I said—and I quote—*we're late for Cissy*. So obviously, someone's with me. Now open up already."

A drumroll of footsteps sounds from inside the house. At last, the door swings open. Inside the threshold, there stands Zeke in full purple body armor, complete with the crest of Purgatory's New Republic on his bicep. Beside him stands a very red-faced Cissy in a purple skirt suit. She's panting. No doubt, my bestie sprinted to the door.

"I'm so sorry," says Cissy. To emphasize her worry, she wrings her hands. On anyone else, that move would look totally fake, but my bestie sells it like a pro. That's why she's so good at the diplomacy thing.

"It's fine," I say. *And it is.* Cissy's working her ass off these days. Incredibly sweet of her to come by early just so Lincoln and I can bypass my worshippers. Sure, Walker gives my followers little projects to stay out of my hair, but Purgatory's a massive place. There's always someone who doesn't get the memo, if you know what I mean.

Lincoln nods regally. "Greetings."

"Hey, Lincoln." Cissy turn to Zeke and freezes. She looks him over from head to toe. Twice. It's as if she's seeing her boyfriend for the first time this morning. Which is probably the case.

"You're wearing body armor today," says Cissy.

Zeke puffs out his chest. "It just came in. Official guard armor. Thought I'd try it on and practice, you know?"

I raise my hand. "True story. Zeke was being totally annoying at the door. For the record, there's no password system here."

Cissy and Zeke ignore me because that's what they do sometimes. Zeke arches his right brow. It's what Cissy calls his 'delicious' look. He then gestures across his body armor. "What do you think?"

A long pause follows while Cissy says nothing. My

bestie is like me in one respect. Both of us love ourselves a man in body armor. Cissy has dropped all pretense of hand-wringing and has segued completely into guy-ogling.

"I like it." Cissy drags out the word *like* for like five seconds.

I clear my throat. "Cis."

My bestie doesn't even look in my direction. "Hmm?"

"We're supposed to meet that Hanner guy," I remind her.

Cissy stays in eye-lock with Zeke. "His name's Herbie."

"Right." I make *twiddle fingers* at her and Zeke. "So the first step in the process is for the two of you to move backward so Lincoln and I can enter the mansion."

"What?" Cissy blinks hard. "Oh, right."

Together, Cissy and Zeke retreat into the reception area. Then they start ogling each other some more. Zeke's eyes flare red. That means his lust demon is active.

Yipes.

There are some memories that are so disturbing, I'd like to burn them out of my brain. Many of them involve Cissy and Zeke making out. Even thinking about it makes me shiver. Next my tail gets into the act. It arches over my shoulder to point at my face. The arrowhead end the wags from side to side, meaning *no, no, no.*

I couldn't agree more.

Grasping Lincoln's wrist, I yank him into the building, through reception and then straight down the hallway leading to the diplomatic wing. As we speed away, I call over my shoulder. "I know where, uh," *what's that name again?* It's too stressful right now to remember, so I take a wild guess. "I can find Hanford on my own so … buh-bye!"

Lincoln narrows his eyes into what I call his *contemplative face*. This happens a lot when he asks me questions about quasi life. "I thought you were part lust demon."

Suddenly I realize how I've lost some cool factor here. The Cissy-Zeke thing freaked me out. Releasing my vise-like grasp on Lincoln's wrist, I force a more leisurely sashay-style pace down the hallway. "What do you mean?" I ask, very casually and with the utmost level of awesome possible. Maybe.

"Cissy and Zeke are about to kiss," says Lincoln.

"Eew."

"And there's my question. Why would that be upsetting?"

Stopping, I fix Lincoln with my most serious stare. "Two words: spit strings." I hold up my palms so they're about three feet apart. "Of like, epic proportions." Okay, that was six words, but hopefully my guy will get the idea.

And does he ever.

Lincoln's face contorts into a look that can only be described as, *disgusted*. Little lines form between his eyebrows and everything. "You are a goddess among women," he states solemnly. "Thank you for sparing me that sight."

At this point, it's worth noting that Lincoln did not even wince when we exploded Simia demons the other week. There were blue guts in our hair and everything.

Therefore I find his reaction to the *spit string* situation to be totally validating.

"You're welcome." I grin. "Now let's go talk to, uh, Hector."

"It's Herbie."

My guy and the names. He's a wizard when it comes to memory. Which is one of many reasons why I'm glad Lincoln's here today. My eyes widen. In all the excitement between Zeke and Cissy, I've gotten distracted from the real purpose of our visit.

Meeting a key witness.

Getting evidence against Acca.

Then using said facts to lock Aldred up in his *forever-jail.*

Oh, yeeeeeeeeah.

2

A few minutes later, Lincoln and I stand before another closed door. This time, it leads to a chamber in the diplomatic wing of the Ryder mansion. I knock gently.

"Who is it?" The voice is young, male and decidedly shaky. Must be Herbie.

"It's Myla Lewis."

"Who?!" A crash sounds through the door as Herbie knocks something over.

Yipes. I keep forgetting how no one connects my real identity with my deity alter-ego. "I mean, it's the Great Scala."

"Oh," says Herbie. "Come in, please."

I push open the door to witness one of the most unexpected sights ever. A scrawny teenager sits at a massive oak table surrounded by empty chairs. *Herbie.* The kid's got a long nose, spikey brown hair, huge brown eyes and a T-shirt that reads 'I heart the Human Channel.' But that's not the surprising part. Nope. What's an eye opener is how white ceramic bowls cover the tabletop. And all those containers are filled with tiny yet disgusting food items.

Ick. And I thought the spit strings were bad.

Lincoln steps in beside me. "Greetings."

"Who are you?" Herbie cranes his neck. "You don't have a tail."

"He's my fiancée," I explain.

Herbie scrunches up his face, as if contemplating this news very carefully. "And you're the Great Scala."

I shoot him a thumbs-up. "Bingo."

Herbie shrugs. "Then I guess it's okay then." He pulls a fresh bowl closer. "You don't kind if I eat, do you?"

I make shoo fingers at him and try not to look too closely. "Nope. Knock yourself out."

Lincoln makes his *contemplative* face again. "What are you eating there, Herbie?"

"Baby hot dogs. Want one?"

I stifle the urge to barf. "No." In my mind, that word came out all low and smooth. But based on how everyone is staring at me with wide eyes? I might have screamed it a bit.

Herbie grabs his baby hotdog bowl and scooches back his chair. "Maybe I should leave."

"No, please." I take the seat across from Herbie and try to ignore the twenty-odd bowls filled with baby hot dogs. "Here's the deal. I had an awful baby hotdog incident in the second grade at Purgatory Prep." I set my hand on my heart. "True story."

"I'm listening." Herbie pops another baby hotdog into his mouth. I really wish he'd use utensils, but I'm in no position to make demands right now. I need Herbie giving evidence more than I want sanitary eating practices.

"It was our end of school party," I begin. "We got one of those super humid days where the temperature was about a gazillion degrees. You went to school with ghoul teachers, right?"

"You know it." After stuffing his mouth with five baby hotdogs at once, Herbie then he leans back in his chair. I take this as a good sign. The guy's getting comfortable.

"Well," I continue. "There were a lot of games, most of which sucked. But one was Dunk The Ghoul Teacher. You know the one? The teacher sits on a ledge-y thing over a pool. If you hit a bull's-eye, they fall in."

Herbie rolls his eyes. "Like anyone would do that to a ghoul. Everyone was too afraid of our overlords."

"No one did." I point at my face. "Except me."

"And I believe it." Lincoln slips onto the chair beside mine. Based on the light in his mismatched eyes, he's loving this story.

"So, my eight year old self then dunked ghouls for like five hours straight. Then the school shut down the game and I realized I was super hungry. There wasn't much food left by this point, only some scraggly baby hotdogs at the bottom of a random bowl. Even worse, they'd been sitting out in the sun and were swimming in some kind of green ooze. But I was super-hungry so I ate them all. Then I puked my guts up."

Herbie stops chewing. "Should we end this? You hate baby hotdogs. I'm part gluttony demon. I can't focus unless I'm eating. I have a doctor's note and everything."

"No, it's fine." I lie. "I just got a little shocked when I first walked in. Now I'm great."

"Really?" asks Herbie.

I rub my tummy and fake it. "Mmmm, baby hotdogs."

Herbie offers me the bowl. "Want some?"

I tap my chin, as if considering this instead of trying not to barf. "Nope, I'm good." I turn to my guy. "Lincoln, how about you?"

"I ate before we get here," says Lincoln smoothly. "Maybe next time."

"You're loss," says Herbie.

I rub my palms together. With the greetings over, it's time to focus on getting Aldred incarcerated. "Let's get to the reason we're here." Hoisting my super-sweet leather satchel, I set it onto the patch of tabletop not covered in baby hotdog bowls.

Lincoln raises his pointer finger. "Before we do that, may I ask a question?"

Herbie talks through a mouth of *yuck*. "Sure."

Lincoln tilts his head. "Not sure how to ask this, but shouldn't gluttony demons be..." he scans the room, as if looking for the word.

"A lot bigger than me?" suggests Herbie.

"That," confirms Lincoln.

"Gluttony is just about major intake of food," explains Herbie. "I've got an amazing metabolism."

"What kind of tail are you packing?" I ask.

"Hummingbird." Herbie stands up and turns around. Sure enough, he has a cute little tail of green feathers sticking out the back of his jeans. "Hummingbirds eat their weight in insects every day. For me, it's baby hotdogs."

"Your weight every day," says Lincoln. "Thank you for explaining."

Things are veering back into scary baby hotdog territory, so I decide to get us back on track. Reaching into my satchel, I pull out a leather book. "This is a codex. It's why we're here."

Slam!

The door bursts open.

I groan. Now what?

3

Cissy rushes into the room. Her blonde ringlets are a mess and her lips look like she just got Botox injections. No question what that means. My bestie and Zeke have been all kinds of busy. In an act of kindness from the universe, there are no spit strings dribbling from her chin.

And no, I'm not kidding. It's happened before.

"So sorry I'm late," says my bestie.

"It's fine." I wave her off. "We met Herbie and we're ready to roll. No need to stay if you're busy."

Cissy plunks herself down onto the empty seat to my right. "I'm not going anywhere. This is so important." While fanning herself with her hands, my bestie turns to Herbie. "Normally, I'm very good at hiding my emotions, but you'll just have to excuse me."

Whatever concerns Herbie had before, he's definitely moved on from them. Cissy's worry doesn't even seem to register with the kid. Herbie just stacks his latest (and now empty) bowl onto the floor, yanks over another container, and chows down.

"You see," says Cissy. "It's really-really-really important that you're here today. Myla is my best friend."

"Who?" asks Herbie.

"She means *the Great Scala* is her best friend," I say. Clearly, Herbie's not great with memory, unless sit involves lunch. Goes with the hummingbird-and-gluttony combo.

"Right." Cissy exhales a long breath. "So this is super hard for me. She and her fiancée are here to gather information about Lady Adair and the House of Acca."

All the color drains from Herbie's face. "Lady Adair is dead, right? She's not doing diplomatic stuff anymore." The hummingbird side of Herbie's personality must be taking over, because the kid starts talking super fast. "I'm not Adair's intern anymore. I don't have anything to do with that crazy lady."

My brows lift. For a while, Adair acted as Antrum's diplomat to Purgatory. Seems like Herbie has quite the experience her Adair's diplomatic. Whenever we get to the evidence portion of the day, things are sure to get interesting.

"It's all right," says Lincoln soothingly. And he has that Princely way of saying things like that where you totally believe him. "Adair is gone."

"Gone where?" asks Herbie. He's wobbling a bit in his chair now. I wonder if the guy's about to pass out. That could get ugly. I decide to step in. I've dealt with guys like Herbie before. It's best to be super clear. "Lady Adair is dead. Lincoln and I totally chopped her head off."

Herbie sighs. "Good. Right. So what do you need me for again?"

And so we return to the downside of a hummingbird profile. Amazing metabolism. Short memory span.

"Adair's comes from this clan called Acca," says Cissy. "Their leader, Aldred, want to kill Myla and Lincoln. I mean, the Great Scala and Prince Lincoln."

"Truth," I say.

Cissy sets her hand on my shoulder. "My best friend wants to take Aldred to court and make him pay for his crimes. To do this, she needs magically recorded evidence in this book." To emphasize the point, Cissy then pats the top of the leather volume with her free hand.

Lincoln and I share a pleased look. The acknowledgement is there, if unspoken. *Cissy is handling this super well.*

"And if the evidence isn't enough to win the day in court?" asks Cissy. "Then Myla and Lincoln will be locked up in a jail forever. They'll be underground with worms and nasty stuff, never to see the light of day again. I'll lose my best friend." Cissy turns to me, tears streaming down her face. "I can't lose you, Myla."

Herbie frowns. "Myla?"

Damn, this guy has a short memory.

Lincoln and I speak in unison. "Great Scala."

I press my lips together hard. Cissy is going off the rails, big time. Lincoln and I share another look. My guy angles his head toward the door. The implication is clear. *You want Cissy out of here?*

I nod quickly. *Yes, yes, yes.*

Unlike me, Lincoln is a smooth liar. He cups his hand by his ear. "Oh, my goodness. Is that Zeke?"

Cissy sniffles. "I don't hear anything."

I decide to play along. "Oh, his voice is totally clear. Zeke says he has another suit of armor to show you."

"Really?" She dabs her cheeks with her fingertips.

Lincoln fixes her with his most believable and regal stare. "Absolutely. You better hurry. I think I heard a female voice down there. Someone named Paula?"

For the record, this is super impressive. Paula Richards is Cissy's old envy nemesis from high school. Even worse, Paula used to date Zeke. I mentioned that fact to Lincoln like once three weeks ago.

Cissy hops up to stand. Her eyes flare envy red. "Okay, you seem fine. I'll take off now."

I twiddle my fingers at her. "Buh-bye."

Cissy rushes from the room. Once the door is shut, Lincoln places a strip of purple tape on the handle. That's no ordinary cellophane. It's a magical charm from Striga. I've seen Lincoln use this particular item before. It's a locking ward, so no one can disturb us again. Nice idea.

Key fact: Herbie is so into his baby hotdogs, the kid doesn't even notice Lincoln setting up the charm.

My guy retakes his seat and turns to me. "Shall we?"

"Absolutely." I refocus on Herbie. "Are you ready to tell your story?"

"Adair's dead right?"

"Totally."

Herbie shoves a fresh handful of baby hotdogs into his mouth. "Then, lets do this."

I grin. *Let's do this indeed.* Once we lock in this evidence, we're one step closer to taking Acca down.

About time.

4

At last, we're about to lock in our first anti-Acca interview. Squirming in my chair, I try to focus on a single thought.

Do not look at the baby hotdogs.

Do not look at the baby hotdogs.

Do not look at the baby hotdogs.

Crap, I looked. *Whoa, that kid can pack in the grub.* Honestly. We haven't been here that long and already, Herbie's halfway through the bowls.

Note to self: thank Cissy later for rounding up so much food. Because once these containers are empty? Herbie will be gone so fast, little poofs of smoke will appear behind him as he runs.

"Let's start with the basics," says Lincoln. "The process of recording your testimony is unique to my people."

"What do you mean?" For someone with a mouthful of food, Herbie speaks pretty clearly. Guess he has a lot of practice. "I watch Mortal's Court. People give testimony all the time."

Yet again, my many hours of television watching prove crucial to my adult life. "It's like this," I say to Herbie. "When humans have a trial, witnesses take the stand in court. In Antrum, you must be thrax to enter the courtroom." Or in my case, a demigoddess who hates rules. But I won't go into that much detail with Herbie. After all, the guy has a hummingbird attention span. "So for your testimony to count, it must be recorded in this particular book." I gesture to the leather volume. "The Rixa Codex."

"So you write what I say in the book?" asks Herbie.

"No, the process involves magic," explains Lincoln. "But it will not affect your person. Is that acceptable?"

Herbie grips his current bowl, dragging it across the table with long screech. "What about my food?"

"The magic won't affect it," clarifies Lincoln.

Herbie shrugs. "In that case, we're good." In a surprise move, Herbie then goes back to eating.

Lincoln lifts the codex. "I, Lincoln Vidar Osric Aquilus from the House of Rixa—"

"Hold on," says Herbie. "That's a lot of names for just a guy. Is this another thrax thing?"

A heavy pause fills the air. My eyes widen. *That's right.* I only introduced Lincoln as my fiancée, and my guy's not in formalwear today. I wince, debating whether to tell Herbie everything. Trouble is, this kid seems easily derailed.

Evidently, Lincoln has the same idea.

"That's exactly what it is," says my guy. "A thrax thing."

Stretching out his arms, Lincoln balances the codex on his palms. "Let the recording begin." The codex rises from Lincoln's hands and then hovers in the center of the room. A flare of white light pulses across its cover.

Herbie stops eating for a whole hot second. "Cool."

"First question," I say. "How did you became Adair's intern?"

"It's like this," says Herbie. "I eat a ton of Happy Piggy baby hotdogs. Those are gourmet. Really expensive. I needed summer job to help pay my bills. The rest of the internships here paid next to nothing. Working with angels was the worst. Only minimum wage."

I nod. *That makes sense. Angels can be cheap sometimes.*

"But interning for the Thrax Diplomat paid major money. I guess Adair went through twelve interns, and every time one left, they upped the salary. So I applied for the job. Sure, I heard she was a little loco. Still, I thought that as long as I got my Happy Piggies, everything would be fine."

"Let me guess," I state. "There was a reason it paid so well."

"You got that right," says Herbie. "All Adair did was yell at me. I couldn't do anything right. She kept saying how I'm a demon so her family would kill me for screwing things up so much. Which is really anti-quasi." Herbie rolls his eyes. "We are not demons. Quasis mostly human with a tiny bit of demonic DNA."

I raise my hand. "Testify." Leaning forward, I rest my

chin on my palms. *Things are getting interesting.* "So what kind of work did she have you do?"

Herbie runs his tongue over his teeth for a moment. I think the move helps him think while simultaneously picking bits of hotdog off his gums. "Adair took milk baths in the morning, and I had to fill the tub. That took tons of my time every day."

My mouth falls open. "She what?"

"Made me get a ton of milk cartons and pour it into a bathtub," sys Herbie.

"No way." I'm having trouble with this concept for some reason. *I mean, milk baths? Who does that?*

"Oh, yeah. There's a diplomatic suite in the mansion. Comes complete with a tub and everything. I had to clean up after she was done." Herbie sticks out his tongue in the universal gag-face. "Never drinking milk again, I'll tell you that."

"I don't blame you." Purgatory milk tends to curdle fast. That cleanup must have been a bitch.

"And what else did you do for Adair?" asks Lincoln.

That's my guy, moving things on from the milk conversation. Clever.

"Adair had me tie her shoes. I made sure her office was filled with fresh flowers every morning. She wanted crystals put all over the place too. Oh, and every day I got her really specific lunches that she never ate. And no matter what I did, she screamed at me for screwing it up. Those death threats from her family." Herbie shivers. "Working for her was terrible. I stopped eating. Sleeping. My hair started falling out."

"So you were a diplomatic intern who did nothing related to diplomacy," I recap.

"That's it." Herbie eats another handful, his eyes lost in thought. After a pause, he snaps his fingers. The movement sends a shower of hotdog juice over the table. "Oh, yeah. I almost forgot. Adair would talk at me all the time. The other interns, too. I mean, if she caught you by the snack machine, she'd talk your head off."

"About diplomatic stuff?" I ask.

"No. About how she really wanted to marry her *Angelbound love*. Yakkity yakkity yakkity. Non stop. *Angelbound love, Angelbound love, Angelbound love*. All the interns called him the *Miserybound loser*."

There's a long moment where the words hang out there.

Miserybound loser.

Oh, this is too good.

I pretend to cough, but the sound comes out sounding a lot like, *told you so*. I still give Lincoln crap about even considering marriage to Adair. Talk about a horror show.

Lincoln gives me the side-eye while smoothing his brow with his middle finger. *Classic.*

"Back to Adair," says my guy smoothly. "Did she say anything about unsanctioned alliances with Hell?"

"Oh sure. She said she was sharing blood with the King of Hell. Armageddon. He was going to possess her and in exchange, she'd be able to steal the powers of the Great

Scala and marry her Miserybound loser." Herbie makes little air quotes with his fingers when he says Miserybound loser.

"Unholy Hell." I gasp, because this news is just so crazy pants. "Did you tell anyone?"

"Why would I?" asks Herbie. "Who would believe that someone was crazy enough to share blood with the King of Hell? I just thought it was Adair being Adair."

"And did Adair say who set up this deal with Armageddon?"

"Sure," replies Herbie. "It was all brokered by Adair's own father, the Earl of Acca. Or so she said. Like I told you before, it was just so nutty it couldn't be true. Was it?"

I hold my thumb and pointer finger an inch apart. "It was a little true."

"Whoa." This time, Herbie jams so many baby hotdogs in his mouth, he actually has trouble speaking. "Wath happenth?"

"The dead thing," I reply. "But back to Adair. Anything else about her and Hell that you want to share?

"Mmm," Herbie finally chews and swallows his bite-a-saurus. "Adair talked all the time about how she was close to Armageddon. That if she ever went to Hell, the place would be a vacation for her. I thought for sure it was a joke."

"It wasn't," I say. "Long story."

Lincoln then launches into a ton more questions about Adair, Armageddon and Aldred. My guy's able to get some more details out, but there are no more major revelations like the whole Miserybound loser thing. Eventually, it gets really clear that we're out of useful queries.

"That's all we require from you," says Lincoln.

"Are you sure?" asks Herbie. "I can give you more details on the bath-thing."

"Nope, we're good," I say. I really don't want to know more about Adair's bathing habits.

"Whatever you say." Reaching over, Herbie drags the final bowl in front of him. Wow. How did the guy eat so quickly?

Oh, right. Gluttony demon.

"One last thing," says Herbie. "This Miserybound loser guy, do you know him?"

Lincoln nods. "I do."

"Pass along a message for me. Adair said that if the Miserybound loser ever married someone else, she'd find a way to drag him to Hell and make his after-life terrible. Same thing with her father. If Miserybound loser married not-Adair, then Aldred had plans for the guy, too. Adair wouldn't say what the schemes were, but the way her eyes got all glazed over with a sick kind of happy? It wasn't good."

"I'll pass it along," says Lincoln. "Although I don't think he'll be concerned."

Now Lincoln may not care about that news, but my insides twist with worry.

"In my opinion," continues Herbie. "That Miserybound loser guy should never walk down the aisle. Total disaster." Herbie looks down at his bowl. Somewhere along the line, he finished off his last baby hotdog. “I’m empty.” His eyes bulge. “I’m empty!” Rising, he rushes from the room.

For a moment, I consider following him. After all, Herbie just helped us out. I want to make sure the kid is okay. That said, the Herbie’s been dealing with his gluttony side for years. No doubt, he has a stash of baby hotdogs somewhere. And there are more important concerns.

Like what Herbie said about Adair and marriage.

Are Lincoln and I making a mistake?

5

Even with Herbie gone, all this talk about my marriage and Acca-related doom keeps buzzing around my head. Not to mention the part about Adair vacationing in Hell? Seems totally fake.

I turn to Lincoln. "Adair in Hell ... does that worry you at all?"

"Not in particular. In fact, I just got some news on that topic this morning. Would you like to hear it?"

We'd been concerned about Adair ever since she chose yelling at Lincoln and me over going to Heaven. Lincoln knows some fallen angels in Hell. My guy reached out for information. Tilting my head, I consider whether or not I want the update. It's already been a lot of Adair this morning. In the end, I decide it's best to get it over with.

"Sure," I reply.

"As it turns out, Adair's relatively comfortable for now. I wouldn't call her stay in Hell a vacation, but Armageddon is protecting her from the worst. The King of Hell wants to keep making deals with Acca. Torturing the Earl's favorite daughter won't necessarily help in that regard."

I think this through. "But once the Earl is dead, things could change for Adair. Eternity is a looooong time."

"Correct. Yet she made her choices. Just as we're making ours."

A weight of worry settles onto my shoulders. I curl forward, resting my elbows on the table before me. "Maybe this is a bad idea. Going after Acca. Getting married."

Lincoln's face turns unreadable. Amazing how he can do that in a second flat. "Because your feelings for me have changed?" he asks.

"Never." I huff out a breath. "It's Aldred. He'll never give up."

Lincoln shifts in his chair, moving to face me. Little by little, he takes my hands in his. The movement makes me turn to face him straight on. My guy meets my gaze straight on before speaking once more. "I have a duty to my people. It will be performed better with you at my side. But I also have an obligation to myself. To us. My father lives in fear of Aldred. I won't do that. More than anything, I want a future with you."

What sweet words. I should feel all better now. Yet I don't. If anything, my weight of worry only seems to grow heavier. "But you know Aldred will scheme about our wedding. Herbie is right. It could be a disaster."

"Whatever happens, we'll face it together. That's what this is about, isn't it?"

In this moment, Lincoln is all princely determination. Some of my anxiety fades. My guy and I have faced down a ton of stuff. Maybe we can ace this as well.

"Be my wife, Myla." Leaning in, Lincoln brushes the gentlest of kisses across my lips. The sensation makes my insides turn all warm and lovey. "Say yes. Again."

And because Lincoln's not the only one who wants this more than anything, I reply with one word. "Yes."

—The End—

The story continues in ACCA, Book 3 of the Angelbound Origins series. Read on for a sample chapter.

ALSO BY CHRISTINA BAUER

ACCA

Myla's adventure continues with ACCA … find out more at bauersbooks.com!

LINCOLN

Enjoy Lincoln's perspective with the Angelbound Lincoln series … more at bauersbooks.com!

FAIRY TALES OF THE MAGICORUM

Modern fairy tales that *USA Today* calls a 'must-read!' More at bauersbooks.com!

DIMENSION DRIFT

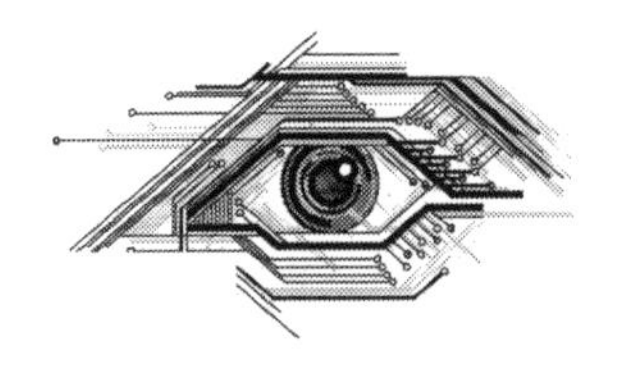

DIVERGENT meets OCEAN'S EIGHT in this dystopian adventure … more at bauersbooks.com!

BEHOLDER

Like GAME OF THRONES? You'll love the BEHOLDER series ... more at bauersbooks.com!

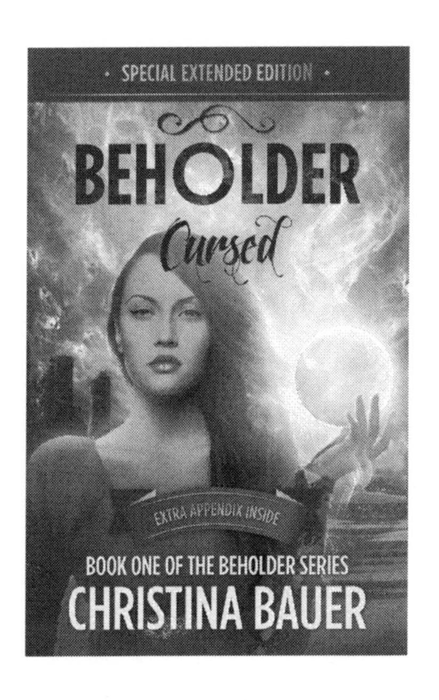

SAMPLE CHAPTER - ACCA

BOOK 3 OF THE ANGELBOUND ORIGINS SERIES

I haul ass across a tenement rooftop. The sky threatens rain, but what else is new? This is Purgatory, after all. Land of Blech. On the next building over, Desmond the Klepto demon scrambles his lizard-like butt off as he attempts to escape. "Attempts" being the key word in that sentence.

At every step, my fiancé Prince Lincoln keeps a steady pace by my side. A warm sense of happiness seeps through my chest.

We're demon hunting together again. At last.

Ahead of us, Desmond leaps onto another rooftop. This part of town is cramped and deserted, so he can easily scramble around without freaking out the general populace. Desmond's a lanky dude with green skin, a flat nose, and an enchanted book in his possession that he just snatched from me when I exited my limo.

What a douche.

Anger pulses through my bloodstream. Desmond stole the Rixa Codex—a small book of evidence that's hugely important.

I want it back like now.

I force my breathing to slow. Even though the book is crucial, I need to be patient. Plus, the chase is all part of the fun, right? And hell knows I haven't had any demon-fighting fun in ages.

Speaking of which, what's the rush to grab Desmond anyway? It's not like he stands a chance against both Lincoln and me.

From the corner of my eye, I give my guy a quick once-over. Hmm. Someone looks mighty spicy in his new black body armor.

Maybe if I let Lincoln run ahead a little, I can get a quick peek at his butt.

I take care to pant excessively while slowing my pace across the uneven shingles. Sure, it's unlikely that I'd actually be tired at this point. Like every native of Purgatory, I'm a quasi-demon. That means I'm mostly human with a little bit of demon DNA. It's what gives me a kick-ass tail as well as powers across two of the seven deadly sins, namely lust and wrath. My lust side grants me a pretty face, curves that stop traffic, and auburn hair that looks amazing without any product. Thanks to my inner wrath demon, I can fight like hell and run full out for days.

Even so, sometimes a girl just needs to slow down and check out her fiancé's butt, so that's what I do right now. Carpe assem.

Lincoln runs ahead of me. "For the record, I know what you're up to."

"Sure, it's called conserving energy. Why should we kill ourselves to catch Desmond?"

"Ah, then this is only about the klepto demon?" Lincoln leaps super-high over some kind of ancient television aerial. From this angle, it's a mighty lovely sight. "Not my glutes?"

I'm so shnagged.

"Fine. I like the view."

"We're hunting a demon, Myla." There's no missing the smile in his voice. Lincoln loves it when I'm sassy.

"Hey, I can multitask."

More smiling-voice-ness. "I've noticed."

Here's the deal. Six months ago, I was the baddest-ass warrior in Purgatory's Arena. Then, I got transformed into a supernatural called the great scala, which means that I'm the only being who can permanently move souls to Heaven or Hell. Trouble is, if I'm hurt, it's a showstopper for the spirit world. Long story short, until a Scala Heir is named, I have to be a responsible demigoddess. That means working behind a desk instead of killing things. It sucks. Hard.

"I concede your multitasking skills." Lincoln makes another mouthwatering leap. "You've got two minutes to dawdle."

Whoa.

"Did you just say dawdle?" I put on a tone of mock-outrage. "What are you, eighty?"

"I'll pass along your critique to my royal tutors."

"Like they'll listen." I snap my fingers. "Hey, I've got an idea. How about you watch some television?" Or any, really. "That'll help you sound like you're from this century."

"Last time I checked, resembling a young human wasn't one of my life goals, and you're not changing the subject. One minute of dawdle time remains." He places extra-emphasis on the word dawdle, the cheeky monkey.

"Eh, bite me."

"No comment." He looks back over his shoulder and winks. When the situation calls for it, Lincoln does love to use his teeth, and not in a bad way. At all.

After that, my guy goes quiet, so I return to ogling mode. Lincoln is tall and broad-shouldered with strong bone structure and messy brown hair. He's twenty—a year older than me—which some say is too young for us to get hitched. Whatever. I can't wait for our wedding. Plus, Lincoln's a kind of demon hunter called a thrax. His people are part angel, obsessed with tradition, and live deep under the Earth's surface. Lincoln's their high prince. More importantly, he's whip-smart, honest, noble almost to a fault, and a great kisser. Now that we're engaged, we've been working up to bigger things than kissing. It involves a lot less body armor and tons more skin.

Mmmmm, a partially naked Lincoln is a beautiful sight.

"Time's up," says Lincoln.

"Boo."

"Honestly, we have to hustle. We need that codex."

Okay, Lincoln has a point. The Rixa Codex is where we've been storing up evidence for a trial against Acca, a House of thrax asswipes who need to be brought down. Once we get that book back from Desmond—and use it to record our last interview for the thrax court—then we'll finally have enough proof to officially tear Acca apart. And after what those freaks put me through last month, I really want to destroy them. I mean, who enters into a secret pact with none other than Armageddon, the King of Hell?

Acca, that's who.

Lincoln and I almost died cleaning up that particular mess. In fact, Lady Adair of Acca did end up dead. She might have been a bit of a bitch, but still. The whole situation isn't something we can let slide.

I pick up the pace so I'm running shoulder-to-shoulder with Lincoln once more. "For the record, you spoil all my fun."

"Huh." Lincoln glances in my direction while arching his brows ever so slightly. "I know for a fact that I'm your main source of fun."

I stick my tongue out at him. He's totally right.

Lincoln laughs, which is a rich and rolling sound that makes everything in Purgatory seem a little less crappy. Together we leap toward another rooftop and land in perfect sync. A few pigeons flap off. When Desmond sees us closing in, he pulls a vial from his pocket, downs the contents, and picks up his pace. For a demon who has to waddle-walk everywhere, that guy sure starts hustling. The vial probably contained a velocity potion.

That said, even if Desmond can go extra fast, I'm not worried that he'll actually escape. While most full-blooded demons fall into the not-too-bright category, Desmond brings dumbass to an entirely new level. He can't stop stealing junk, dresses like a homeless clown, and has stalker issues with my family. Yet the biggest giveaway of Desmond's stupidity is the fact that he's running away from us right now.

Come on, showing your back to a pair of hunters? Seriously? That's like predator crack. The dude must have a death wish.

Desmond jumps off the roof to land on the pavement in a roll. That's no easy feat when your spine's extra long. Interesting. I've never seen Desmond so motivated before. Lincoln and I share a puzzled look before leaping off as well. We sprint a few blocks in silence.

"Does any of this seem odd to you?" Lincoln finally asks.

"I was thinking the same thing. This isn't Desmond's MO."

"Precisely."

For months, Desmond's been trailing my family in the hopes of stealing random bits of our junk. No real shocker there. Mom's the President of Purgatory and I'm the Great Scala. As a result, we both have our share of stalkers. Some are cute, even if they do rummage through our trash, looking for keepsakes. Others are creepy.

Like Desmond.

I shake my head. "Normally, Desmond never runs. He just hands over whatever he stole. Which is what should have happened back at the limo."

"It's what he did last time, and without any complaint."

"Yeah, that was at the Toys for Quasi-Demonic Tots thing."

Last week, Desmond lifted some stuff from Mom's purse while she was speaking at a fundraiser. Not a great idea. While Mom's the President of Purgatory, my father's a badass archangel. All Dad had to do was glare at Desmond, and the klepto handed over what he took. That time, it was Mom's brush and an old Tic Tac from the bottom of her purse. Like I said, Desmond's not the brightest star in the demonic sky. Sure, it's in his nature to steal, but most klepto demons are a little more strategic about it.

Okay, a lot more strategic.

A sinking feeling runs through my belly. Maybe Desmond isn't too smart, but someone else is. "He could be a pawn here, you know. Who would expect Desmond to get mixed up in something seriously evil?"

Lincoln's voice gets crazy calm. "Go on."

"Let's look at the facts. Desmond is running from us. You know we can't resist that."

"True."

"Next, how does a klepto demon go so fast on those

stubby little legs? That vial must have contained a velocity potion. Enchantments like those are pricey. You don't pay for them with stolen Tic Tacs. And then there's what he took. To grab the Rixa Codex, Desmond had to know when and where we'd be…And whether we'd have the book."

"All of which requires some serious scheming."

"Exactly. The whole thing is totally out of character. Desmond's a demon who spontaneously grabs junk. He doesn't plan complex heists."

Lincoln's full mouth thins to an angry line. "And now, he's lifted our codex, the very evidence that we need to put Acca behind bars." Thrax are all about tradition. Since we've challenged the House of Acca to court, thrax rules state that one side must go to jail. If it isn't Acca, then it's Lincoln and me.

Prison. What a sucky way to spend your honeymoon.

The more I think about it, the more I'm convinced. "Desmond is doing someone else's dirty work. Guess who."

A muscle ticks by Lincoln's jawline. That means he's pissed. Only one group gets him this angry. "Acca."

"Yup." Boy, do I ever hate those fuckers.

The House of Acca wants to rule the thrax homeland of Antrum. Since Lincoln's next in line to the throne, my guy stands in their way. Which is why Acca tried to marry Lincoln off to their Lady Adair. Too bad for them, Lincoln fell in love with me first, mostly because an oracle angel named Verus stuck her nose in our business. Long story. Anyway, not only does Acca still want the crown, but they also really, really, really want me dead. Meh.

More silence follows as we run along and ponder. Lincoln's the first to speak again. "There's a flaw in your logic. Acca must know that we'll get the codex back from Desmond."

He's got me there. Even if Desmond has a dozen spells on him, we'll still take that klepto down. I mean, I haven't even called on my little supernatural buddies for help yet. To move souls to Heaven or Hell, I have power over tiny lightning bolts of energy called igni. If worse comes to worst, I can summon my igni to send Desmond back to Hell, and keep the codex right here. Sure, that would be a total pain in the ass—once igni start moving souls, it's hard to get them to stop—but I have that option as a last resort.

So what's Acca really up to?

My tail arches over my shoulder. It's a beauty, what with being all long, black, and covered in dragon scales. The arrowhead-shaped end jabs in Desmond's direction. That's its way of saying we need to grab the klepto, fast.

"Don't worry, boy." I give my tail a comforting pat. "We'll get him."

Desmond rounds a corner, and the street turns from bad to worse. The downgrade in neighborhood quality is awesome, in my humble opinion. Here's why. Most of the after-realms have issues with demons sneaking in and causing trouble. On Earth, it's the thrax who clean things up. In Purgatory, that work falls to our police. However, our government's still reeling from Armageddon's recent invasion (I kicked his ass back to Hell, by the way). As a result, our police haven't been cracking down on demonic squatters.

Long story short, crappy areas like this one? They're classic hangouts for the truly evil. My heart thuds faster in my chest. Deserted ruins filled with über-nasty demons?

The day's looking up.

I grin from ear to ear. "I think I know what plan Desmond was given."

"Do tell."

"We're not supposed to fight a klepto demon."

"Could've fooled me."

"Desmond's leading us somewhere else."

Lincoln nods slowly. "Such as straight into a Class A battle." Thrax categorize demons by letter. Class A are the hardest to kill.

"Fighting a Class A would be soooooo awesome." I shoot Lincoln a sly look. "Maybe we'll get to take down another tinea." I let out a wistful sigh. "Together."

Lincoln chuckles. "I love your idea of date night." I know that laugh. Lincoln is as excited as I am.

"How about we make this even more interesting?" I ask.

"What are you thinking?" The husky tone in Lincoln's voice says that he knows exactly what's on my mind.

"We bet on who makes the killing blow to the Class A."

"And the prize?"

"Same as always. The winner names the next kiss."

This is my favorite game in the history of ever. Whoever wins the bet gets to demand when and where our next kiss will take place. And no matter what the time or location, the so-called loser must comply. Typically, these interludes don't end with kissing, either. Our last bet was who could first cross the Plains of Rixa on horseback. Lincoln won and demanded a kiss in the royal stables. We ended up naked, and I was picking hay out of my hair for days. The whole thing was beyond great.

I wag my eyebrows. "So, what do you say?"

"You're on."

Sweet.

Desmond turns down another deserted road. Actually, road is a generous word. It's more of a pathway through piles of rubble. Lincoln and I speed along behind our prey. I would skip-run if it didn't slow me down.

I am so winning this bet.

Bring it on, Desmond.

—End Of Sample—

~

To find out more about ACCA, visit:

https://tinyurl.com/baueracca

APPENDIX

IF YOU ENJOYED THIS BOOK...

...Please consider leaving a review, even if it's just a line or two. Every bit truly helps, especially for those of us who don't *write by the numbers,* if you know what I mean.

Plus I have it on good authority that every time you review an indie author, somewhere an angel gets a mocha latte. For reals.

And angels need their caffeine, too.

ACKNOWLEDGMENTS

If you're reading my freaking acknowledgements, chances are, I should thank you for something. So, for the record: you are awesome, dear reader.

That said, huge and heartfelt thanks must go out to my husband and son for their rock-solid support. Writing *Angelbound* meant a lot of early mornings, late nights, long weekends, and never-ending patience. You two are the best guys in the universe, period.

After that, I must thank the extensive network of reviewers, friends and colleagues who helped me build my writing chops in general. Gracias.

Finally, deep affection goes out to my late, much loved, and dearly missed Aunt Sandy and Uncle Henry. You saw the writer in me, always. Thank you, first and last.

COLLECTED WORKS

Angelbound Origins

About a quasi (part demon and part human) girl who loves kicking butt in Purgatory's Arena

1. Angelbound
2. Scala
3. Acca
4. Thrax
5. The Dark Lands
6. The Brutal Time *(2019)*
7. Armageddon *(already here, long story!)*
8. Quasi Redux *(2020)*

Angelbound Lincoln

The Angelbound experience as told by Prince Lincoln

1. Duty Bound
2. Lincoln
3. Trickster *(forthcoming)*

Angelbound Offspring

The next generation takes on Heaven, Hell, and everything in between

1. Maxon
2. Portia
3. Zinnia
4. Kaps *(forthcoming)*
5. Huntress *(forthcoming)*

Beholder

Where a medieval farm girl discovers necromancy and true love

1. Cursed
2. Concealed
3. Cherished
4. Crowned
5. Cradled

Fairy Tales of the Magicorum

Modern fairy tales with sass, action, and romance

1. Wolves and Roses

1.5 Moonlight and Midtown

2. Shifters and Glyphs
3. Slippers and Thieves *(forthcoming)*
4. Bandits and Ballgowns *(forthcoming)*

Dimension Drift

Dystopian adventures with science, snark, and hot aliens

Prequels

1. Scythe
2. Umbra

Novels

1. Alien Minds
2. ECHO Academy *(forthcoming)*
3. Drift Warrior *(forthcoming)*

ABOUT CHRISTINA BAUER

Christina Bauer thinks that fantasy books are like bacon: they just make life better. All of which is why she writes romance novels that feature demons, dragons, wizards, witches, elves, elementals, and a bunch of random stuff that she brainstorms while riding the Boston T. Oh, and she includes lots of humor and kick-ass chicks, too.

Christina lives in Newton, MA with her husband, son, and semi-insane golden retriever, Ruby.

Stalk Christina on Social Media

Blog:
http://monsterhousebooks.com/blog/category/christina

Facebook:
https://www.facebook.com/authorBauer/

Instagram:
https://www.instagram.com/christina_cb_bauer/

Twitter:
@CB_Bauer

VLOG:
https://tinyurl.com/Vlogbauer

Web site:
www.bauersbooks.com

COMPLIMENTARY BOOK

Get a FREE book when you sign up for Christina's newsletter: https://tinyurl.com/bauersbooks

Printed in Germany
by Amazon Distribution
GmbH, Leipzig